WAYMAN MURDERS

THE WAXMAN MURDERS

Paul Doherty

ISIS
LARGE PRINT
Oxford

First published in Great Britain 2006
by
Headline Publishing Group, a division of Hodder Headline

Published in Large Print 2008 by ISIS Publishing Ltd.,
7 Centremead, Osney Mead, Oxford OX2 0ES
by arrangement with
Headline Publishing Group, a division of Hodder Headline

British Library Cataloguing in Publication Data
Doherty, P. C.
    The Waxman murders. – Large print ed.
    1. Corbett, Hugh (Fictitious character) – Fiction
    2. Murder – Investigation – Fiction
    3. Great Britain – History – Edward I, 1272–1307
    – Fiction
    4. Detective and mystery stories
    5. Large type books
    I. Title
    823.9'14 [F]

ISBN 978-0-7531-8034-1 (hb)
ISBN 978-0-7531-8035-8 (pb)

Printed and bound in Great Britain by
T. J. International Ltd., Padstow, Cornwall

*This book is dedicated to David and Jack Sullivan
of "Birch Hall", Coppice Row, Essex.*

Prologue

Timeo est summersus in undis.
I fear the dark waves break above him.

Medieval lament

The Feast of the Translation of St Edward the Confessor, 12 October 1300

"From the horrors of the sea and its devouring monsters, *Domine libera nos* — Lord deliver us" was a common prayer of those who used the sea lanes from the tip of Cornwall through the Narrow Seas and up to where the waves crashed like demons against the fang-tooth rocks off Farnborough Head. However, no sea monster was more feared than the great soaring, fat-bellied three-masted war cog *The Waxman*, with its jutting prow and high stern castle, fighting platforms and other instruments of war. The terrors of a night squall, the fury of devil-ridden winds, the horrors of the blackest storm and the monstrous soaring waves paled against the speed, savagery and ruthlessness of *The Waxman*, under its master Adam Blackstock, late citizen and burgess of the King's city of Canterbury.

The *Waxman* was well named; she would suddenly appear, then melt away, as if shrouded in some malevolent protective mist, only to reappear off the

Humber, the mouth of the Thames, or prowling off Pevensey or one of the Cinque Ports. Her crew were regarded as fiends incarnate and their evil-looking cog a ship of the damned. Only recently *The Waxman* had taken a wine ship off Bordeaux, seized its precious cargo and valuables, then sunk the craft after hanging its captain and drowning the survivors of his crew. She had even attacked the warlike galleys of powerful Venice and, more importantly, the round-bellied cogs of the German merchants, the mighty Hanseatic League who had their own dock and quayside at the Steelyard in London.

A year ago, around Lammas Day, Blackstock had won his greatest prize, a Hanseatic carrack, *The Maid of Lübeck*, with its cargo of furs and pelts. Even more precious had been that casket, carved out of whalebone, containing the Cloister Map being dispatched to Sir Walter Castledene, knight of Canterbury, providing precise details of a fabulous treasure trove between the Suffolk walks and the River Denham. The map had been drawn in cipher, but Blackstock was now preparing to take *The Waxman* up the River Orwell, past the Colvasse peninsula, to shelter in a tree-shrouded nook, near a ruined hermitage and its derelict chapel, St Simon of the Rocks. Here he could go ashore and meet his half-brother, Hubert Fitzurse, an educated man trained in the cloister school of St Augustine's in Canterbury. Hubert had even gone to the halls of Cambridge before entering the Benedictine order, but that was all in the past, shadows of things which could have been. Now, on the Feast of the Translation of St Edward the Confessor, *The Waxman* was beating her way up the Essex coast towards Orwell for Blackstock's meeting with his half-brother which might change both their lives.

On that freezing October morning, with the clouds pressing down like an iron-grey pall, Adam Blackstock stood staring out across the mist-strewn sea. He was dressed in leather leggings pushed into fur-lined boots, a thick woollen cloak over his shirt and jerkin, the cowl of which was pulled up to protect his head and face against the icy, salted wind biting at his skin. Blackstock seemed unaware of the harsh weather, the straining, swaying ship, the swollen grey seas, the shriek of the gulls or that dreadful mist which seemed to cloak everything. He had ordered all lanterns to be lit and he felt safe enough; few craft would take to the seas in this weather, whilst *The Waxman* was well armed. Blackstock was busy dreaming about the past, speculating on the future and wondering how it would all end. If the Cloister Map was genuine, and Blackstock believed it was, then he and Hubert would become great and mighty men, perhaps even buy pardons from the King — what a change!

Blackstock clung to the ropes of the rigging, letting his body sway with the surge of the sea tossing his ship backwards and forwards. He was used to that and betrayed no fear. Some people claimed he had a hangman's face, dark and sombre, furrowed, with dead eyes and a sharp nose over bloodless lips. Others said the face reminded them of a monk, an ascetic, a man dedicated to the service of God and the love of his brethren. In truth Blackstock cared for no one apart from his beloved half-brother.

As he stood at the rigging, Blackstock reflected like some monk in his stall on how it all had begun. His father had married twice. Hubert's mother, a Fitzurse, had died in childbirth so Blackstock's father had married a local girl, a wench from one of the outlying farms. Hubert was six years Adam's senior, yet they'd spent their childhood, as their father often remarked, as if they were twins, peas from the same pod. From an early age Hubert had proved himself able with the horn book, a clever scholar, so he was sent to St Augustine's Abbey to be taught by the Black Monks. When he returned home, however, he and Adam had enjoyed a veritable paradise of a childhood. Happy days fishing and boating along the River Stour, helping their father on the farm, journeys into Canterbury visiting Becket's great shrine and attending the busy city fairs and markets. In 1272 their paradise had descended into nightmare. In that year old King Henry III had died, mumbling and feverish, at Westminster. His eldest son and heir, Edward, was on crusade in Outremer. In the absence of a strong ruler, the king's peace had been violated in many cities and shires by marauding gangs of rifflers and robbers who attacked isolated manor houses to ransack and loot. The Blackstocks' manor near Maison Dieu was one of these.

On that fateful evening Blackstock's father had come running up the stairs, forcing Adam out of an upper casement, virtually throwing him out on to the hay-filled cart below, shouting at him to flee and shelter

4

in the nearby woods. A time of nightmare! Blackstock had hidden beneath a bush, watching his father being cut down, his mother and her maid raped before they too were killed, throats slit, bellies opened. Of John Brocare, his father's kinsman, there was no sign. At the time Adam believed Brocare had also been murdered, his corpse consumed by the conflagration. The following morning, the sheriff's men arrived to view the devastation and found Adam. Hubert had been in Canterbury at the time, sleeping with the other boys in the scholars' dormitory at St Augustine's. The brothers were taken to the Guildhall, where some grey-bearded, sombre-eyed man had told them the full extent of the tragedy. They'd sat in that dusty room and realised how their lives were to be drastically changed. "Sombre-eyes", perched behind the table, stared at them sadly as he described how their home had been destroyed, their father and mother murdered, the corpses of other victims burnt beyond recognition. He explained how their parents would be buried in God's acre at St Mildred's, beneath the old yew tree where they'd first met at the giving of church-ales. He tried to soften the blow, but Blackstock, sitting beside Hubert and holding his hand, just stared at the mullioned window behind the old man's head, watching the sun-motes dancing in the light piercing the thick glass. Afterwards, it was like a dream. The merchant had taken both boys downstairs, introducing them to other men who explained how their father had been not only a successful yeoman farmer but a member of the powerful Guild of Furriers and Skinners in the city, which meant that they had a solemn duty of care towards both Hubert and his younger brother. Hubert seemed to understand and later explained it all to Adam, adding in halting sentences what was to happen in the future.

The next morning they'd attended their parents' requiem mass in St Mildred's and watched both coffins, specially purchased by the Guild, being taken out to God's acre to be buried. Wooden crosses were immediately thrust into the freshly dug mounds of earth. The Guildsmen solemnly promised that, within a year and a day, these would be replaced by marble crosses cut by the finest stonemasons. Adam didn't care. All he could remember were his mother's screams, the flames shooting up through the roof of the house and his father lying on the cobbles, legs kicking, clutching his stomach. He tried to explain all this to Hubert but his brother didn't seem to understand; he would just stare, shake his head and press his fingers against Adam's lips as a sign to keep silent.

After that, they were like ships becalmed after a fierce storm. Hubert continued with his studies and proved himself to be an adept scholar in theology, philosophy, grammar and syntax, a young man with what one magister called "the gift of tongues", not only the classics, Latin and Greek, but Norman French and German. Adam, in the mean time, had been apprenticed to the trade of a skinner and leatherer. He proved himself skilful but soon won a reputation for being distant and aloof, keeping himself to himself. The only person with whom he would relax was his brother on his infrequent visits back to the city from the halls of Cambridge. Hubert eventually entered the Benedictine order, while Adam became a tradesman in his own right, a citizen inheriting what was left of his father's money and estate. Never once did he ever go back to the family manor farm, and through the Guild he salted money away with goldsmiths in the city.

Adam always felt as if he was separate from the rest of mankind, even here on the ship; it was as if a great gulf yawned between himself and God's other creatures. Now and again he had visited his parents' graves in St Mildred's but never once went inside the church. He found the mass and other ceremonies boring, and where possible he excused himself from the mysteries of the Guild: their annual ceremonies, parades, festivities, the offering of votive candles, what Adam secretly called "their empty mummery" at the various churches in Canterbury or its great cathedral. On occasion he visited Becket's magnificent shrine, but even then he was more interested in how much it was worth. He'd stare greedily at the great jewels gleaming in the gold sheeting and wondered how easy it would be to steal them.

At other times Adam felt a seething anger which he couldn't express until one night, just after Michaelmas, he'd been gambling in a tavern in the Mercery. A quarrel broke out and his opponent had called Adam "a whoreson". Adam couldn't really remember what happened next; all he could recall was his opponent's slobbering mouth in his unshaven face. The man leaned across, repeating those foul curses, those awful words about his parents, then Adam's knife was in the man's throat and Adam was fleeing for his life. He eventually sheltered in London, but found it difficult as he wasn't a member of a Guild to secure any meaningful employment, so he drifted down to Queenshithe and secured passage aboard a wool ship sailing for Dordrecht. There, amongst that foreign port's inns and shabby alehouses, he discovered his true calling. He was a natural-born seaman, a sailor. He loved the sea and studied its ways, its cruelty, the fury of the winds, the management of a ship and the organisation of its crew. At first he applied his skill with a coven of river pirates operating off the mouth of the Scheldt, but due to his cunning, ferocity and bravery soon won the attention of others and became a privateer sponsored by the powerful merchants of Hainault to sail out with letters of marque to intercept, pillage and destroy enemy ships.

Some years ago Blackstock had bought *The Waxman*, selected his crew and declared war against all men, having no fear of God or his own kind. At the same time news came from England that Hubert had abruptly fled the Benedictine community at Westminster and urgently wished to meet his half-brother. One August night Blackstock took *The Waxman* up the River Orwell and met his brother at the deserted hermitage. They had embraced, clasped and kissed each other. Hubert had confessed that he had little time for God and certainly none for the Benedictine order. He declared that the death of his monastic calling had been due to a visit from Brocare, their father's kinsman.

Brocare had survived the massacre by fleeing, and out of shame and fear had kept himself hidden until remorse and a desire for revenge had driven him back into what he called the daylight of their lives. Brocare was full of guilt, desperate to do something to avenge the great wrongs perpetrated. No one had ever discovered who was responsible for the attack on the Blackstock manor and the bloody massacre that followed, but Brocare had his own suspicions. He had produced a list of possible suspects which he shared with Hubert, and the monk realised he had been living a fool's life in a world where cruel rapacity was the order of the day. He and Adam agreed that the night their parents died, their own souls had also died. God had taken everything from them so they would give nothing to God. Hubert explained how he was now hired by mayors, sheriffs and bailiffs as a *venator hominum*, a hunter of men, tracking down outlaws, bringing them to justice and claiming the reward. He had even hunted members of the coven who had murdered their parents, though in the main, death had placed most of these beyond his reach. He confided to Adam that some had been Canterbury men, which only deepened the brothers' hatred and contempt for that city.

In the end, Hubert and Adam spoke little about the past but planned for the future. They agreed to meet more often. Both men realised that what had happened so many years ago outside Canterbury had scarred their lives and only vengeance could purge their anger. Taken up by the surge of life, they could do nothing but go with it. Over the succeeding months they grew even closer. Hubert would often share information with his brother, who would reciprocate by handing over plunder for Hubert to sell to the denizens of the underworld in London, Bishop's Lynn, Bristol and Dover, where goods could be moved and sold without any questions asked . . .

Blackstock hung grimly to the rigging ropes, straining against the sway of the ship. He glanced over his shoulder at Stonecrop, his lieutenant and manservant, a dour man who stood hunched, head and face almost hidden by his deep-cowled cloak.

"You are sure of this, master?"

Blackstock turned. Stonecrop approached, pushing back his cowl to reveal black hair closely shorn over a lean, spiteful face. Blackstock had met him in Dordrecht some years ago and saved him in a tavern brawl. Stonecrop had proved to be his man, body and soul, in peace and war. He had eyes as dead as night, black and lifeless. Hubert didn't like him, adding that he certainly didn't trust him. Blackstock did. He recognised himself in Stonecrop, a man who cared for nothing and no one.

"I've told you." Blackstock turned away. "I met Hubert in Wissant; he confirmed the treasure must exist." He pointed through the grey, misty drizzle towards the coastline. "We will soon make landfall at Orwell and thread our way up to the hermitage. Hubert will be there."

"Why didn't he come with us?"

Blackstock laughed. "Hubert doesn't like the sea. Anyway, he had other business to do, a matter between him and me, not you."

Stonecrop pulled his cowl back over his head and turned away whilst his master stared up at the great mast, its canvas sail furled back. Once again Blackstock looked round, making sure all was well, lookouts posted in the prow and stern vigilant for rocks.

Now his thoughts turned to the Cloister Map; that was what its owner, the German merchant Paulents, had called the ancient manuscript. The map had been sketched in the form of a cloister and marked an area of wasteland in Suffolk around a cluster of ancient barrows near the River Denham. According to the map, one of these barrows contained the vast treasure hoard of some barbarian king buried in a longship packed from prow to stern with gold, silver plate, precious jewels and costly armour, a king's ransom waiting to be claimed.

"A ship on land, buried near a river," Blackstock pondered the riddle posed by the map, "but out of the swing of the sea."

"What was that, master?" Stonecrop called.

"Nothing." Blackstock grinned to himself. There'd be time enough, he reflected, to inform Stonecrop and the rest of the crew.

He moved as the ship swayed, buffeted by the powerful north-easterly wind which raised curtains of misty salt-edged spray. Blackstock looked up once again at the raven's nest on the mast, then around at the men slopping water from the bulwarks. He strained as he always did to hear the music of the ship. Never mind the storm; it was the ship that mattered! Blackstock had been well taught by the skilled privateers who prowled the Narrow Seas between Dover and Calais, as well as the trade routes to the wine city of Bordeaux and further south to the ports of Spain, or even — as he could do now, if he struck north-east — the frozen ports of the Baltic. Andit de Bodleck, master and captain of *The Soul in Limbo*, out of Brabant, had been his principal mentor. Yes, Andit had been the best teacher, despite being captured by two royal cogs of Edward I of England, his ship sunk and the life strangled out of him on a gallows overlooking Goodwin Sands on the eve of Reek Sunday. Blackstock had heard how Bodleck had refused the ministrations of the local parson; the privateer was a self-professed pagan who made offerings to an eerie war goddess called Nenetania.

"Strange old life," Blackstock mused aloud.

"What is, master?"

This time Blackstock thought it tactful to reply. "How few people, Stonecrop," he shouted back above the creak of the ship, "truly believe in priests; they'd rather be thrashed than make their confessions to them."

Blackstock peered towards the prow. At least five of his crew were former clerics who'd committed some crime and were now dressed in serge leggings and leather jerkins, hair and beard matted, their tonsures long gone. He wondered how many of them, if captured, would plead benefit of clergy. Would Hubert do that? But of course, such dangerous living was going to end once they found that treasure ship and the precious hoard it contained. At first Hubert had been sceptical, but Blackstock had insisted that if a high-ranking Hanseatic merchant like Paulents and Sir Walter Castledene, merchant prince and knight, believed in it, there must be some truth to the story. Then, by mere chance, Hubert had been hunting a goldsmith out of Bishop's Lynn, a collector of books and manuscripts. The man had killed a priest in a tavern brawl and been put to the horn as *ultegatum* — beyond the law. Hubert had eventually tracked the felon down and captured him in the small village of East Stoke on the River Trent near Newark in Nottinghamshire. He had bound the man's hands, tied his legs beneath his horse and begun the journey back to Bishop's Lynn. On the way the two men struck up a friendship. Hubert talked about a great treasure ship buried somewhere in Suffolk, and to his astonishment the goldsmith said he'd heard similar rumours and legends. He offered Hubert a manuscript on condition that he cut his bonds and let him go, and eventually Hubert agreed. They slipped by night into Bishop's Lynn and the goldsmith returned stealthily to his house. They'd broken down the boards, forced the shutters, snapped the sheriff's seals and opened a coffer of manuscripts. The goldsmith had collected other possessions then left. In a tavern the following morning, he'd handed a piece of parchment over to Hubert, who quickly realised that this extract from an English chronicle did indeed refer to a treasure hoard buried somewhere in Suffolk. He released the goldsmith, though much good it did the fellow, as he was later taken by the sheriff's comitatus and hanged out of hand. Meanwhile Hubert used the manuscript to reflect on the Cloister Map and eventually concluded it would lead them exactly to where the treasure hoard was buried.

Blackstock had kept such information, as well as the map, to himself. He'd not even shared it with the villainous Canterbury merchant Sir Rauf Decontet, one of his manucaptors, who'd advanced some of the money for him to buy *The Waxman* and who still took a share of whatever plunder he seized. Blackstock licked his lips. In fact he'd kept a lot back from Decontet. One day he and Hubert would settle their final account with that miserly rogue. Most importantly, the two brothers had made a compact that once they had the treasure there'd be no more hunting by land and sea. They would quietly disappear and re-emerge in some other town, perhaps some other country, as prosperous wool merchants. No more filthy bilges, dirty taverns, vermin-infested alehouses; no more water or wine from clay-lined tubs or hard bread alive with weevils or sea biscuit which stank of rat urine.

"Land, land to the west!"

Blackstock whirled around. He could make out the faint outlines of cliffs and hills before the mist closed again. He smiled and fingered the charm, a gargoyle, an imp with one leg crossed over the other, nailed to the mast. Soon they would make landfall.

"Master! Master!"

Blackstock stared up as the horn wailed the alarm from the raven's nest above him.

"What do you see?" he called.

The ship fell silent. No slap of bare feet against the sea-salted deck; no timber creaking or waves crashing. Some demon cloaked in the mist seemed to trail its fingers along Blackstock's flesh.

"What is it?" he bellowed.

"Ship to the north-east, an armed cog."

"What device?"

"I cannot see."

"Damnation to you!" Blackstock shouted back.

Stonecrop needed no second bidding. Ram's horn already to his lips, he blew three wailing blasts and the crew scrambled for weapons: bows, quivers, long pikes, swords, daggers and shields, whilst small pots of burning charcoal were brought up from below. Those who had them donned helmets, hauberks and other pieces of armour. Blackstock hurried up into the prow and stared through the mist boiling above the grim grey sea. Some distance away, sails billowing, a war cog was using the easterly wind to bear down on them. It was a ship very like his own, though slightly bigger, with raised stern and jutting poop. Again the horn wailed from the raven's nest.

"Master, south-east another ship."

Blackstock could hardly believe it. He went down the slippery steps from the prow and slithered across the deck, pushing and shoving his crew aside, up into the stern where the rudder men fought to keep the ship on a straight course. By the face of Lucca! Blackstock tried to quell his surge of fear. Another ship was heading out of the mist like an arrow. A cog of war, surely? Merchantmen would not be so bold. A king's ship perhaps, but why now, on a freezing October day? They were here deliberately, they'd come to trap him! They must have left the mouth of the Thames and stood far out to sea, knowing the planned time and date of his landfall at Orwell. He had been betrayed!

Blackstock screamed at Stonecrop to bring his war belt. He strapped this on and gazed wildly around. Never in his worst nightmare had he envisaged this, being trapped by two cogs of war, fully armed, against the English coast! The east wind was against him; it would be futile to try and slip between his opponents. He could run for land, beach his ship on the rocks, but what then? This had all been well plotted. The local sheriff and his comitatus would be waiting. Blackstock realised he had no choice but to fight.

"Master!" the lookout shouted. "The first one to the north is *The Segreant*; its pennant shows a green griffin rampant."

Blackstock clawed his face. Paulents! That powerful merchant of the Hanseatic League had decided to take his revenge.

"And the other?" Blackstock shouted back, though he already knew the answer.

"*The Caltrop*," the lookout shouted back. "It flies the silver wyvern."

Blackstock staggered to the taffrail and held it; staring down at the swelling sea, he felt sick. Von Paulents the German and Castledene the Canterbury merchant, the Kentish knight with fingers in every pie cooked in England, had plotted to trap him.

"They are flying the Beaussons," Stonecrop yelled.

Blackstock, peering through the haze, could now see both ships clearly as they closed, sails billowing, poop and stern crammed with fighting men. From the masts of both cogs floated blood-red ribbons, a sign that it would be a fight to the death, no quarter given, no terms, no mercy offered.

Throughout that grim grey afternoon, Blackstock used every trick, every device he knew, but it was futile. The two ships were intent on a fight *à l'outrance*, to the death. Blackstock was beside himself with fury; it clouded his mind and dimmed his wits. He had certainly been betrayed, but by whom? Somebody on board? His brother? Had Hubert been taken, had he been arrested and tortured? The pursuers closed mid-afternoon, eager to bring their prey to battle before darkness fell. Blackstock's only hope vanished. Despite rallying his crew, he knew it would be a futile fight. He swiftly clattered down to his small, narrow cabin to collect his armour before being summoned back by the cries of Stonecrop. *The Segreant* was now approaching rapidly, sails furled; it was trying to swing alongside. *The Caltrop* was still some way off. Blackstock donned his mailed hauberk and his helmet with its broad noseguard. He drew both sword and dagger, steadying himself against the sway of the ship. All around him massed his crew, attired in the most grotesque collection of rusty armour and animal pelts, the heads of dogs, wolves, foxes and bears still attached to them.

The Segreant approached, turning slightly under the watchful eye of its rudder men; Blackstock realised these must be skilled seamen. The cog was broad-bellied but swift, and slightly higher than his; the men on board were dressed in dark brown or Lincoln green. Blackstock suppressed a shiver of fear as he glimpsed longbowmen amongst the enemy; Paulents must have the support of royal troops. Blackstock turned. *The Caltrop* was doing a broad sweep to pass *The Waxman*'s stern and approach from the other side. Something was wrong! Castledene was taking his time. *The Segreant* was closer. Blackstock stared across. The enemy were all hooded and masked; they looked like a horde of sombre, ghostly monks. Why were they wearing those masks across their faces? Then he saw one of the enemy urinating on to a piece of cloth before putting it over his face. Immediately he recalled what old Dieter had told him, about how the great privateer Eustace had been captured and defeated during the minority of the present king's father. Blackstock gazed wildly around.

"Lime!" he screamed. "Lime!"

Already the archers on *The Segreant* were leaning back, yew bows bent, yard-long shafts notched. They loosed and the arrows fell like a deadly rain amongst *The Waxman*'s crew; some of these staggered back or twirled round as the goose-quilled shafts thudded into face, neck and chest. Blackstock ran forward, turning his face away. Too late: men-at-arms on *The Segreant* now released small sacks of lime. They'd taken careful note of the wind direction and the powder flowed across to sting the eyes and clog the mouths of *The Waxman*'s crew. The lime caused chaos. More arrows fell. *The Segreant* drew alongside, crashing into *The Waxman*, its men pouring across. Blackstock, eyes sore, mouth burning, ran to the other side as *The Caltrop* closed the trap, its captain using the powerful surging tide to come alongside, shattering the side rails of the enemy ship. Boards were lowered. Men-at-arms and archers poured across from both sides. The deck of *The Waxman* soon ran with blood from the vicious mêlée of hand-to-hand fighting with club, mace and dagger which ensued. The enemy, screaming and shouting, pushed Blackstock and the surviving members of his crew back towards the stern. Blackstock, standing on the tops steps, stared down at the enemy pressing close. Paulents was there, small and balding, his smooth round face wreathed in smiles as if already savouring his triumph. Beside him was Castledene, in full armour except for a helmet, his chest covered in the livery of a silver wyvern couchant against a green background. The merchant prince's sallow, pointed face beneath a mop of wiry grey hair was splattered with blood. He was already directing his men to finish off the enemy wounded with a swift thrust across the throat with a misericord dagger.

Blackstock watched all this as he and what remained of his crew were forced back up on to the stern castle. At last the fight petered out. *The Waxman*'s crew were exhausted; eyes streaming, their skin blighted by the lime, they threw down their weapons and were dragged away. Blackstock, armed with sword and dagger, remained alone on the deck of the stern castle. He glanced around. Both rudder men were dead, arrows deep in neck, chest and face. Castledene and Paulents approached, the German slipping on the blood-soaked deck. Castledene shouted at his own men to sluice the lime from the boards. He came to the bottom of the steps and glared up.

"Finished, Blackstock!" he yelled. "I'll take you back to Orwell to hang, your brother next to you." He stroked his neatly clipped grey moustache and beard, his watery blue eyes flinty-hard as he glared hatefully at this pirate who had sunk three of his ships. "The Cloister Map!" he demanded. "Hand me that and I'll give you a swift death."

"How did you know?" Blackstock countered, staring round. Behind the two enemy captains, his men were being bound hand and foot. Stonecrop, however, remained unfettered, standing apart from the rest. Blackstock had his answer. He glared down at Castledene and Paulents. "Hang?" He smiled. "No, I'll not hang, nor will my brother. You are both marked and sealed by the Angel of Death."

Blackstock lunged forward, the image of his brother bright in his mind as the longbows twanged and the deadly shafts pierced his face and neck. His life was over even as he tumbled down the steps. Castledene turned the body over with the toe of his boot and stared down. Blackstock's eyes were already clouding in death, blood gushing out of nostrils and mouth. Castledene knelt down, pulled back the mailed hauberk and rifled through the dead man's clothes and wallet. When he found nothing, he shouted at his own lieutenant to go down to the cabin and search. The man came hurrying back up the steps, an empty coffer in his hands.

"Nothing, sir, nothing at all. What shall we do with these?" He pointed at the prisoners.

"Hang them all!" Castledene shouted. "From stern and poop! Especially this." He kicked Blackstock's corpse.

Stonecrop came forward, hands extended.

"You promised me my life."

"So I did." Castledene, suffused with anger, walked to the side. He turned and gestured at Stonecrop. "I promised this man his life. I keep my promises. Throw him overboard; he can swim to the shore."

CHAPTER
ONE

Quis sait, si veniat.
I do not know whether he will return.

Medieval lament

Canterbury, December 1303

The three horsemen made their way along the old Roman road to Harbledown Hill. They'd sheltered at the priest's house of St Nicholas's church, using the royal seal to gain warmth and some food before continuing their journey. Now they were approaching the summit of the hill overlooking Canterbury and its splendid cathedral. Snow had fallen. The leaden grey skies threatened more. As they passed the crossroads with their empty gibbets and stocks, the lead rider reined in. Sir Hugh Corbett, Keeper of the Secret Seal of Edward I of England, soothed his skittish horse and pushed back the cowl of his cloak to reveal a long, olive-skinned face. Some men called it hawkish, with its deep-set dark eyes, sharp nose above full lips and firm chin: a watcher and a brooder, or so they said, like a falcon upon its perch, an aspect enhanced by Corbett's raven-black hair, tinged with grey, swept back and tied tightly in a queue on the nape of his neck. Corbett was tall and slender, careful and fastidious about what he ate and drank. He usually made a joke about this, saying that he would like to regard himself as ascetic; in truth, his stomach was delicate after long and arduous campaigns in Wales and Scotland, where, with the rest of Edward's troops, he'd drunk brackish water, eaten rotten meat and cut his teeth on iron-hard rye bread. He was dressed in dark red and black, his leather jacket clasped close over a white linen shirt, his dark blue cloak pulled tight over red leggings and high-heeled boots, the best from Cordova, on which silver-gilt spurs jingled. He took off the long leather gauntlet on his left hand and the chancery ring, the symbol of his office, gleamed in the day's dying light. Then he loosened the broad leather war belt round his waist from which sword and dagger hung.

"Now," he leaned forward, gripping the high saddle-horn, "when we reach the top of this hill we'll see Canterbury, and its cathedral, which holds the shrine of the blessed Becket. We'll then sing a pilgrim hymn, or perhaps something more liturgical, appropriate to the season." Corbett had been looking forward to this. He liked nothing better than the plainchant of the Church, the rise and fall of the music emphasising the awesome words and the rolling Latin phrases which conveyed a deep sense of the spiritual, of man's place before God. His companions were not so enthusiastic.

"Master, must we?" Ranulf atte Newgate, red-haired and green-eyed, his thin white face made even more so by the intense cold, pushed back his own hood and glared at Corbett. "We've been travelling," he moaned, "since Lauds."

Ranulf, Senior Clerk in the Chancery of the Green Wax, simply wanted to ease himself out of the saddle, take off his boots and, as he'd remarked to the third member of their party, the mop-haired, moon-faced Chanson, Clerk of the Royal Stables, toast himself in front of a roaring fire. Now he undid the top clasp of his black leather jerkin and pointed across at Chanson.

"Despite his name, he cannot sing. He sounds more like a fiend sitting on a scorching skillet getting his arse burnt."

"At least I'm not terrified of the countryside," Chanson retorted. "He is, you know, master. He believes all sorts of gargoyles lurk in the undergrowth." Chanson nursed the inside of his right leg. "I've a sore here," he groaned. "I need a physician more than I do a hymn."

"We'll sing first," Corbett insisted. "Chanson, you may do so softly. It's all part of the pilgrim tradition, to give thanks when you glimpse Canterbury." He put on his gauntlet and pulled up his hood.

Ranulf quietly cursed and Chanson whispered insults as they made their way up Harbledown Hill. The snow began to fall again, faintly at first, then the flakes became like great white feathers floating down. When they reached the summit, they glimpsed, through the gathering murk, the King's city of Canterbury with its crenellated walls, squat castle, brooding Westgate, lofty church towers, and soaring above all this, the minster of the cathedral, its mass of carefully carved masonry rising like a prayer against the evening sky. The lights of the city glowed like candles about it; the smoke from fires and workshops hung like gusts of incense around this holiest of England's shrines.

For a while, despite the gathering gloom, Corbett tried to point out the principal landmarks, then he dismounted, only to turn abruptly at a sound behind him. Another group was approaching; its leader carried a huge lantern with an enormous fiery candle glowing inside. The strangers passed Corbett's party, pushing their way by. The light-bearer thrust the lantern pole into a deep snowdrift beside the trackway, sending the shadows dancing. The strangers grouped together oblivious to the chaos they had caused. Ranulf's horse whinnied and reared, whilst the pack pony Chanson was leading abruptly moved back on its hind legs. Ranulf, exasperated, drew his sword; the icy scraping sound stilled the chatter amongst the strangers. They looked round, and their leader shuffled back through the snow. He was cloaked and hooded, the lower part of his face hidden beneath broad cloth bands. In the poor light his eyes glittered; when he pulled the mouth bands down, his hot breath burst clear on the wintry air.

"*Gaudium et spes*." He growled the usual Christmas greeting. "Joy and hope."

"*Gaudium et spes*," Corbett replied, indicating that Ranulf should re-sheathe his sword.

"We are Les Hommes Joyeuses — the Joyous Men," the fellow continued, "travelling players. Our carts are somewhere behind us. We have come to give thanks to our patron Thomas à Becket and to God's Holy Mother."

"Then, friend," Corbett hid his smile, "we shall sing together. But why are you travelling to Canterbury in the dead of winter?"

"In thanksgiving," the leader of the Joyeuses replied, continuing the pretence that he did not know Corbett. "To sing a carol to Christ's Blessed Mother. Last month we sheltered in Suffolk." The man, one of Corbett's spies, chattered on. Corbett waited for the real message. "Ah yes, we are glad to be out of Suffolk, with its treasure-hunters, lepers and grisly death. We bring all sorts of news. Ah well," he stamped his feet, "are we to stay here and freeze?"

In the flickering light of the candle, Les Hommes Joyeuses assumed a funereal air lacking any kind of Yuletide cheer.

"By what name are you called?" the leader asked. He wanted Corbett to reassure the rest of his party.

"Sir Hugh Corbett, king's emissary to Canterbury, Keeper of the Secret Seal."

The Joyeuses came forward, their dismal air lifted; hands appeared from beneath cloaks. Corbett heard the scrape of blades being shoved back into sheaths, as cowls and hoods were pushed back.

"I am sorry," their leader confessed, winking quickly at Corbett, "we thought you were different, something else, perhaps outlaws or wolfsheads." He extended a hand. "Robert Ormesby, formerly clerk of Taunton, Somerset, now the Gleeman, poet, mummer and mimer."

Corbett grinned, grasped the Gleeman's hand and squeezed it gently. "Then let us carol merrily together! What chant?"

26

"Advent is drawing to a close," the Gleeman replied, pursing his lips. "Why not one of the O antiphons? 'Clavis David' or 'Radix Jesse'?"

Corbett, much to Ranulf's annoyance, agreed heartily to both and they all trudged to the far side of Harbledown Hill, the snow falling thick and fast. Ranulf was reluctantly coaxed to join in. Tunes were hummed; Corbett conceded the honour of cantor to the Gleeman, whose strong voice broke into the beautiful antiphon: "Root of Jesse, set up as a sign, come to save us . . ."

Corbett and the rest joined in the refrain, "And delay no more, and delay no more . . ."

The deep-throated singing swelled out, under the leaden skies, proclaiming the coming of the Emmanuel, the King of Peace, the Christ child. The words of the antiphon cut through the freezing air, drifting towards Canterbury, the King's own city, which housed the blessed bones of the murdered Becket and where even more hideous killings were being subtly plotted.

Once the singing was finished, Corbett felt better, and again clasped the Gleeman's hand.

"Where will you lodge? Not a stable?" he joked as he pulled up his cowl.

"May as well be," the Gleeman replied. "Perhaps the inn yard at the Chequer of Hope, but if not that . . ." He shrugged.

Corbett stepped closer, peering at the man. The Gleeman was broad-faced, with well-spaced eyes, thin lips, a snub nose and full cheeks, a merry-looking man with a tinge of cynicism. His light hair was shorn to a stubble, his upper lip and chin freshly shaved and scrubbed.

"If you fail there," Corbett whispered, "come to St Augustine's Abbey near Queningate. Use my name, and I'll see what I can do . . ."

Corbett made his farewells and strode across to where Ranulf slumped holding the reins of his horse.

"Ranulf," Corbett murmured, one foot in the stirrup, "Christmas is a time of friendship, bonhomie and good cheer. All pilgrims to Canterbury pause here to say a prayer or sing a hymn." He swung himself up into the saddle. "Now we shall press on."

Corbett spurred his horse forward. Ranulf followed, whilst Chanson on his own palfrey struggled to control the pack pony, which had revealed a wickedly stubborn disposition. Behind them the cries and farewells of the Joyeuses faded as they made their way along the icy trackway.

"It's lonely," Ranulf remarked.

"Winter makes hermits of us all," Corbett retorted. He slouched low in the saddle, bowing his head against the biting wind. In truth, he'd be glad to reach St Augustine's. He was tired of the icy sheets which hung everywhere, the cold-veiled mist, snowflakes flying thick and fast like the white bees of heaven, the earth hard as if clasped in a mail corselet, the sky like a cloak of lead stretching above them. At least, he comforted himself, the King had promised that his senior clerk would be home by the Feast of the Epiphany. Corbett desperately looked forward to that, longing to be closeted in his own private chamber with silver-haired Maeve and their two children, Edward and Eleanor. A time of peace, of roaring fires, hot posset ales, roasted chestnuts and apples, mulled wine spiced with nutmeg, braised beef, and above all, the Lady Maeve. He would lie with her and compose a poem. In fact he'd begun one already:

Strengthen my love, the castle of my heart.
Fortify with pleasure . . .

"Master, this business in Canterbury?"

"The King's business, Ranulf!" Corbett broke from his reverie. "Three years ago, Adam Blackstock, master of *The Waxman*, a privateer, was captured and killed off Orwell. The principal ordainer in this was a Canterbury merchant named Sir Walter Castledene."

"Who is now mayor."

"The same," Corbett agreed. "Now Castledene had, and still has, an intimate friend amongst the Hanseatic mercantile fraternity, Wilhelm von Paulents."

"Who is coming to England with his family."

"Precisely. They will be the guests of Sir Walter and the King, and will lodge at the manor of Maubisson on the outskirts of the city, not far from the Dover Road." Corbett squinted up at the sky. "Paulents, along with his wife, son, maid and bodyguard, a mercenary called Servinus. They are bringing something Paulents once thought he'd lost: the Cloister Map, showing where a great treasure hoard lies buried somewhere in Suffolk. It's written in a cipher. About four years ago Paulents sent the map to Castledene, but Blackstock seized it from *The Maid of Lübeck*, which he intercepted and sank. He planned to take the map to his half-brother Hubert, a subtle and skilled scholar who could easily interpret the cipher and seize the treasure. Blackstock was sailing for Orwell to meet Hubert when he himself was trapped and killed. The original map was never found, and Hubert, a master of disguise even amongst the most cunning of counterfeit men, simply disappeared."

"And no one else survived from *The Waxman*?"

Corbett's horse suddenly started as an owl glided across the trackway, floating like some lost soul into the darkness beyond. He soothed his mount, stroking its neck, then reined it in for a while to let it settle. Behind them Chanson cursed as he fought to control the pack pony, which had also been frightened.

"No one." Corbett threaded the reins through his hands and stared longingly at the distant lights of the city. "The entire crew was hanged. *The Waxman* was ransacked from the top of its mast to its hull, but no trace of the Cloister Map was found. Blackstock must have destroyed it. Anyway, Paulents has been busy searching, and has at last found a copy of the chronicle the original map was taken from. He is now bringing this to England, and he and Castledene will finance the search for the treasure."

"And the King? Us?"

"We act for the King in this matter." Corbett wiped the snow from his face. "We are the King's will. You must have listened to Drokensford, Langton and other officials of the Exchequer: the royal treasury is empty.

30

Edward wages bloody war against Wallace and the kingdom of Scotland."

"And a greater part of any treasure trove belongs to the King?"

"*Tu dixisti* — you've said it!" Corbett quipped.

He urged his horse along the rutted trackway. Now the countryside was not so lonely: houses rose on either side, their gates shut, doors firmly locked against the icy night. The smell of wood smoke, charcoal and fragrant cooking odours urged them on. Somewhere behind a lychgate, a dog barked. Darkness was sweeping in. The moon began to rise and the stars shimmered like pinpricks of light above them.

"In a word, Ranulf," Corbett added, "we are here to help decipher the chart, though I believe it may already have been done. We are to ensure Castledene and Paulents agree to the King's rights, safeguard Paulents, and deal with —"

"The Lady Adelicia?"

"Adelicia Decontet," Corbett agreed. "Soon to be arraigned before Sir Walter Castledene and other justices in the city Guildhall on a charge of murdering her husband, Sir Rauf Decontet. Adelicia was once the King's ward. If Edward of England has a soft heart for anyone, it is Adelicia 'La Délicieuse'. However, her late husband was also a friend of the King. He lent Edward money for his recent wars in Gascony."

"So the King will intervene in this matter?"

"No." Corbett turned in the saddle, sheltering his face against the driving snowflakes. "We are here to see that justice is done. If she truly shattered her husband's skull as you would a nut, then she'll not hang, Ranulf, she'll burn before the city gates."

"And why are we staying at St Augustine's Abbey?"

"Because it's more comfortable; because Hubert once studied there. We might learn something, and . . ."

"And what?"

"Wait and see. Come."

Corbett urged his horse into a canter, and Ranulf and Chanson followed, unaware that ahead of them, those twin disciples of Cain, horrid murder and bloody mayhem, also crept towards the King's city of Canterbury.

Wendover, captain and serjeant-at-arms in the city of Canterbury, was also concerned about murder. So anxious had he become, he truly wished he could slip into the shriving pew at St Alphege's church and confess all his sins to Parson Warfeld. Yet was he as contrite as the rite of absolution said he should be? Indeed, although he was racked by the fear of hell, the allure of Lady Adelicia's soft white body, so smooth and perfumed, her golden hair hanging down, those light blue eyes, her soft speech and elegant gestures seemed a total hindrance to God's grace. Lady Adelicia Decontet had turned Wendover's world upside down. He was reminded of that wall painting in St Alphege's which showed three rats hanging a cat and, in the background, an antelope hunting a fox ridden by a rabbit: a parable of the topsy-turvy world he now lived in. After all, he was supposed to keep the King's peace, not violate it through fornication with a leading citizen's wife, especially one now imprisoned in the dungeons beneath the Guildhall.

Lady Adelicia stood accused of murdering her miserly husband, of smashing his skull with a fire-tong, splattering his chancery chamber with blood and brains. Yet how could she have done that? Wendover knew she was innocent. On the very afternoon the heinous crime had been committed, Adelicia had been with him in his chamber at The Chequer of Hope, ripe and rich, turning and twisting under him. She'd arrived as she always did, in disguise. The tavern was so busy, it was easy for her to slip like a shadow up its outside staircase. Yet such secrecy had not saved her from disgrace. Now she had been imprisoned and accused of murder. So far she had said nothing, yet soon the justices, led by that hard-hearted bastard Castledene, would force her to plead either way under *peine forte et dure* — she would be laid in the cobbled yard of the Guildhall and pressed with wood and weights until she did so.

Wendover was in such an agony of mind, he was hardly aware of his duties or his surroundings. He was oblivious to the biting cold, the stark, empty, white-sheeted enclosure, the soaring curtain wall he was resting against and, in the distance, the brooding manor house of Maubisson. He was truly facing his own sea of troubles. Not only did he have Lady Adelicia's imprisonment to deal with, and the charges which might be laid against him; there was also the business of the Cloister Map and, of course — Wendover shook himself from his day-dreaming — the safeguarding of Maubisson. He left the shelter of the curtain wall and gazed across the hard-packed snow at the manor house, a huddle of dark buildings ranged along the brow of a hill. He could glimpse slivers of light between the shutters over the narrow windows. As he walked closer, straining his eyes, he could make out the outline of the great hall with its gabled wings either end, as well as its porch and steps lit by flickering cresset torches fixed in sconces on either side of the cavernous main door. A strange place, Maubisson. Given a French name by a God-obsessed merchant who had decided to build a church in the old English style that existed before the Conqueror came. A long nave had been raised, really nothing more than a hall; a tower was supposed to be added, but the merchant went to his eternal reward before his idea ever took shape. There had been no consecration and Maubisson had fallen into the hands of the Crown and the city corporation. Over the years other wings had been attached: two-storey buildings of plaster and wood on a stone base which formed a quadrangle with an arched double gateway at the back; that gate, together with the courtyard within, was closely guarded by Wendover's men, as was each side of the building as well as the front door.

Wendover stared up at the sky. Night was fading; soon it would be morning. He moved further away. All was still. The owl in the trees had flown on, whilst the dog fox yipping at the cold as it hunted in the undergrowth along the curtain wall had fallen silent. Wendover began to walk the perimeter. He checked the guards as far as he could see, but the snowdrift was rather too deep for the arduous climb up the hill to the porch, so instead he returned to the main gate, sighing with relief at the shelter it provided. He wondered how the foreigners inside were coping. Had they recovered from their journey sickness? Castledene, as well as that interfering city physician Desroches, had been most insistent that Paulents and his family be kept safe and secure. Wendover suspected that the knight was more concerned about protecting the precious possessions of the merchant than anything else.

Wendover walked across to the campfire, crouching down amongst the other city guards to warm his hands and take his share of the strips of meat cooked to almost black on the oil-soaked pans thrust into the flames. He drank some watered wine and waited. At last it came: the bells of the cathedral, St Augustine's and other city churches tolling the hour for Lauds and the Jesus Mass. He rose to his feet, tightened his belt, pulled his cloak about him and walked towards the main door. He felt tired, and the journey up the slight incline where the snow had drifted deeply seemed to take an age. He shouted at one of the guards on the main steps to come and help him. The man floundered down to meet him holding a lantern.

"Thanks be to God," the guard yelled, extending a staff for Wendover to grip. "At least it's stopped snowing."

Wendover grunted in reply as he grasped the pole and pulled himself forward, free of the drift. He climbed the steps to where the rest of his guards were grouped around the fire at the top, lifted the heavy brass door weight, carved in the shape of a mailed fist, and brought it down. He could hear the crashing echo through the hall beyond, but it brought no response . . .

The dungeons beneath the Guildhall in Canterbury were fetid, rank holes, but Lady Adelicia Decontet had been given the best: this stood at the end of a mildewed passageway, a small, narrow chamber sealed off by a heavy door with a grille at the top. The jailor liked to joke that it was the most luxurious of his lodgings, reserved for prisoners awaiting either trial or their final journey in the hangman's cart to the gallows outside the city gates. Lady Adelicia now sat in the corner of the cell, warming herself over a dish of coals and staring around in the light of a thick, evil-smelling tallow candle which she'd paid the jailor to fix on an iron hook driven into the wall. She had read and studied all the graffiti etched there: names and initials, sometimes prayers — "Jesu Miserere, Maria Mater" — but in the main curses or lewd and obscene drawings. She was manacled like the rest of the prisoners, though the chains were long enough for her to move to the small table and the scraps of food on a pewter dish, shreds of salted beef, rye bread and hard cheese, which she'd also purchased from the jailor. She stared up at the great cobwebs spanning each corner under the filthy roof, and down at the straw on the floor which, despite her pleas, hadn't been changed. It was wet, stinking and rotting black. Thankfully the cell walls were thick and kept some of the cold out, while the chafing dish was generously heaped with sparkling charcoal. The smell of burning was a welcome relief from the foul odours which curled everywhere. She tried to close her ears to the cries and shouts of other prisoners, the banging at doors and the cursing of jailors. She'd been supplied with silver and had bribed her keepers well. At least she could eat, was allowed some form of movement, given a jakes pot and, every third day, handed a bowl of water and a rag to wash and clean herself. The pallet bed had also been sheeted and provided with two woollen rugs to wrap herself in when she eventually did decide to sleep.

Any other woman would have been terrified at the prospect facing her, but Lady Adelicia was cold and impassive, her mind teeming like a busy beehive. She knew she was no murderess. True, she'd hated her husband — who wouldn't? — with his dirty, cunning ways, slobbering mouth, and small hard eyes like two piss-holes in the snow! An old fox, with his pointed face, scrawny red hair and protuberant ears. A man wealthy enough to buy anything he wanted, yet he ate, lived and smelt like the poorest peasant, a miser to the bone, hard of face and hard of heart, with a foul temper and a tongue coated in venom. Adelicia, a royal ward, had been married off to the King's money-lender; she had never forgotten that, and neither had Sir Rauf.

Adelicia shivered, not so much from the cold but at the thought of her dead husband's hands on her, forcing her head down, making her perform all sorts of abominable practices. In despair, she had prayed. She had visited the House of the Crutched Friars, sat in their shriving pew and whispered her confession, but what relief could they offer? She'd gone before the lady altar, lit tapers, prayed her Ave beads, but there was no escape or respite until Berengaria had arrived. She was a foundling raised by the parish who had done great service in the household of one of Sir Rauf's clients. When the man had gone bankrupt, Sir Rauf, true to form, had seized all his goods, and Berengaria, a sly minx of about sixteen summers, with saucy eyes and a cheeky mouth, became part of their household. In a short time she and Adelicia had become allies, though not friends. They understood each other. Adelicia would give Berengaria coins, favour her, and allow her liberties never permitted before, and when she had met Wendover, the girl had come into her own.

Adelicia closed her eyes. The Crutched Friar who'd advised her in the shriving pew was right! The road to hell was broad, easy and slippery. One sin led to many greater. Small gifts, coy glances, secret meetings and furtive kisses: in the end they had become intimate and Wendover had proved to be an ardent lover, a welcome relief from Sir Rauf, though recently Adelicia had grown tired of the chattering youth behind Wendover's tough warrior pretence. Oh, and how Wendover liked to talk, especially about himself and his past exploits as a mercenary, and how they would find the Cloister Map, their path to wealth and riches. What golden prospects the future held! Adelicia would listen to him, as she had on that cold December afternoon before falling asleep. When she'd woken, Wendover had gone. He often did that. Sometimes she found coins or petty gee-gaws missing. At first she couldn't believe he was a sneak-foist, a pilferer of pennies, when he was supposed to be her accomplice in the search for greater things, yet the evidence was there. Was he also a murderer? Adelicia wondered. On that fateful afternoon had Wendover slipped towards her house and killed Sir Rauf? He had often talked of her being a widow, about what she would do if Sir Rauf died. True, the preachers sermonised about God's will, but would a man like Wendover be prepared to give God's will a helping hand? Had Wendover killed Sir Rauf?

Adelicia turned quickly and screamed at the rat racing across the table; she shook her chains and the vermin disappeared. She thought again of that afternoon. She stood accused of murdering her husband after a violent quarrel. She had rejected such a charge, pointing to the nonsense of it all, yet the accusations remained and now hung over her like a hangman's noose. Lady Adelicia was no fool. She was a high-born lady accused of dashing out her husband's brains. Her cloak had been stained with his blood; gore-soaked napkins had been found in her bedchamber, so what hope did she have before twelve good burgesses whose ears would have been bent by their wives as they whispered their honeyed poison?

So far, Adelicia had kept her own counsel. She had said nothing about Wendover, or their trysts at The Chequer of Hope. Who would believe her? She was cunning and quick enough to realise that it would only go against her. She would be cast as an adulteress as well as an assassin. No, Adelicia had other plans. She knew a little of the law; she would turn King's Approver. If Castledene accused her of being an assassin, well, she would accuse Sir Rauf of being a murderer. After all, she knew about Stonecrop, what her husband had done; the evidence was there for all to see, that corpse rotting away in the desolate garden of Sweetmead Manor. She would blame Sir Rauf for that and make no mention of the Cloister Map or her relentless search for it. What else should she fear? Berengaria? The little minx was now lodged with Parson Warfeld, apparently unmoved by the horrors around her. Berengaria acted like a cat who'd licked the cream bowl clean, as if savouring secrets known only to herself. Sharp memories pricked Adelicia's mind, glimpses caught through a half-open door of Sir Rauf stroking Berengaria's hair. Would the girl remain loyal? And Wendover, with his arrogance and pilfering ways, what would he say?

Lady Adelicia clutched her stomach. Whom could she trust? In the end she had made the right decision. Castledene knew she had been a royal ward and had forwarded her petition to the King. Edward was now sending his own man into the city. Adelicia nodded to herself and moved towards the table, eager to take another mouthful of watery ale. She would talk to the King's man and no one else.

CHAPTER
TWO

Ecce, nocturno tempore orto brumali turbine.
Behold, at night-time the storm breaks.

Columba

Sir Hugh Corbett was roughly roused from his bedchamber at the guesthouse of St Augustine's Abbey by a heavy-eyed lay brother, hands fluttering, who stammered the usual monastic benediction before hastily adding that Sir Walter Castledene had arrived. The Mayor of Canterbury was deeply agitated, so the lay brother declared, waiting below with his retinue in the refectory. Castledene was insisting that the King's emissary accompany him immediately to Maubisson.

Corbett aroused Ranulf and Chanson in the adjoining chamber, going in and out as he hastily dressed, kicking Chanson's bed, leaning over Ranulf to shout at the heavy-eyed clerk to prepare himself. Corbett pulled on his spurred boots, gathered up his war belt and cloak and hurried down the torchlit staircase. Sir Walter had left the refectory and was waiting impatiently in the hallway; his horsemen milled in the cobbled yard beyond, their mounts snorting and kicking at the cobbles. The torches carried by the riders spluttered sparks through the freezing cold air, making the horses even more skittish. The greetings between mayor and clerk were brief but cordial. Corbett knew

Castledene of old. They'd fought in Segrave's mounted brigade at Falkirk five years earlier. Corbett would never forget that fight. The English longbowmen had broken Wallace's schiltrons and the heavy mailed cavalry of Lord Segrave had poured in, phalanx after phalanx of armoured knights, to bring the remnants of the Scots to battle, mace against club, sword against stabbing dirk, a frenzy of blood-spilling which still haunted Corbett's dreams.

"Sir Walter." Corbett stepped back. "What is the matter?"

Despite being a wealthy man, a powerful citizen, Castledene looked dishevelled and tired; his wiry frame cloaked in a simple cote-hardie, quilted jerkin and hose above battered riding boots, his lean face drained of all colour.

"You'd best come to Maubisson, Sir Hugh. I have dreadful news." Castledene glanced fearfully over his shoulder at his retinue. Mailed men-at-arms clustered in the entrance; others stood outside amongst the horsemen. The mayor hardly gave the guest master, who now came hurrying down, a second glance whilst he curtly nodded at Ranulf and gestured at the door.

"Sir Hugh, come, for God's sake! We have to go to Maubisson! Paulents and all his family are dead!"

"Dead?"

"Hanged like a coven of felons! Do you understand me, Sir Hugh? Hanged here within the King's peace and under our protection!"

"How?"

Castledene didn't answer; he was already moving towards the door. All thoughts Sir Hugh had had of joining the good brothers in their stalls and participating in the glory of plainchant were quickly forgotten. He muttered his apologies to the guest master and followed Castledene. Horses were hastily trotted out and saddled, the yard noisy with hooves clattering over cobbles. Ranulf shouted at the grooms to check girth and stirrups. Corbett, half asleep and freezing cold, mounted, gathered the reins and then they were away, cantering out of the abbey yard along a narrow icy lane leading down to the Dover road. Corbett was aware of the jingle of harness, the snorts of horses and the quiet curses of men cantering through the freezing grey dawn. They passed carts lumbering into the city. He glimpsed lantern lights, flickering flames, a lonely lamp glowing in an arched window, but then the dark swept in around them. The road was slightly raised; carts and wagons had already shifted the fallen snow but it was still dangerous going. Two horses went down and they and their riders had to be left behind. At last the comitatus reached the trackway stretching down to Maubisson. Here the snow was so deep they had to dismount and walk their horses towards the iron-studded gateway in the curtain wall of the manor. This was ablaze with torchlight from flambeaux fixed in sconces or on poles driven into the ground. More guards clustered here, all wearing the livery of the city beneath their cowled cloaks: three ravens against a blue and gold background.

The captain of the guard, Wendover, hastily introduced himself and led them along a narrow path, still buried deep under snow, up the main steps and into the manor hall. The rest of the retinue hung back. Castledene went forward, followed by Wendover, Ranulf and Chanson. As Corbett entered, he gazed around and gasped. He had experienced all forms of horror: he had wandered battlefields where the dead lay thick like some blood-coated robe strewn across God's earth; he'd stumbled over corpses hacked and cut, past cadavers swinging from trees, eloquent witness of man's cruelty to man; he'd ridden through villages annihilated like any City of the Plain in the Old Testament, where cottages and houses were blackened shells and the wells were crammed to the brim with the blue-black remains of the decomposing dead.

Maubisson Hall, however, possessed a unique, frightening dreadfulness. At first glance the chamber was an exquisitely comfortable one, with dais, tables, benches and chairs; tapestries and coloured stiffened cloths hung against the walls. Candlelight glittered from precious vessels, whilst smoke still curled from the mantled hearth and the air was faintly sweet with the odours of cooking. These just emphasised the hideousness of the corpses: silent, twisting shadows hanging by their necks, held tight by thick tarred rope. Dangling from ugly iron brackets driven into the wall, the corpses were suspended like half-empty sacks; legs, feet, arms and hands trailing, heads slightly turned as if peering into the darkness beyond.

Corbett ignored the exclamations of those around him and walked across. He studied the stout L-shaped brackets, pieces of iron hammered into the wall either side of the shuttered windows from which lanterns could be slung. Near each corpse a stool or chair had been pushed away. Corbett had seen enough hanged men and women to last him a thousand lifetimes: corpses blacker than charcoal, cavities carved from their eyes by yellow-beaked crows, faces pitted and holed by kites, hollow bones rattling beneath tattered rags. In contrast the Maubisson corpses seemed almost alive, except for those half-open glassy eyes, gaping mouths and protuberant tongues.

"An entire family," he murmured.

"Where is Servinus?" Castledene exclaimed. "Their bodyguard? He's not here!"

Corbett only half heard him, eyes straining up through the darkness. He wanted to catch the expressions on those dead faces, to remember their ghastliness so that when he began to pursue their assassin he would never forget, show no mercy, offer no pardon.

He stepped back. "Cut them down!" He gestured at Ranulf, shaking his head in an attempt to clear from his mind the nightmare image of his own family in such a hideous situation. "For God's sake, man!" he added to Castledene. "This is an abomination! Have them cut down."

They all helped. Tables, chairs and stools were pushed close, daggers drawn. Corbett tried to ignore the hiss of trapped air from the corpses as the nooses

round their necks were cut. At length all four —
Paulents, his wife, their son and their young
flaxen-haired maid — lay side by side on the floor.

"I've sent for Parson Warfeld from St Alphege's,"
Castledene declared, "as well as the city physician Peter
Desroches. They'll both be here soon."

Corbett crouched at the feet of the row of corpses.
Paulents' face was slightly contorted; his wife and son
and the maid looked as if they were asleep: so young,
yet they were all marred by that gruesome purple-blue
circle round their throats, the strange colour of their
skin, the way their lips appeared swollen. Corbett tried
to ignore the dead faces as he carefully inspected wrists
and nails, the backs of hands and heads, sniffing at
parted lips. He pressed his hand against Paulents' face,
then felt the muscles of the shoulder, chest and
stomach.

"They must have been dead some hours," he
declared. "At least to my reckoning, their corpses are
beginning to stiffen."

"Desroches will examine them," Castledene declared.

"Aye, and so will I, Sir Walter." Corbett continued
his scrutiny. "*Mirabile dictu!*" he exclaimed, getting to
his feet.

"What, master?" Ranulf came over, beads of sweat
lacing his brow, his usual reaction to the sight of any
hanging. It was a fate he himself had almost suffered
many years earlier, being saved only by Corbett's
intervention.

"*Mirabile dictu,*" Corbett repeated. "Marvellous to
say! I've inspected the corpses, at least cursorily, yet I

can detect no mark or blow, no sign of force or poison." He shrugged. "As I've said, at least to my scrutiny." Corbett walked towards the dais, ever watchful of who was now in the hall. Castledene was standing over the corpses. Wendover and Chanson guarded the doorway; the retinue stood behind them staring in at this abomination.

"No one has touched anything?" Corbett turned to Wendover.

"Nobody, sir," the captain retorted. "I'll go on oath. I came in." He gestured across to the corpses. "I saw those. I immediately left and sent a message to Sir Walter. Everyone had to wait outside until my lord arrived."

Corbett noted Wendover's obsequiousness to Castledene. He stepped on to the dais and stared at the table laid out so elegantly.

"Everything can be accounted for," Wendover sang out. "Not a porringer, goblet or platter will be found missing."

Corbett grunted and moved along the table: five chairs, no sign of a sixth. Paulents must have occupied the thronelike chair in the centre, his wife on his right, his son on his left; further down the maid and the hired mercenary Servinus. They'd apparently eaten well: the main platters bore the remains of pastry, chicken, slices of beef and some sauce now dried hard. The tablecloth was of shimmering white linen. Corbett glimpsed stains, some minuscule black dots. He bent down and studied one of the platters. Mice and other rodents had apparently been busy. He scrutinised the wine goblets, jugs and water beakers. He could neither smell nor detect anything tainted. No sign of disturbance was evident. The chairs were pushed in to the table whilst the rushes on the floor betrayed no marks of bodies having been pulled from the table, dragged off the dais towards those dreadful iron brackets.

"Master?"

"Yes, Ranulf." Corbett turned.

"Do you think it could have been suicide?"

Corbett shook his head. "No, this was foul murder, a massacre." He pointed down at the corpses. "Their killer isn't trying to mislead us but terrify us. This, he or she is saying, is how I deal out death."

"She?" Castledene came over.

"No." Corbett shook his head. "That was a mistake. A man, a powerful one, cunning and deadly, is responsible for this."

"But how?" Castledene hissed.

"Sir Walter, I need urgent words with you alone. Ranulf, guard the hall. Allow no one but the parson and physician to enter." Corbett extended a hand. "Sir Walter, there must be a chamber above stairs? Ask for braziers to be placed there, fired and glowing, but no wine or food, nothing from here." He walked over to Wendover. "You've searched the rest of the manor house?"

"Once I sent the messenger, yes, sir, from attic to cellar, stable and outhouse. We found nothing untoward, nothing sinister, no sign of forced entry."

"And when you came in, no one could have slipped out?"

"My lord," Wendover gestured at the men thronging behind him, "they're all city guards wearing the corporation livery."

"So?"

"And we had a password."

"Which was?"

"Maubisson," Wendover replied. "One guard always called that out to any other. No stranger, no intruder was seen either entering or leaving."

"So where is Servinus, Paulents' bodyguard?"

"Nowhere," Wendover gabbled. "God knows, Sir Hugh! We've searched, we were vigilant. There is, was, no sign of him!"

Corbett nodded. Whilst Castledene hurried to prepare an upstairs chamber, Corbett returned to the corpses. In truth, the more he observed, the longer he walked that darkening chamber with those gruesome corpses laid out stark on the floor, the more mystified he became. It certainly wasn't suicide, yet there was no mark of violence, of intrusion, no sign of any assassin. Nothing except the four corpses and the fact that Servinus was missing. He turned round. Wendover was standing in the doorway talking to one of his guards.

"You, sir." Corbett called him over. "Why were Paulents and his family so closely guarded?"

"They had fallen sick, my lord."

"What do you mean?"

"They had some sickness. That is why Sir Walter had them housed safely here."

"But they were supposed to lodge here anyway."

"Yes." Wendover shrugged. "Sir Hugh, you must ask Sir Walter that yourself."

Corbett stared at the captain as if seeing him for the first time. Wendover shuffled his booted feet, plucked at a loose thread on his woollen legging, then adjusted the battered war belt round his waist. Corbett crouched down by one of the corpses and continued his close scrutiny. Wendover, he believed, was highly nervous. He was youngish-looking, with curly brown hair, fair-faced and bright-eyed, but a man who probably hid behind his livery. The weapons, the leather hauberk, even Wendover's neatly clipped dark brown moustache and beard, indicated a man in love with the pretence of himself. Corbett glanced sideways. He noticed the cheap rings on the stubby fingers, the leather brace around Wendover's left wrist, the gleam of oil on his hair and beard. A lady's man, he concluded, a boaster who revelled in his own calling and status.

"My lord, what do you think?" Wendover asked, eager to break the silence.

"Murder," Corbett replied. "Heinous murder. And as the old proverb has it, murder will out. There's also another saying, Master Wendover." He watched the captain gulp nervously. "Evil shall have what evil deserves." Corbett rose to his feet.

Wendover tried to control his fear. As first he'd regarded this royal clerk as a May-day boy, but now, standing there cloaked like a raven, black hair swept back, those sharp eyes staring at him from that sombre, watchful face, Corbett frightened him, as did that other one, similarly dressed, with his red hair and keen green eyes. Wendover heard a sound and glanced over his shoulder. Ranulf was standing close behind him.

"So, sir," Corbett took a step closer, plucking at the cords on Wendover's leather jerkin, "did you see anything untoward here? Anything, sir, on your allegiance to the King. After all," Corbett added coldly, "you were on guard."

"I saw nothing!" Wendover spluttered, stepping back, but Ranulf pushed him forward again.

"Sir Hugh?" Castledene was standing in the doorway to the kitchen. "No need for your games here, Sir Hugh, or yours, Master Ranulf."

"No games." Corbett went over to the merchant prince. "Oh no." He shook his head. "No games, Sir Walter, I assure you. Someone will hang for this!"

A short while later Corbett made himself comfortable in the high-backed chair in one of the upper chambers. Castledene sat facing him across the long, narrow table. Beside either chair was a warming brazier full of sparkling charcoal. A six-branched candelabra, each spigot holding a pure beeswax taper, glowed lucidly, the flames dancing like angels in the cold air of the chamber. On the wall behind Sir Walter was a triptych depicting Simeon and Anna greeting the Divine Child in the Temple of Jerusalem. Corbett studied this as he deliberately allowed the silence to continue. Then he glanced round, taking in the heavily draped cot-bed in the corner, the bedside table with its chequered top, the mullioned glass door-window high in the wall, the turkey rugs on the floor, the coffers, and caskets grouped around the iron-bound chest at the foot of the bed.

"Sir Hugh, you have questions?"

"I certainly have, Sir Walter. A comfortable chamber," Corbett observed. "Every luxury for your friend."

"The King commanded it."

"The King commanded it," Corbett echoed. "You have checked Paulents' treasure chests and coffers?"

"I . . ."

"Sir Walter," Corbett leaned forward, "you are Mayor of Canterbury. Paulents was your friend and I mourn for him as I do for his wife, son and maid, but you also act for the King in this matter, as do I." He held up his left hand, displaying the chancery ring. "I am not your friend, Sir Walter. Nevertheless, you and I," he gestured across the table, "have fought for our lives on the battlefields of Scotland and Wales, so let's not play the clever man of law, the shrewd merchant. Tell me honestly: after he arrived here, did Paulents show you the secret coffer in his private chamber?" He let his hand fall with a crash. "Please, Sir Walter, the truth."

"I am not a plaintiff before King's Bench."

"You could be." Corbett shrugged. "I could serve writs on you for refusing to answer. Sir Walter," he leaned across the table, "four of God's children lie foully murdered downstairs. Servinus their bodyguard has disappeared. They were all the King's guests, foreigners who entered this kingdom with royal approval and licence. They fell under the Crown's protection. Edward will want answers. So, are we going to engage in cat's cradle? Hodman's bluff? Answer and question? Point and counterpoint? If we are, Sir Walter, I'll take you back to London and loose Berenger, Staunton and the other royal justices on you. They'll savage you like mastiffs."

"Sir Hugh?" Castledene held his hand up.

"From the beginning," Corbett warned. "The truth, simple and stark; no fables, no subtle deceits."

"It's true what you say, Sir Hugh," Castledene began slowly. "We have fought on the same battlefields. I am the King's man but I'm also a Canterbury man. My grandfather's father was born here. I was raised here. I went to school in Christchurch Cloister. I love this city. Being a second son," he sighed, "gave me little advantage, so I joined the King's household and, as you know, showed courage — or at least didn't betray my fear — in Wales and Scotland. I won the King's favour and a number of valuable ransoms, and I came back to Canterbury, where I married. My poor wife died; she now lies buried in God's acre at St Dunstan's. I put all my energy and talent into building up trade and business; you name the item and I sell it, especially wool. Sir Hugh, the markets of France, Brabant, Hainault and Italy are greedy for our wool. I bought land. I raised sheep. I sold wool then I bought ships. Merchants from different countries, Sir Hugh, have a lot in common with chancery clerks. We speak the same language." He flailed his hand. "We meet and talk to each other. There are no differences when it comes to trade, be it Germany, Brabant, Castile or Aragon.

Money always talks, it breaks the barriers; it is almost as powerful," he smiled thinly, "as God's grace.

"In London I met Paulents, a Hanseatic merchant. I liked him, I visited him and he visited me. We entered into trade negotiations, nothing remarkable. Now Paulents was also a scholar very interested in the history of England, particularly its eastern shrines. He was always fascinated by the stories of how his ancestors, the Angles, Saxons and Jutes, invaded this island. Anyway, about four or five years ago Paulents found an entry in a chronicle apparently written by some warrior who'd fled from England to Germany, where he later took vows and entered a monastery. When he was in England this former warrior had attended the funeral of a great Saxon king which was celebrated with fabulous ostentation. He talked about a ship of gold, laden with treasure, buried beneath the fields of eastern England. Now the chronicle he wrote," Castledene held his hand up, "contained a map in the shape of a monastic cloister: a square with pillars around its garth. According to Paulents, this Cloister Map shows the treasure to be buried beneath wasteland somewhere in south Suffolk near the River Denham. Paulents trusted me fully; he copied this map and sent it to me, but it never arrived. You see, Sir Hugh, the richer I became, the more I attracted the attention of other people. In the year of the Gascon War, 1296, an audacious privateer had appeared on the sea-roads, a man I knew vaguely: Adam Blackstock, a former citizen of Canterbury, half-brother to Hubert the Monk. You know the details of their past. The chancery at

Westminster must have informed you. Well, Blackstock proved himself to be a ruthless, indomitable fighter as well as a most skilled mariner. Eventually he owned his own ship, *The Waxman*. Now here is a problem, Sir Hugh . . ." Castledene paused.

"What problem?" Corbett asked.

"Blackstock and *The Waxman* were certainly patronised by leading merchants, even here in Canterbury. I always suspected Sir Rauf Decontet secretly supported him."

"Was there any personal animosity," Corbett asked, "between you and Blackstock?"

Sir Walter shrugged. "Blackstock was a citizen of Canterbury, as was I, but we never met. He became a pirate and lived beyond the law. He sank some of my ships. He also attacked Hanse merchant cogs." He smiled wryly. "It became personal when *The Maid of Lübeck*, belonging to Paulents, was attacked and plundered, for it was also carrying the precious Cloister Map. Paulents, myself and Edward of England decided to act."

"But something went wrong."

"No," Castledene replied with a sigh, "something went right. Paulents came across Blackstock's lieutenant, a sly, eerie man called Stonecrop, in a Brabantine port. Blackstock had dispatched him there on some errand. Now Paulents could have hanged Stonecrop out of hand; instead the man turned traitor and told us exactly what had happened. First that Blackstock had intercepted the Cloister Map. Second that he had communicated this valuable find to his half-brother.

Third that he was planning to sail back to Orwell to meet Hubert and unearth the treasure. It was easy to establish the times and dates of his proposed landfall."

Castledene paused at a noise below.

"Parson Warfeld and Desroches the physician have arrived," he declared.

Corbett shrugged. "They have their tasks to do and so have we. Please continue."

"We trapped and boarded *The Waxman* and subdued its crew, but Blackstock refused to surrender —"

"Was he hanged?" Corbett intervened.

"No, we killed him and gibbeted his corpse."

"And Stonecrop?" Corbett asked.

"I threw him overboard," Castledene declared. "He was worthless. I could have hanged him but he deserved a slight chance. I've never heard or seen of him since. He probably died in the swollen icy seas. We searched Blackstock's cabin but found nothing. The Cloister Map had disappeared; there was nothing but an empty coffer fashioned out of whalebone."

"And then what?" Corbett asked. "You must tell me, Sir Walter! Be precise, because I believe all this has a bearing on what we've seen tonight."

"I was angry," Castledene confessed. "We took *The Waxman* in tow and sailed up the Orwell, but when we reached the Hermitage there was no sign of Hubert." He shrugged and spread his hands. "That was the last we ever heard of him or the treasure."

"Were there any survivors," Corbett asked, "apart from Stonecrop?"

"No." Castledene shook his head. "Those who weren't killed were hanged. We showed no mercy to anybody."

"And then what?"

"Paulents returned to Germany and began searching for a fresh copy of the Cloister Map. The chronicle he'd first discovered was very ancient. It had passed through his hands and he had copied it. You know what it's like, Sir Hugh: precious manuscripts are jealously guarded by the scriptoria, libraries and chanceries of monastic houses. Paulents thought he would never find it again, but even so he searched furiously for it. The problem was that he could never tell people why he needed it. Eventually he found a copy of the manuscript in the library of the Shrine of the Three Kings at Cologne. He transcribed the map again, then wrote to me suggesting that he come to England and, with my help and that of the King, search for the treasure."

"Were Paulents and his entourage ill when they landed at Dover?" Corbett asked. "Wendover claimed they were suffering from some sickness."

Castledene shrugged. "They were certainly ill, though of what I am not sure. I sought the advice of the city physician, Desroches. Paulents' family said they felt clammy and tired. I certainly wished to keep them safe."

Corbett studied this cunning merchant carefully. "That's not entirely true," he declared. "There was something else, wasn't there?"

Castledene looked as if he was about to deny it, but then he opened the wallet on his belt, took out two pieces of parchment and slid them across the table to Corbett.

"Read them."

Corbett picked up the scraps of manuscript; the words on them were carefully written in a clerkly hand.

Thus says Hubert, son of Fitzurse, the Man with the Far-Seeing Gaze. You have been weighed in the balance. Your days have been numbered. You have been found wanting.

The other piece of parchment bore the same message. Corbett glanced up. "When were these delivered?"

"One to Paulents at his tavern in Dover; the other was handed to me in Canterbury. Hubert Fitzurse, Blackstock's half-brother, must be responsible."

"I thought you said he'd vanished?"

"He had, but apparently he has now reappeared. True, Paulents and his family felt ill, but the guards at Maubisson were not posted against sickness . . ." Castledene gestured at the parchment. "Rather against those threats, as well as to protect the precious manuscript Paulents had brought."

Castledene excused himself, got to his feet, scraping back the chair, and left the chamber. He returned with an exquisitely carved whalebone coffer set in wood with moulded clasps on the front. He fished a bunch of keys from his robe, opened the lock and undid the clasps.

"Those are Paulents' keys?" Corbett asked.

"Yes," Castledene confessed. "I found them in the pocket of his robe."

"You should have told me!" Corbett warned. "I never saw you do that."

"Sir Hugh, I cannot trust everybody. When we examined those corpses, others were milling about. I had to make sure. I took the keys and searched Paulents' chamber. You can see that for yourself. Nothing has been disturbed and neither has this coffer." He pulled back the lid and drew out two rolls of parchment. The first was a list of monies Paulents had in England. Corbett could make no sense of the second document; various letters and symbols were strewn across a drawing closely resembling the cloisters of a monastery.

"The Cloister Map," Castledene murmured.

"I'll keep this," Corbett retorted. "Ranulf will make a fair copy and return it to you, but I must keep the original."

Castledene reluctantly agreed. Corbett slipped the manuscript into his own wallet.

"These warnings," Corbett leaned across the table, "were delivered both to Paulents and to you?"

Castledene nodded.

"So . . ." Corbett picked at a wax stain on the tabletop. "Paulents arrives in England, he feels unwell. In Dover he receives a threatening message; in Canterbury you receive the same, which means that Hubert, Blackstock's half-brother, must be hunting both of you."

"Which is why I had to keep my guests safe. Paulents and I discussed the warnings. We concluded that the safest place was Maubisson, with a strong guard around the hall and in its courtyard. No one could hurt them here."

"You could have moved them elsewhere: the castle?"

"No, no!" Castledene shook his head. "Paulents was very determined on that. He believed he was safe under my protection. Maubisson is on the Dover Road, close to Canterbury, and can be easily guarded."

"And how was that arranged?"

"Furnishings were brought in." Castledene gestured around. "Food and provisions. The guards were always here. Nothing untoward happened. Paulents arrived late yesterday morning. I and Physician Desroches greeted him and his family. We brought them in here and housed them securely. I took Paulents around the manor, showing him where things were. Desroches then left, and I followed soon afterwards."

"And yet," Corbett declared, "within hours Paulents and his family were brutally murdered. But how? That provokes further mystery. Paulents was not an old man; he was strong, so was his wife, his son, even the maid; yet no one resisted. No one raised the alarm. How could anyone have got in here and hanged all four without being detected?"

CHAPTER
THREE

Quod non vertat iniquia dies.
And so it comes, the wicked day.

Rabanus Maurus

Corbett scratched his chin, trying to ignore the cold, prickling fear in his stomach. He felt heavy-eyed, repelled by the lurking menace of this desolate manor house, now reeking of a mysterious malevolence.

"There's Servinus," Castledene remarked, "the bodyguard: a tall, burly man, head all shaven, dressed in black leather and armed to the teeth."

"Did Paulents trust him?"

"Yes, Servinus had worked for at least a year in his household: a Brandenburger, a mercenary who'd fought with the Teutonic knights. Servinus was sober and taciturn; he'd stare at you but hardly speak, a shadow who knew his place. He too had suffered from the rough crossing, complaining in broken English about the sea salt getting everywhere. He seemed pleased to be here, satisfied with this house, calling it a 'donjon' — a place of safety."

"So where is he now?" Corbett wondered aloud. "Is he the killer? Did he flee? But how? Why? A Brandenburger, a foreigner in Canterbury in the depth of winter, would find it difficult to hide." Corbett moved restlessly. "And how could he kill four people so silently and escape so easily from what he himself called a donjon?"

"I have issued a description . . ." Castledene murmured, his voice trailing off.

"Let's return to the obvious," Corbett insisted. "We know that Blackstock had a half-brother. We know that you sailed down the Orwell to the Hermitage with Blackstock's corpse dangling by the neck from the poop of *The Caltrop*. This must be Hubert's vengeance. Paulents hanged his brother, so he has now hanged Paulents' family."

"But why? I mean why now?"

Corbett shook his head, picked up the Cloister Map and stared at it. "I'll try and decipher this, discover what the truth is. For the moment, let us return downstairs."

They left the chamber, going down the rickety wooden staircase into the kitchen and buttery, then back into the hall. Parson Warfeld, a rubicund, smooth-faced man, was busy amongst the corpses. He'd brought a boy holding a taper and was now anointing the corpses with holy oil, dabbing their heads, eyes, lips, chests, hands and feet whilst he whispered the sacred words, urging the souls of the dead to go out and be greeted by the angels. Another man was sitting in the throne-like chair behind the dais. Castledene took Corbett over and introduced Peter Desroches, the city physician, former scholar of Salerno and Montpellier. Desroches was of medium height, thick-set, with blond hair neatly cropped above a pleasant, smiling face. He was dressed in a dark blue serge tunic gathered around his waist by a silver cord; precious rings winked on his fingers as did a bracelet about his wrist. He was clean-shaven, fresh-faced, eyes twinkling with amusement as he clasped Corbett's hand.

"I've heard of you, Sir Hugh. Your reputation precedes you."

"In what connection, sir?"

"Oh, this and that." Desroches smiled. "I follow the affairs of the court most closely. One day I hope to obtain preferment there. Now this matter, it is heinous and hateful." He pushed back the chair and got to his feet. "Sir Hugh, all four were hanged. None of them resisted; there were no scuff marks, no signs of violence. And look at this."

He led Corbett out of the hall into the small porch. Two of the city guards were sitting on the stone bench just inside the doorway, intently watching a rat scrabble around in a wire-mesh cage, its sharp little claws pattering on an empty wooden platter.

"When I arrived," Desroches explained, "I asked one of the guards to catch a rat. I put it in the cage, and mixed a platter of every scrap from the different dishes, then laced it with wine and water. Paulents and his family ate and drank the same. Look, there's no ill effect."

"So they weren't poisoned or drugged."

"Precisely," the physician agreed. "Nothing at all." He crouched down, staring at the rat, a fat brown rodent with curling tail and aggressive snout. "So far, no signs of any poisoning." Desroches rose to his feet. "I have used this method before. If food is tainted or poisoned, the rat will soon manifest symptoms, but not here. Indeed," he lifted a finger portentously, "some people even maintain that a rat can smell tainted food and will avoid it. That is certainly not the case here."

Corbett walked back into the hall. He stood just within the doorway, hands on his hips, and stared at the four corpses now hidden under blankets on the floor. He could make no sense of this. "Wendover," he called over his shoulder. The captain of the guard came hurrying up. "You were responsible for preparing Maubisson?"

"Yes, my lord," Wendover agreed quickly. "We began yesterday morning. Everything was ready as you see it now: kitchen provisions, buttery stores, rooms furnished, the walls adorned with hangings, braziers filled ready to be fired, the hearth cleaned, everything Sir Walter wanted."

"And then what?" Corbett asked.

"We left early yesterday," Wendover replied. "Everyone withdrew. I personally checked every chamber. There was no one here. We all gathered at the gateway, waiting for Sir Walter's guests to arrive. They did so around midday. Sir Walter himself brought them here."

"And then what?"

"Monsieur Desroches visited them."

"Master Physician," Corbett called, "would you join us here?"

Desroches walked over.

"You met Paulents and his family here?"

"Yes, that's right, early in the afternoon. They complained of seasickness, of feeling hot and feverish. I didn't know whether it was due to the dire conditions at sea or if they'd been infected by some contagion. I thought it best if they stayed here. Well," he amended, "Sir Walter and Paulents insisted on that, but they all seemed in good heart."

"They certainly recovered their appetites." Corbett gestured at the table. "They ate and drank well."

"As I said," Desroches smiled, "it may have just been the rigours of the journey. They seemed in good humour."

"And you noticed nothing untoward?"

"Nothing at all," Desroches agreed. "I left shortly afterwards."

Corbett crossed to the mantled hearth and stared down at the smouldering fire. Here was a manor, he reflected, closely guarded, its entrance, curtain wall, even the courtyard within the enclosure, all locked and barred. Little wonder: Paulents had realised he was in danger; he had been warned and threatened. And yet in one evening, he and his family had been massacred.

"Sir Walter," Corbett called over his shoulder, "you are sure nothing is missing?"

"Nothing at all," the merchant replied.

Corbett turned to Ranulf standing by the wall and gestured him over.

"Let's walk this house," he murmured. "There must be something."

They left the rest and went up the stairs to the bedchambers ranged along the murky, freezing gallery.

Corbett inspected each chamber carefully, both windows and doors, but soon recognised it was a fruitless search. He could find nothing out of place. He went back down, out into the courtyard, and stared at the guards milling around a fire, warming themselves. Why had Paulents been killed? Revenge? Certainly not for the manuscript. If Hubert was the killer, perhaps he did not need it. Corbett walked back into the hall, where Castledene and Desroches were in deep conversation.

"Sir Walter?"

The merchant prince came over.

"If Hubert has deciphered the manuscript," Corbett enquired, "why hasn't he dug up the treasure? If he had, Hubert would be long gone."

"We don't know if he even has the map," Castledene replied. "All we do know is that the original was somehow taken from *The Waxman*."

"Do you think these murders could be his revenge?"

"I certainly do."

"Which means," Corbett laid his hand gently on Castledene's shoulder, "that he also intends to take vengeance on you. Remember that, Sir Walter."

Corbett made his farewells, promising Castledene he would join him at the Guildhall later that day to investigate the matter of Lady Adelicia Decontet. Physician Desroches also declared himself finished and offered to accompany Corbett as far as St Augustine's before journeying on into the city. Corbett thanked him and pointed out that he would like Desroches to attend to Chanson, who had developed an ulcer on the inside of his leg. Desroches declared that Maubisson was, perhaps, not the best place for medical inspection or treatment. He could do that at the guesthouse in St Augustine's. Corbett agreed and offered to pay, but Desroches shook his head.

"Just give my good wishes to His Grace the King." The physician smiled. "Flatter my reputation and who knows what patronage I may gain? No, don't mistake me, Sir Hugh," he laughed, "I am not one of these physicians who loves gold more than physic, but I never refuse a kind offer or an open door."

Corbett glanced once more at the corpses and crossed himself. "Sir Walter," he called out, "I would like to carry out my own searches, just once more!"

Castledene shrugged. "Do so, Sir Hugh."

Accompanied by Ranulf, Chanson and the city physician, Corbett revisited the cellar, the various chambers and galleries above the hall as well as the other wings of the house. He still could find nothing amiss. Assisted by his companions he especially checked windows, doors and shutters, ever vigilant for any sign of violence, yet there was none. Paulents' baggage and that of his family was in their chambers. Beds had been prepared, water poured into lavarium bowls, goblets and cups left on tables. Paulents' wife had already begun to unpack, laying out a triptych celebrating the life of St Anne as well as a tray of unguents, creams, oils and perfumes. Corbett felt he was in that twilight gallery between life and death. Silent chambers full of relics belonging to men and women snatched so violently from life. The preacher's phrase: *in media vitae sumus in morte* — in the midst of life we are in death — echoed like a funeral bell through his mind. What horror had walked these galleries? What hideous plot had been devised and brought to fruition here?

Corbett and his two companions, together with Desroches, put on their cloaks and went outside, crossing the inner courtyard where the city guard had built their fire. The cobbles were still strewn with ash and scraps of food. They walked round the outside of the manor; the sky, still threatening more snow, hung grey and lowering. The wind was biting cold, even the ravens and crows had ceased their marauding to shelter in the nearby trees. In some places the snow was at least a foot deep. Corbett found that a help, because it made it plain that there was no evidence of intruders approaching or leaving by any window; the only noticeable disturbances were along the pathways leading up to the main and rear doors. During their walk Corbett was diverted by Desroches, who proved a genial companion, chatting about some of the mysterious deaths he'd examined in Canterbury as well as what he had seen during his military service in Gascony under Lord Bearn.

"You are Canterbury born?" Corbett asked as they went back to the stables.

"Yes and no," Desroches replied. "My family originally came from Ospring to settle here. My father was a wine trader so he moved us all to Bordeaux. The years passed, and my parents returned to Canterbury, where they died. I was not the sharpest of scholars, but

I managed to gain entrance to the medical schools and halls at Montpellier and Salerno. I journeyed around Europe, then returned to Gascony about ten years ago, when Philip of France was beginning to threaten the duchy. I did my military service, and really imagined myself as a soldier, but," he shook his head and shrugged, "so much death," he whispered, "the futility of it all!" He paused, staring out across the snowlocked fields of Maubisson. "No one came here." He sighed. "If they had broken in, Paulents and his son would have resisted, the alarm would have been raised. And if the assassin was hiding here, sooner or later he would have to reveal himself. Again, the alarm would have been raised." He turned, rubbing his face to restore the warmth. "Sir Hugh, do you agree?"

Corbett shook his head. "Nothing," he confessed. "I can find nothing!"

"And Castledene?" Desroches asked.

"He is as mystified as I am. I think he's told me the truth. Paulents brought something very special here, yet it wasn't stolen. So the motive for the murder was pure revenge. You are a physician, Master Desroches; do you know anything about Blackstock, the privateer?"

The physician pulled a face and shook his head. "I've heard chatter about him and his half-brother Hubert, the former Benedictine. People claim Hubert is a truly evil man, someone who's in love with death. Castledene has told me about what happened. You do know Sir Walter has been threatened by him, the Man with the Far-Seeing Gaze?"

69

"And I wonder why?" Corbett murmured. He paused and stared at the physician. "Do we have the full truth?"

Desroches simply shrugged. They made their way back to the stables. Desroches collected his palfrey and sumpter pony, which, as he joked, was his assistant, for it carried his pannier bag and small coffers full of the mysteries of physic.

"You take no weapons?" Corbett asked.

"Never." Desroches swung himself into his saddle. "In the past I have; now I never will. The best treatment for disease, Master Corbett, is good health. If there are no wounds, there is no need for cures. I have seen enough violence, but if I'm attacked," Desroches stroked his horse's neck, "I am a good rider on a fleet horse." He grinned. "Everything else I leave to chance. Moreover, I am well known in Canterbury. I treat the poor as well as the rich, and both in the main leave me well alone."

They organised themselves and made their way out along the trackway between the trees down to the main gateway, past the guards and on to the road leading back to St Augustine's. The thoroughfare was now busy with carts laden with produce making for the city markets. Progress was slow as carts became stuck or draught horses, their hogged manes frozen, skittered and slithered on the ice. Conversation was impossible. The freezing cold clung like a veil around them. The tips of Corbett's ears were like ice and frost formed on his face, biting at the tip of his nose and stinging his lips. He thought of Leighton Hall, of a roaring fire,

70

cups of posset, and Maeve sitting in the chair beside him, all peace and quiet. He tried to hide his discomfort by recalling the verses of a carol, but he could only reach the second line so he gave up, concentrating on the journey, watching his horse's head bob, half listening to the sounds around him.

They turned off the thoroughfare and took the road leading down to the cavernous gateway of St Augustine's Abbey. Desroches, to lighten the mood, began a pithy and humorous description of the ambitions of the present mitred abbot, Thomas de Fyndon, but the misty cold eventually silenced him, his witty remarks fading away. As he fell quiet, he kept reining in, pulling at the leads of his sumpter pony. Now and again he'd turn in the saddle and stare back. He seemed uneasy. Ranulf needed no such encouragement. He was highly nervous of the countryside swathed in white, with its gaunt trees, their black branches stretching out like tendrils over the strange noises echoing from the snow-caked gorse and brambles.

"What is it, man?" Corbett asked.

"I'm sorry," Desroches spluttered. "Are we being followed? I just . . ."

Corbett reined in, turning his horse as the bells of the abbey began to mark the hours for the dawn Mass and the office of Prime. He glanced to the right and left: nothing but frozen trees, snow-draped bushes, the mist drifting and shifting like vapour; a perfect place, he reflected, for an ambush. Corbett realised he'd been in a similar place before: those ice-bound Welsh valleys, waiting for the enemy to creep closer, to spring up and deal out sudden death. Still the abbey bells tolled. Corbett recalled the words of a sonnet: *See how the wicked are bending their bow and fitting arrows to their string.* Desroches was correct: something was wrong. A crow burst from a branch directly to his right, followed by the whirr of a crossbow bolt; it streaked through the mist and slammed into a tree behind them. Corbett drew his sword and struggled to quieten his startled horse. Chanson was cursing. Ranulf had already dismounted. Desroches was muttering under his breath. Corbett waited for a second bolt, but then started in surprise:

"Listen now!" The strong voice echoed from the mist directly to his right. "Listen now, King's man, to the oracle of Hubert, son of Fitzurse, the Man with the Far-Seeing Gaze. Meddle not in what is not yours."

"God's teeth," Corbett shouted, "show yourself!"

"I have and I will, King's man."

Ranulf made to leave the trackway, sword drawn, ready to flounder through the snow towards the sound of that voice.

"Stay!" Corbett ordered. "Stay, for the love of God."

Corbett's horse moved restlessly as the clerk, sword drawn, peered through the misty whiteness. He knew it was futile. A rook cawed mockingly, then all was still.

"Whoever he was," Corbett declared, "he's gone. If he meant further mischief, we'd have known."

They continued their journey. Corbett was relieved to glimpse the soaring walls of the abbey. Its great gates swung open at their approach, and as they clattered

72

into the great yard, lay brothers hastened across to take their horses. Corbett slid from his mount and eased the tension in his back and legs. He told Ranulf to take Desroches and Chanson to the guesthouse.

"Where are you going, master?"

"Why, Ranulf," Corbett pulled off his thick leather gauntlets and beat them against his thigh, "I am going to kiss my Lord Abbot's ring, present my credentials, flatter him, praise him, his abbey and his guesthouse, and thank him profusely." He walked off towards the arched porchway leading to the cloister and the main abbey buildings.

Ranulf helped Chanson stable the horses and then took Desroches into the guesthouse. Once they'd settled into their chambers, Ranulf brought up the physician's panniers and coffers and Desroches tended to the ulcer on Chanson's leg. He cleaned the wound with wine and a herbal poultice, smearing on an ointment and lightly bandaging the open sore, whilst giving clear instructions on how and when the dressing was to be changed. To distract Chanson he chattered about other ailments he was treating, particularly a case of St Anthony's disease where the skin reddened, dried and cracked.

"Strange," Desroches murmured. "I believe it's the food my patient eats: oats and maize which are no longer wholesome."

"Did you treat Paulents?" Ranulf asked.

"No," the physician replied over his shoulder, "I did not. Castledene and I went out to meet them at Maubisson. They simply felt unwell. I personally thought it was due to the rough sea crossing, which would have disturbed the humours of an ox, though by the time they'd reached Maubisson, they were sweating and feeling nauseous. I simply counselled them to keep within doors." He shrugged. "The guards and their close watch were Castledene's idea."

"Were they frightened?" Corbett came through the doorway. "I mean Castledene and Paulents?"

"Oh yes." Desroches patted Chanson on the knee, rose and went across to the lavarium to wash his hands. "They were often closeted together, whispering to each other. Paulents' son, the maid and his lady wife were pleasant enough, quiet, rather fearful at being in a strange country. They said nothing untoward. I suspect they knew that Paulents was concerned and, of course, why not? Both he and Castledene had been threatened."

"But that only began when Paulents arrived in this country."

"Yes," Desroches conceded. "By then I suppose it was too late to return home."

"And the first warning was delivered in Dover?"

"From what I can gather." Desroches screwed up his eyes and peered at the ceiling. "Yes, Paulents arrived on Monday. He received the warning as he entered the tavern where he would stay overnight before his journey to Canterbury. We met him yesterday afternoon, Tuesday. I believe that Sir Walter also received a warning, at the Guildhall. In both cases a scrap of parchment. Paulents' was pushed into his hands. Castledene's was found amongst a number of petitions presented to the Mayor by various citizens. Of course, there was no indication of who wrote them or where they came from. Ah well," he gestured at his panniers, "Master Ranulf, if you could help me with these, I'd be grateful."

"Monsieur Desroches?"

The physician turned.

"Can I pay you?" Corbett repeated his offer, gesturing at Chanson.

Desroches simply waved his hand. "A pleasure," he smiled, "and don't forget to mention my name at court. The ulcer is not serious, a little infected but I have cleaned it. Chanson can now take care of it himself. I'm sure the good brothers in the infirmary would also help. Sir Hugh, perhaps I will see you later in the day?"

The physician left. Corbett heard him patter down the stone steps. Ranulf, cursing quietly under his breath, followed laden with panniers and coffers. Corbett went across to where Chanson was already acting the invalid, stretched out on the bed nursing his leg. Corbett smiled and patted him on the shoulder.

"You will be well enough, Chanson. Try not to tease Ranulf about those woods."

Corbett returned to his own chamber. Once inside, he locked and bolted the door and stared around. He was glad he'd come here, though he was fearful about what he had to do. He always stayed at abbeys or priories, and this chamber showed why, being clean, sweet-smelling and well swept. The furnishings were simple but pleasant, the walls decorated with coloured cloths bearing the symbols of Christ's Passion, a wooden crucifix and a gold-edged diptych. The sheets on the bed looked clean and crisp. There was a table pushed under the mullioned glass window and the chamber boasted a stool, coffer and aumbry. Corbett looked at his own coffers, caskets and leather chancery bags piled in a heap in the far corner. They would have to wait. He pulled back the hangings on the bed and sat down on the edge, easing off his boots. He wondered what Maeve would be doing at Leighton Manor. She'd be up early as always, busy about this or that, going into the chancery room or out into the yard. He closed his eyes, swept by a deep sense of homesickness, even though he was here in the comfortable chamber of an opulent abbey.

Corbett sat for a while trying to collect his thoughts. From below he could hear Ranulf coming back into the guesthouse, Desroches shouting cheerful farewells. He was about to rise and undo the clasps of one of the chancery coffers when he heard a thud on the shutter against one of the far windows. He hastened across and carefully pulled back the thick wooden slats. A blast of cold air blew in. This window was empty of glass or stiffened parchment. He was wondering what could have caused the noise when he glimpsed the crossbow bolt embedded deep in the wood. He immediately stepped to one side and stared out. Below stretched a courtyard, and some distance away thick vegetation and bushes draped in heavy snow. The mysterious archer must lurk there, though Corbett could glimpse no movement or tracks. The attacker must have come over the curtain wall of the abbey or slipped through a side gate. He must also know where Corbett lodged. The clerk glanced at the crossbow bolt and noticed the piece of parchment fastened to it. Crouching down, turning his head slightly against the cold, he undid the twine and pulled the parchment off. He quickly pushed the wooden shutters closed, went across to the glass-filled window and undid the parchment. It contained a further warning:

Thus says Hubert, son of Fitzurse, the Man with the Far-Seeing Gaze. I have warned you once, King's man! I now warn you a second time. Do not meddle in affairs which are not your concern. Tell Edward of England that he is not, as yet, on my reckoning.

CHAPTER
FOUR

Postquam primus homo Paradiseum liquerat . . .
Gravi peonas cum prole luebat.
Ever since man first lost the garden of Paradise, he
has paid for it with bitter sorrow.

"On the killing at Lindisfarne" Anonymous

Corbett stared at the piece of parchment, yellowing and
well thumbed. It could have been ripped from any
manuscript or book, whilst the pen strokes were clumsy
and almost illegible. On peering closer, however, he
noticed how each word, as on the warning sent to
Castledene, was carefully formed, as if the writer was
trying to imitate a young scholar with his horn book.
He had little doubt that the would-be assassin in the
forest had followed him here and struck again. He
placed the piece of parchment on the table and sat
down on the stool, stretching his hands out to welcome
the crackling warmth from the small brazier. For a
short while his unease, that nagging, numbing fear,
returned. He hated this uncertainty. It evoked
memories of fighting in Wales, of the sudden ambush: it
was what he feared most, imagining some messenger
galloping along the snow-clogged lanes to Leighton to
inform Maeve she was a widow, their children
fatherless.

Corbett took a deep breath, murmured a prayer and began to hum the Salve Regina to comfort himself, to dispel the darkness from his mind. Time passed. He dozed for a while, being roused by the abbey bells clanging out a fresh summons to the monastic community.

"It must be time," he whispered to himself. "Knowing Master Griskin, he'll be early rather than late."

Corbett stood up, pulled his boots towards him and put them on, hopping from foot to foot. He opened a coffer and took out his war belt with sword and dagger in their sheaths, as well as a small arbalest and a quiver of bolts. Picking up his cloak, he doused the candle under its cap-guard and went to the next chamber. Ranulf was busy teasing Chanson about his leg. Corbett quickly told them what had happened. Ranulf wanted to see the scrap of parchment, but Corbett just shook his head. "Leave that for a while. If the assassin wanted to kill me he would have tried harder. He is attempting to frighten me."

"Is he succeeding?"

Corbett smiled drily. "To a certain extent, yes, but I suspect it is only fear he wishes to create. He dare not kill the Keeper of the Secret Seal here in Canterbury; that would bring the King's wrath down upon this city. Hubert Fitzurse, the Man with the Far-Seeing Gaze, understands that. No, no, he wants me to stay out of what he calls his affairs, not to meddle; which means, Ranulf, that he has unfinished business in this city."

"Are we for the Guildhall, master?"

"No, Ranulf, we are for the Chantry Chapel of St Lazarus here in the abbey. I have to meet an old friend."

Corbett turned on his heel. Ranulf pulled a face at Chanson, shrugged, grabbed his own war belt and cloak and followed quickly after.

They went along the freezing cloisters, across snow-bound gardens and through the Galilee Porch into the abbey church. Corbett paused to admire the magnificence of its nave, a miracle of airy vaults, sweeping arches, squat columns, transepts, ambulatories, chantry chapels, stone-eyed statues, grinning gargoyles and sombre table tombs. The light was poor, so the stained-glass windows were dull, turning the nave into a place of shifting shadows, a true antechamber between life and death; a field of souls where the spirits of the dead swirled whilst tapers and candles glowed like heaven's beacon lights. Gusts of shifting incense trailed their fragrance, and the sound of their boots echoed strangely on the stone-paved floor.

Ranulf shivered. He stared down the nave at the soaring rood screen with its stark cross bearing a tormented Saviour. Through the doorway beyond he could glimpse the choir stalls and a gilded corner of the great high altar. Corbett adjusted his sword belt and walked through the half-light. Ranulf followed, aware of the tombs either side almost hidden by the gloom. Despite his attempts to educate himself, to model himself upon his master and deal with facts and hard evidence, he was still plagued by the nightmares and experiences of his childhood. By stories about armies of demons prowling through the twilight looking for their quarry, and gargoyles in churches which, at certain times, sprang to life, ready to swoop upon their unsuspecting victims.

"Master," he asked, "what are we looking for?"

"Griskin," Corbett replied over his shoulder.

"Griskin?" Ranulf laughed. "Little pig? Who is that? Why?"

Corbett held his hand up for silence. They crossed the nave and entered a gloomy chantry chapel. A small altar stood to the left at the top of some steps; before this were two prie-dieux with a bench behind them. The narrow window in the far wall was glazed, yet the light was poor. Ranulf stared round at the wall paintings depicting Lazarus being raised from his tomb, Christ healing lepers, Namaan the Syrian bathing in the waters of the Jordan on the instruction of Elijah.

"Griskin?" Corbett pulled forward his sword and sat down on the bench. "I knew him in the halls and schools of Oxford. We called him 'little pig' because of his love of pork, and to be honest," Corbett grinned, "because of his looks." He glanced up at Ranulf. "You may remember him? You met him once at the Exchequer of Receipt in Westminster."

Ranulf nodded, though for the life of him he couldn't recall Griskin.

"Anyway," Corbett continued, "Griskin was no scholar of the quadrivium and trivium. More importantly," his smile faded, "his parents became lepers. He left the halls and schools to look after them. He never finished his studies. A good man, Ranulf, with a fine voice, slightly higher than mine, but when we sang the Christus Vincit . . ." Corbett shook his head and Ranulf suppressed a groan. He could never understand his master's love of singing. "Anyway, Griskin's parents died in a Bethlehem hospital outside London, and Griskin applied to the Chancery for a post. He became a nuncius, a messenger. Griskin enjoys one great talent: he is an excellent searcher-out." Corbett tapped his foot on the hard paving stones and stared at the cross on the small altar. "If anyone can find anyone, it's Griskin. Now when we returned from the West Country and His Grace the King," Corbett tried to keep the sarcasm out of his voice, "wanted me to go to Canterbury, he gave me some of the facts about what had happened here, about Blackstock and his half-brother Hubert. Before I left Westminster, I dispatched a letter to Griskin telling him what I knew and asking him to search the countryside north of Orwell, as well as here in Canterbury, for any trace of Hubert the Monk. To cut a long story short, Ranulf, I said I would meet him here on this day, between the hours of eleven and twelve, in the Chapel of St Lazarus at St Augustine's. Griskin would like that. He has a special devotion to that saint because of his parents' condition."

"And it is now between the hours of eleven and twelve," Ranulf declared, "and he has not yet appeared. Perhaps he has been delayed because of the snow?"

"No." Corbett shook his head. "I received confirmation from Griskin that he'd be here. He always keeps his word. He'd have told me if he couldn't." Corbett was about to get to his feet when he gasped and pointed at the altar. "Ranulf!"

At first Ranulf couldn't see what he was indicating. Then he saw it, on the white lace-edged altar cloth: a small golden cross on a silver chain.

"*Jesu miserere!*" Corbett breathed, getting to his feet. He pushed between the prie-dieux, strode up the steps and grasped the chained cross, turning it so it glittered in the poor light.

"What is it, master?"

"This cross! Griskin's mother gave it to him when he left his village in Norfolk for Oxford. He regarded it as his greatest treasure. He was always fingering it, never took it off, not even when he washed, shaved or changed his clothes."

"Perhaps he left it as a token, master?"

"No." Corbett opened his wallet and placed the chain within. "It can only mean one thing, Ranulf: Griskin will not be . . ." His voice trailed off. Corbett returned to the bench, sat down and put his face in his hands to quell his own fears. For just a brief moment he recalled Griskin and himself staggering along Turl Street in Oxford singing their heads off. They'd both joined the choir of St Mary's Church to carol lustily. Other memories flooded back: Griskin, with his wit and ready laugh, his love of a cup of claret and a slice of pork roasted to crispness. Corbett felt the tears well in his eyes. In his heart he knew Griskin would never, ever give up that chain. Only if he'd been ambushed . . .

"Who killed him?" Ranulf asked harshly.

Corbett kept his hands to his face, waiting until the tears dried, then he glanced up. "*Facile dictum*, easy to say, Ranulf. If Griskin was searching for Hubert the Monk, sooner or later his quarry found out. Somewhere, either here in Canterbury or in Suffolk, Griskin was murdered. He would have had his wallet on him, and in that, letters from me containing details of our meeting here. His killer — and I suspect it was Hubert the Monk — left this chain as a mocking message." Corbett tried to control his trembling. Abruptly he felt very cold. He was deep in the dark of this matter. Often he felt there was a gap between him and his quarry, those criminals, wolfsheads and outlaws he pursued on behalf of the Crown, but this was different.

"Why?" Ranulf asked, as if suspecting what Corbett was thinking. "Why kill Griskin?"

"Why?" Corbett stared up at the crucifix on the wall. "Adam Blackstock was killed by Paulents and Castledene, but they were supported by His Grace the King. He loaned them a company of Welsh archers, longbowmen, and allowed them the use of charts, and harbour facilities at London, Dover and the Cinque Ports. Hubert is waging a war of vengeance; this is not only about lost treasure, but revenge! Revenge against Paulents, which has already been carried out. Against Castledene . . ."

"And against the Crown?" Ranulf asked.

"Yes, Ranulf." Corbett turned. "Against the King. I warned Castledene to be careful, yet it would seem we are as vulnerable as he."

Corbett stared round the chantry chapel, then rose and left. For a while he stood in the nave, staring up at the rood screen, lips moving as he mouthed a silent prayer. Griskin's fate was his own nightmare: of being involved in secret, murky business until one day a knife or an arrow came whipping out of the darkness. He fought to control his own fears. Behind him Ranulf stood watching his master carefully.

"If he is hunting us, let us hunt him," he whispered.

Corbett nodded, crossed himself, genuflected towards the high altar and left the church.

A short while later they had saddled their horses and were about to leave the slush-strewn stable yard when the guest master came hurrying up.

"Sir Hugh," he gasped, "there's a company here called Les Hommes Joyeuses . . ."

Corbett leaned down and pressed his gauntleted hand against the guest master's shoulder.

"It's Brother Wolfstan, isn't it?"

"Yes, Sir Hugh."

"Where are Les Hommes Joyeuses?"

"They are camped out in the cemetery near the Langport Road . . ."

"They've come for shelter," Corbett declared. "Please, Brother . . ."

"They cannot stay here," Brother Wolfstan murmured, bitten fingers to thin lips, his pale, bony face twitching; then his watery eyes smiled. "Ah, there is the old priest's house near St Pancras' Church. I am sure they could settle there. My Lord Abbot will surely agree. It lies to the southeast of here. I'll see what I can do, and Sir Hugh," he gabbled on, "there's someone else."

Corbett suppressed a groan.

"A leper," the guest master exclaimed, his hot breath hanging in the icy air. "He calls himself the Merchant of Souls and the Keeper of Christ's Treasury. He left this message with the doorkeeper of the Aefleg Gate: tell Sir Hugh that he will pass our house on the trackway to Queningate; tell him I have a message." Brother Wolfstan opened his eyes and screwed up his face. "Ah yes, that's it, say to him I have a message from Griskin."

Corbett needed no second bidding. He thanked the guest master and left by the Theodore Gate, skirting the high curtain wall on to the main thoroughfare leading down to Queningate, the great eastern entrance into Canterbury. The broad trackway was still ice-bound, and iron-studded carts slowly creaked their way down to the city markets. It was just past midday and the bells of the city were tolling out through the murky air, marking the hour for all workers to rest, to recite one Paternoster and five Aves then break their fast. Ranulf remembered this as he stroked his rumbling stomach. However, Old Master Long Face was intent on business, so business it would be before they ate and drank again. They passed the crossroads. Beneath the broad-beamed gallows, a friar of the sack perched on a wheelbarrow. Either side of him a shivering boy held a glowing lantern horn. The friar, peaked face hidden deep in his cowl, recited the office of the dead, an act of mercy for those who'd died on that scaffold during the previous month. His words rolled awesome and heart-chilling:

He has broken my strength in mid course,
He has shortened the days of my life.

Corbett recalled poor Griskin, and as he passed, quietly finished the verse of that psalm.

And I pray to God, don't take my life away,
Before my days are complete.

He pulled the folds of his cloak up over his mouth and nose and glanced warily to his right and left, where snow-filled fields stretched to frost-covered trees.

A short while later, muttering at the cold, Corbett took directions from a tinker shuffling towards the city. They turned off the thoroughfare, following a lane down to the leper hospice. Ranulf was full of objections. Corbett pulled down the folds of his robe, leaned across and patted his companion on the shoulder.

"Don't worry, Ranulf, your death is not waiting for you here; the contagion is spread only by touch and close familiarity, so we will be safe."

The grey ragstone wall of the hospice came into view. The lychgate was closed and barred though the narrow path leading up to it had been cleared of snow. Corbett dismounted and pounded on the gate. Immediately a bell tolled within and Ranulf heard the fearful clicking of the leper clappers. The gate rattled as bolts were drawn back. Corbett returned and mounted his horse. Three dark-garbed figures slid through the half-opened postern door as both Ranulf and Corbett fought to control their horses. All three were dressed in motley rags, mantles about their shoulders, hands and faces swathed in bands with only slits for their eyes and mouths; their fingers were similarly covered whilst their feet were protected by heavy wooden galoshes.

"What say ye?" The figure in the middle walked forward.

"I am Sir Hugh Corbett, king's emissary to Canterbury . . ."

"Well, Sir Hugh, king's emissary to Canterbury," the man declared, his voice soft and mellow, "I am the Merchant of Souls and I hold," he stretched out a hand, "the key to Christ's Treasury, namely His poor."

Corbett opened the leather bag fastened to his saddle horn and drew out a small purse of clinking coins. He edged his horse forward, dropped the pouch into the man's outstretched hand and stared down at eyes full of laughter.

"Why do you call yourself the Merchant of Souls?"

"Because, Sir Hugh, I promise those who care for us, as any good merchant vouches, that I will sell their souls to God." He held up the purse. "I thank you for this. These," he gestured to his companions standing slightly behind him, "are Christ's poor. Fill their bellies, Sir Hugh, and you fill Christ's treasury. For if you give a cup of water to one of these, then you have given it to Him."

"And Griskin?" Corbett asked. "You said you had a message for me."

"I knew Griskin," the Merchant of Souls replied. "I met him."

"You met him." Corbett closed his eyes and smiled. "Of course," he whispered.

"Griskin's parents were lepers," the Merchant of Souls continued. "He looked after them and suffered no ill effects, no contagion. He was not frightened of us."

Corbett nodded. He had forgotten about his former comrade's complete lack of fear of other lepers.

"That is how he travelled the countryside," the Merchant of Souls went on. "Who would approach a leper? We stand outside city gates, we beg for alms. Our ears may be rotting, but we hear about this person or that. I can tell you all about Canterbury, Sir Hugh. How Lady Adelicia Decontet is held in the dungeons in the Guildhall accused of murdering her husband, as well as that other great abomination perpetrated at Maubisson Manor. You see, Sir Hugh, all things come to us. People think we do not exist. We are like the trees, something they pass and ignore, yet we stand and listen. Master Griskin travelled the countryside. He visited our brothers in Suffolk, its towns and villages, and then he came back to Canterbury. At times he played the boisterous clerk, but when he wanted to, he assumed the garb of the leper." The Merchant of Souls tapped the yellow star sewn on his left shoulder. "Then he would come here. He was a good man, Sir Hugh."

The Merchant of Souls grasped the reins of Corbett's horse.

"And what did he say?" Corbett asked.

"He believed he had found the truth about some matter from a hermitage near Orwell." The leper looked down at the trackway. "Ah yes, he said he was going to meet his good friend, though he never gave your name, Sir Hugh. I learnt that later. He said the secret was bound up with the hermitage and its chapel, St Simon of the Rocks, and that's all he would say."

"And then what happened?" Corbett asked.

"He left us. He said he was going back to Suffolk. Why, Sir Hugh? Will he return?"

"No," Corbett replied. "Brother Griskin is dead."

The Merchant of Souls hastily crossed himself. "Then God assoil him," he whispered. "How, Sir Hugh, an accident?"

"Murder!" Corbett replied. "But I am God's vengeance." He leaned down and patted the leper on the shoulder. "I promise you that, Merchant of Souls. Remember me in your prayers, and here." He opened the leather bag again and pressed another small purse into the man's hand. "Give that to Christ's Treasury."

He was about to turn his horse when the leper spoke.

"Sir Hugh, have you forgotten something?"

Corbett soothed his horse. "What, sir? What have I forgotten?"

"Brother Griskin was searching for a man called Hubert the Monk, a man who hunted down outlaws, half-brother to the pirate Blackstock."

90

"Do you know of him?" Corbett asked. "Indeed, how do I know you are not he?"

The Merchant of Souls laughed, a merry sound. "Trust me, Sir Hugh, I am not Hubert the Monk. Griskin talked about him and said he was a man of great deceit and subtle wit. They say he, too, was one of the few men not frightened by the likes of us."

"Have any of your brothers ever met him?" Corbett asked.

"Many, many years ago. One of our brothers, now deceased, went to the cloister school with him; Magister Fulbert taught them both. That is all. But as I said, we stand by gateways and porchways; we listen to the chatter of everyone. You are hunting him, aren't you, Sir Hugh? I wish you well. God's grace go with you, for I have told you all I can."

Corbett thanked him and rejoined Ranulf, and they made their way back up towards Queningate. They passed through that yawning arched entrance into the city and Ranulf stared around. He'd been to Canterbury with Corbett once before, but that had been through the outskirts, not the city itself. This was a stark contrast to the silent countryside. Despite the snow and ice, the place was busy as an upturned beehive. The broad pathways and lanes were packed with people, a sea of surging colour as the crowds moved to and from the markets. Corbett and Ranulf had no choice but to dismount and lead their horses, forcing their way through, following the old city wall down beneath the glorious massy-stoned cathedral and on to Burgate Street, which cut through the centre of Canterbury.

On either side of this main thoroughfare rose the beautiful mansions and stately homes of the merchants and burgesses of the city. These were sumptuous houses of pink and white plaster and black beams, each storey jutting out above the other and resting on a solid stone base. The doorways and gables of these mansions, carved, gilded and painted, overlooked the cacophony of sound along Burgate as pantlers, grooms, buttery boys and other servants bustled out to buy provisions for their masters. Herb wives and milkmaids were eagerly selling their produce. Apprentice boys scampered up to attract their attention by plucking at their sleeves before retreating back behind the broad stalls, erected against the front of houses under their billowing striped awnings. The poor clamoured for alms as the rich, with sparkling eyes, red lips and lily-white skin, processed by in their satins and samites, heads covered in short hoods with the liripipes wrapped around their necks, their shoulders mantled in wool, their waists girdled with belts studded with silver and gold. Dirt-smattered blacksmiths in bull's-hide aprons stood outside their smithies shouting for custom, whilst beside them water boiled in buckets from the red-hot irons thrust there. Merchants' wives in costly robes furred with ermine, multicoloured and lined with soft vair, surveyed the stalls and made their purchases. A jester offering to do a somersault wandered amongst them, his head, completely shaven, covered in glue and decorated with duck feathers. An old woman with a tray shrieked how she had night herbs which would cure all ailments. Beside her a chanteur, a professional story-teller, explained how in Ephesus the Seven Sleepers had turned on to their left side, a gloomy sign of how the times were growing more perilous. Carters tried to force their way through, whilst more enterprising citizens pulled sledges full of produce. Dogs yipped and yelped; a piglet, specially greased, had been released by a group of children and ran loose across the thoroughfare, pursued by a legion of its young tormentors.

They passed the main entrance to the cathedral. Ranulf wished to go in but Corbett replied that they would visit it later. They continued on their way up into the great courtyard of the Guildhall, a three-storey building, wattle-daubed and timbered on a honey-coloured stone base. Servants ran up to demand their business, but as soon as they saw Corbett's warrant they immediately became obsequious, offering to take his horses. Once Ranulf had dealt with this, they entered the Guildhall, turning right into the main chamber, a long, draughty room, its doorways and windows protected by heavy cloths.

For a while they just sat on a bench whilst a common serjeant loudly listed the goods of some dead citizen: "three canvas cloths, twelve barrels, two tubs, four bottles, six leather pots . . ." Corbett listened to the man's sonorous voice rise and fall. He could have stood upon his authority, showed his seal, demanded immediate access to the Mayor, but he wanted to collect his thoughts, and looking at Ranulf, he believed his companion felt the same. At last the cold began to seep out of his fingers and he relaxed in the glow of warmth from the braziers, piled high with charcoal, which spluttered and sparkled in every corner. He was about to rise to his feet when an usher suddenly burst through the door and gestured frantically at them.

"Sir Hugh, Master Ranulf!" he gasped. "His Worship's apologies, please, please follow me."

He took them up some stairs to a richly furnished room draped with thickened arras and warmed by chafing dishes laid out along the great table which ran down the centre. Corbett and Ranulf had scarcely arrived and taken off their cloaks when Sir Walter Castledene entered. He was dressed in a long robe of dark murrey, a silver cord around his waist, a gold chain of office about his neck, soft buskins on his feet. He had shaved, his hair was freshly oiled, and he looked more calm and composed than earlier in the day. He greeted Corbett and Ranulf and gestured to the high-backed chairs placed before a specially carved brazier; this was capped with a pointed lid and perforated with small holes to allow the sweet fragrance of the herbs sprinkled on top of the coals to seep through the room. Once seated, ushers served them biscuits sweetened with saffron together with mulled wine smelling strongly of cinnamon. After the usher had left, securing the door behind him, Sir Walter explained that this was his own private parlour. He pointed out its various treasures: the gilt-edged jasper salt-cellar; the spoons, porringers, dishes, ewers, bowls, cups, jugs and goblets, all precious metalled and studded with gems, which adorned the open-shelved aumbry against the far wall. He then described the origins of the diptychs on the tables and chests as well as the pictures on the embroidered arras, which depicted the city arms, those of Castledene as well as grisly scenes from the martyrdom of Becket.

After these pleasantries had finished, Corbett politely brushed aside Castledene's speculations on what had happened at Maubisson and succinctly informed the Mayor about what had occurred since he left that brooding manor earlier in the day: the attack in the woods, the crossbow bolt smashing into the shutter of the guesthouse chamber, the disappearance of Griskin and the strong possibility that he had been murdered. Castledene grew agitated, lacing his fingers together, and now and again leaning forward towards the brazier to catch some of its warmth.

"You have been threatened again?" Corbett asked harshly.

Castledene nodded. "You know I have, the same as Paulents." He closed his eyes. "'You have been weighed in the balance . . . you have been found wanting.' I am to be punished for the death of his brother." He opened his eyes and glanced at Corbett. "Beneath this robe, Sir Hugh, I wear a shirt of light chain mail. I carry a dagger, and where I go, Wendover or my guards always follow. This is a time of judgement." He tried to keep the desperation out of his voice. "Hubert has come back to harvest his revenge against Paulents, against me and against the Crown. He intends all three to suffer."

He paused as an usher came in to announce that the physician Peter Desroches was waiting downstairs.

Castledene lifted a hand. "Ask him to wait for a while," he called over his shoulder. "Then he can join us."

"Paulents wasn't threatened in Germany?"

"No," Castledene agreed. "It was only when he arrived in Dover."

"And you?"

"Yesterday, and again this morning," Castledene replied. "The same way: a small scroll of parchment was found lying in the hallway below amongst other common petitions. The tag on a piece of string bore my name. A clerk brought it up. You wish to see it?" Without waiting for an answer, he rose and moved to the small side table, unlocking a coffer and bringing back what Corbett had expected: a yellowing piece of parchment which could have been cut from anything. The words inscribed in thick ink, like those in a child's horn book, repeated the earlier warnings.

"Anyone," Castledene muttered, "could have written that."

"Do you have a description of Hubert the Monk?" Corbett asked. "If he was Canterbury born, people must know him."

"As a young man in the Benedictine order," Castledene sat down, "they described him as comely faced, always personable, courteous, a brilliant scholar. He later joined the community at Westminster but left to become a *venator hominum*. One thing I have discovered: Hubert very rarely, at least to our knowledge, came in to Canterbury. He tended to prowl between the Cinque Ports on the south coast and as far north as Suffolk, around the town of Ipswich: good hunting ground for the likes of him. He would trap outlaws and bring them in. Of course when he did, he would always be hooded and visored; there is no law against that. After all, he could argue that he needed to disguise his appearance so as to apprehend those who lurk in the twilight of the law."

"So you have no real description of him?"

"None whatsoever," Castledene conceded. "Nor have we discovered anything about his habits, where he eats, drinks or sleeps. Does he own property? What shire or town does he live in? He is a veritable will o' the wisp, Sir Hugh; he comes and goes like the breeze."

"But how can he be in two places at once?" Ranulf asked. "A message was delivered at Dover on Monday to Paulents, and around the same time to you in Canterbury." He shrugged. "Of course, it's possible for someone, despite the snow, to travel from Dover to Canterbury and deliver both messages."

"Or arrange for them to be delivered," Corbett declared. "I could go down into the street and hire a dozen boys who are prepared, in return for a penny, to take a missive to this person or that."

"But the abbey?" Castledene asked. "How could he get into the abbey church of St Augustine?"

"Again very easy," Corbett conceded. "I suspect our Master Hubert is well disguised. He can dress as a lay brother and scale the curtain wall. It wouldn't be difficult. People are going to and fro, a busy place Canterbury, and St Augustine's is no different."

Castledene nodded and stared at the crucifix on the wall.

"And you believe he murdered your man Griskin?"

"I do," Corbett replied, "but God knows where or how or why. Griskin would have made enquiries; sooner or later some of this must have reached Hubert. I suspect he pays taverners and alehouse masters to keep him informed. He would have to, wouldn't he, if he was hunting an outlaw? Griskin is dead," Corbett declared. "That golden cross, he would never give it up! Not in this life."

He rose, stretching his hands above the brazier, savouring its warmth, then glanced at the window. He'd been in Canterbury for some time. He needed to think, to reflect, to discover where the enemy really was, and then plot.

"Sir Hugh? What are you thinking?"

"The business at Maubisson will have to wait a while. Lady Adelicia Decontet?"

"She should be committed for trial," Castledene declared. "The King has asked me to delay it until you have investigated the case. However, come the New Year, certainly once Epiphany is over and the twelve days of Christmas are finished, I and two justices must sit, certainly no later than the Feast of Hilary."

Castledene got to his feet. A frightened man, he kept plucking at his fur-lined mantle, staring anxiously towards the door.

"What I have done," he continued in a hurry, "is to invite Master Desroches and Lechlade here." He glimpsed Corbett's mystification. "Sir Rauf Decontet's manservant, though I am afraid you will not find him much use. He is a toper, a drunkard born and bred. Lady Adelicia will also be brought up. I have had fresh robes sent down to her, and she has been allowed to wash and prepare herself. Her maid Berengaria will accompany her." Castledene went across and stared at the hour candle fixed on its iron spigot. "The day is fading," he murmured as if to himself. "Sir Hugh, we'd best begin now."

CHAPTER
FIVE

Regis regum rectissimi prope est Dies Domini.
The day of the Lord, of the most rightful King of
Kings, is close at hand.

Columba

Corbett sat at the top of the table, Ranulf to his right,
their sword belts on the floor beside them. Ranulf
opened his chancery bag, taking out quills, ink pots,
pumice stone, a sand shaker, fresh rolls of parchment
and strips of green ribbon. The chamber became busy.
Desroches bustled in. He smiled at Corbett and Ranulf
and took his seat on the bench. He was followed by
Lechlade, a grimy, grey-haired, shuffling figure, his
swollen red face marred by a broken nose and ugly
warts. He was unshaven, slobbery-mouthed, bleary-
eyed and reeked of ale fumes. His cote-hardie was
blotched and stained with dried food, his thick, dirty
fingers protected by ragged mittens. He bowed towards
Corbett and sat down next to the physician, who
wrinkled his nose in disgust at the other man's rank
smell.

A short while later, Lady Adelicia and her maid
Berengaria entered, flanked by city guards. Corbett
rose, bowed and gestured at them to sit at the other end
of the table. He glanced sideways at Ranulf and

suppressed a grin. The Senior Clerk of the Chancery of the Green Wax was known for his deep veneration of any beauty, and Lady Adelicia was certainly beautiful. She was of medium height, with a willowy figure and a lovely swan neck. Her face was almost perfect, framed by a simple white linen veil. She reminded Corbett of one of those damsels in a church fresco, with her smooth forehead, arching brows, beautiful wide-spaced eyes, pale ivory skin and lips as red as a luscious rose. She was dressed simply in a blue silver-edged gown bound by a gold cord; no rings or bracelets glittered, yet she seemed to brighten the room with her sweet smile and elegant gestures. Berengaria, her maid, was a complete contrast: red-cheeked, auburn-haired, with a mischievous face; her bold blue eyes fluttered at Corbett before she simpered at Ranulf and, turning sideways, glanced teasingly at him out of the corner of her eye.

Finally Castledene entered the chamber in a cloud of scarlet robes of office. He sat opposite Ranulf as Wendover closed the door and took up guard against it.

"Lady Adelicia," Corbett began, "I regret to find you in these circumstances, but as you well know, you have been charged with the foul crime of the murder of your husband. You have petitioned the King, so His Grace has asked me to investigate the matter. However, I must advise you that once the Holy Season is over, certainly by the Feast of St Hilary, you must go on trial before Sir Walter and two other justices of oyer and terminer."

"I know well the heinous allegations levelled against me," Lady Adelicia replied, her voice surprisingly strong, her face no longer sweet but hard and resolute. "I am innocent of any charge."

"Lady Adelicia," Corbett declared, his voice carrying, "that will be a matter for the jury and the royal justices. You were married to your husband for how long?"

"Over two years."

"And your marriage?"

"Was a May to December alliance," she snapped. "I was the King's ward. I did not wish to marry Sir Rauf, but," she fluttered her long fingers, "I had no choice in the matter. The King was insistent." She paused. "I hated Decontet, I admit that. I found his touch foulsome."

"But not his money!" Lechlade slurred.

"Shut up!" Lady Adelicia's face became red with anger; she glared at Lechlade slumped against the table. "You are nothing but a toper drinking from morning until night. You stumble about, you smell!"

Lechlade just smiled tipsily, rocking backwards and forwards on the bench.

"Did your husband ill-treat you?" Corbett asked. "Beat you?"

"I told him that if he laid a finger on me I would kill him." Adelicia's voice was steely.

Corbett tried to hide his sense of despair. This was a beautiful young woman, married against her will to an old miser whom she had hated. If she repeated the same before His Majesty's justices of oyer and terminer and a jury of twelve good men and true . . .

"Lady Adelicia." Corbett held up his hands, aware of Ranulf's quill skimming across the parchment. "I must advise you to be more prudent."

"I am prudent," she retorted. "I am also innocent. I may have hated my husband, disliked him intensely, his lewd ways, his meanness, but I did not murder him. I was not in the house that day."

"And this house?" Corbett asked.

"Sweetmead Manor." She laughed sharply, as if mocking the name. "A mansion, a fine town house, Sir Hugh; it stands between the Templar priory and the Abbot of St Augustine's mill."

"And on that Thursday," Corbett asked, "the Feast of St Ambrose: what exactly happened?"

"I rose early in the morning and broke my fast. I returned to my chamber to wash, change and prepare for the day. Afterwards Berengaria and I decided to visit the market outside St Andrew's church. I left just before noon."

"And when you returned?"

"It must have been between the hours of four and five. I remember the market bell tolling."

"So, on a cold December day," Corbett said, "you spent almost five hours in a market? You went nowhere else?"

Lady Adelicia stared coolly back.

Corbett saw Berengaria momentarily flinch and promised himself to return to that matter.

"So what happened then?"

"I came back to the house. Darkness was falling. Berengaria carried a lantern horn before me. We had hired two link boys from the market to escort us. When I returned to the main door of my house, Physician Desroches was waiting. He had roused Lechlade and summoned Parson Warfeld."

Corbett held up a hand. "You, sir." He pointed at the manservant, who was busy wiping his nose on the back of his hand. "Your mistress left at noon. What did you do then?"

"You should ask her where she went!" Lechlade replied.

Corbett had to bang the table to restore order. "Sir, limit yourself to my questions otherwise you will spend some time in the dungeons beneath this Guildhall. What did you do that afternoon?"

"Well," the man sniffed, "I knew my mistress had left and that Sir Rauf would be in his counting house, so I went down to the Green King — it's a nearby tavern — and bought myself a jug of ale."

"Didn't Sir Rauf have ale in his house?"

"No, sir, just wine in his cellar, and he kept a very strict eye on that. Anyway, I brought the ale back, took it to my chamber, locked the door, drank and fell asleep. I was as happy as a pig in its muck until this busybody" — Lechlade jabbed the physician on the arm — "turned up banging on the doors."

"Were all the doors locked?"

"All. My master was very strict on that. Morning, noon and night, whatever the weather, if we were in, the doors were locked and bolted. If somebody left, the doors were locked and bolted after them. The same was true of Sir Rauf's chamber, though only he had the key to that."

"And Lady Adelicia's chamber?"

"Oh, she owned a key to that, as did the master."

"Continue," Corbett demanded.

"Well then, I am aroused from my sleep. I open the window. I look down. I see the physician here shouting up at me. 'Lechlade,' he calls, 'what is the matter? I wish to see Sir Rauf!' I reply, 'There is nothing the matter.' I come downstairs, unlock the front door, and in he comes, all high and mighty, sniffing like he always does."

Desroches remained impassive in the face of such insults.

"And?" Corbett asked. "Master Desroches, perhaps you had best explain why you were there."

"I was Sir Rauf's physician," Desroches replied slowly. "I often visited him. He paid me good silver. He was worried about this ailment or that. I would just sit there and chat to him, then I would leave. Now, Sir Hugh, Rauf Decontet very rarely left his house. I decided to visit him mid-afternoon on the Feast of St Ambrose, but when I arrived there was no Sir Rauf to greet me. I believed something was wrong. I eventually roused Lechlade, who came down and let me in. To the right of the entrance is the hall of the house. Sir Rauf had his chancery chamber on the left. I knocked on this door but there was no reply. The windows were all shuttered, but going outside and looking through a gap, I caught the glow of candlelight. Sir Rauf would never leave a candle glowing if he had gone out. He was a very careful, how shall I say, prudent man. We banged on the door, but again, no answer. I suspected something terrible had happened. However," Desroches gestured at Lechlade, "he's a born toper. I wanted another witness present. I left the house and hired a farmer's boy. I gave him a penny and dispatched him across the wastelands to fetch Parson Warfeld from St Alphege's."

"Why?" Corbett asked.

"As I said, I wanted a witness. Decontet was a very wealthy man. I did not wish, later on, to face spurious allegations about my own honesty."

"Very well," Corbett soothed. "Do continue."

"Once Parson Warfeld arrived, Lechlade and I took a bench from the hall and forced the chancery door. Inside, on the floor near his counting table, was Sir Rauf. He lay face down in a widening pool of blood. The back of his skull" — Desroches tapped his own head — "was smashed like a jug. Nearby was a set of blood-stained fire tongs, powerful pincers used to move coals in the fire, which, by the way, had died down. Sir Rauf was obviously dead. His flesh was cold, the blood beginning to congeal. I glanced quickly around but noticed nothing missing or disturbed."

"And the keys to the chamber?"

"They were still on Sir Rauf's belt. Lechlade and Warfeld will testify to that."

"Then what?"

"Parson Warfeld immediately knelt down and whispered the act of absolution into the dead man's ear to shrive him of whatever sins he carried."

"But he was definitely dead?" Corbett asked.

"Oh yes. The soul had gone, though perhaps it still hovered there, hungry for absolution, if God's mercy permitted. Sir Rauf," the physician added wistfully, "certainly had a great deal to answer for."

"He did indeed!" Lady Adelicia snapped. "His treatment of me."

"And then you arrived, my lady?" Corbett continued.

"Yes. I went into my husband's chancery chamber and saw his corpse sprawled there. I was shocked." She gestured at her maid. "Both of us were." She paused to clear her throat. "When I'd entered the house, I'd taken off my cloak and laid it over a bench." She pointed to Castledene. "Physician Desroches had sent for him and the city guard. It was . . ." Her voice faltered.

"It was dark when I arrived." Castledene took up the story. "I found Master Desroches, Lady Adelicia, Parson Warfeld and Berengaria sitting before the fire in the small parlour. I too checked the chamber and had the corpse immediately taken to the mortuary chamber at St Alphege's church so it could be dressed for burial. I then questioned Lady Adelicia about where she had been, what she had done and what time she had arrived home. I carefully checked the house; there was no sign of any forced entry. The windows were shuttered, the rear and front doors had been locked and bolted. I could see very clearly where Master Desroches and Lechlade had broken down the chancery door."

"And the key?" Corbett intervened. "The key to Sir Rauf's chamber?"

"It was certainly on a hook on his belt when I discovered the corpse," Desroches repeated. "Lechlade and Parson Warfeld can testify to that."

"I saw it too," Castledene added, "and took it into my keeping." He chewed on his lip. "Sir Hugh, you, as a royal justice, know the *forma inquisicions* — the kind of formal interrogation I must carry out. Lady Adelicia's answers about her whereabouts were ambiguous. I asked to see her hands and examined the gown she was wearing. She objected —"

"I am a lady!"

"Hush." Corbett held a hand up warningly.

"I found no bloodstains," Castledene continued, "but when I demanded to see her cloak, I found dried blood on both the right side and the left sleeve."

"I don't know where they came from." Lady Adelicia was flustered. "I must have brushed a butcher's stall or a flesher's wall in the shambles."

"So that's where you were!" Lechlade slurred mockingly.

Corbett quickly quelled further outbursts.

"I then asked to see her chamber, which is above the stairs," Castledene continued. "This was locked. Lady Adelicia declared there were two keys to that chamber, one held by herself, the other by her husband. I asked her for the key and she handed it over. I unlocked the chamber and went in. It looked as if someone had left it in disarray."

"I don't know," Lady Adelicia protested. "I never —"

Corbett gestured at her to be silent and nodded at Castledene to continue.

"I found a bloodstained napkin on the floor and more pushed behind the bolsters on her bed. I gave these to Master Desroches to scrutinise. He agreed the napkins were blood-soaked so I returned to Lady Adelicia and asked her where she had been? What part of the market? Whom she had conversed with? Could anyone bear witness that when her husband was killed, she was still in the city? She could not reply. I then asked Berengaria if she could support her mistress's story. I reminded her that she would go on oath and that punishment for perjury in such matters is a horrid death. She could easily be cast as an accomplice."

"I told the truth!" Berengaria interrupted, her voice rising to a screech. "I told you, Sir Walter, I left my mistress for a while. She went to make her own purchases, and so did I."

"How long?" Corbett asked. "How long were you absent from your mistress?"

Berengaria gazed fearfully at Lady Adelicia, then stared down at the table.

"Hours?" Corbett asked.

Berengaria nodded without raising her head.

"The bloodied rags," Sir Walter declared, "are in a canvas bag in my own private chamber here; they will be produced in court. Lady Adelicia has recognised them as napkins from her own store. She cannot explain how the blood got on them."

"So." Corbett straightened up in the chair and glanced across at the thick mullioned glass window. Even though it was early in the afternoon, the darkness was creeping in. He stared around the chamber.

Despite its luxurious hangings and costly furnishings, this was a sombre place, made more so by the young woman at the end of the table whose life now hung in the balance. Corbett disguised his own unease. According to the evidence, Lady Adelicia must be lying. She could not explain where she had been or what she had been doing that fateful afternoon.

"Lady Adelicia?" Corbett smiled. "You claim you left your house about noon?"

"That is correct."

"Before you left, did you quarrel with your husband? Were you cross with him? Lady Adelicia, one day you will go on oath. You must tell me the truth."

"I went to his chamber." Lady Adelicia paused, blinked and stared hard at Corbett. "We had the most bitter quarrel."

"Over what?"

"Over the usual, money! I wanted to make certain purchases for myself. He refused."

"Did you scream at him?"

"Of course she did," Lechlade intervened. "Her voice could be heard all over the house. Ask her maid."

"Then what?" Corbett asked.

"I left my husband's chamber."

"And he locked it behind you?"

"Yes, he did."

"What did you do then?"

"I hurried up to my own chamber. I did not wish to be late —" She stopped abruptly.

"Late?" Corbett intervened. "Late for what, Lady Adelicia?"

"It was time to leave." She was flustered. "I took my purse and my cloak. Berengaria was waiting in her chamber — it's a small closet room near mine — then we left."

"And you, sir?" Corbett turned to Lechlade, who was now slumped half asleep.

"I've told you," the man slurred, "once the lady of the manor left, Sir Rauf locked himself in his counting chamber. What more could I do? I went and bought a pot of ale, drank it and fell asleep until I was aroused by a knocking which would have raised the dead."

"We must visit Sweetmead," Corbett declared. "Even though the hour is late, I wish to see this house. You, Lechlade and Berengaria, where are you staying now?"

"Parson Warfeld," Berengaria replied, "is a good man. He has given me and Lechlade comfortable lodgings in the priest's house. He said we can stay there."

"Sweetmead and all its possessions," Castledene intervened, "have been sealed and placed under heavy guard. No one can enter until this matter is resolved."

"Ah well." Corbett straightened in the chair. "Lady Adelicia, I ask you formally. On Thursday afternoon, the Feast of St Ambrose, you were absent from your house, according to your own statement, for at least four or five hours. There is every possibility that you returned, killed your husband and left again. This matter could be very quickly cleared up if you could prove exactly where you were."

The silence in the room became oppressive. Faint sounds echoed eerily from the street; the drapes on the wall rippled under an icy draught; a candle flame abruptly guttered out. Lady Adelicia sat with both palms flat against the tabletop, staring at some point beyond Corbett's head. Only once did she glance swiftly at her maid, who nodded imperceptibly.

"At this moment in time, Sir Hugh, I cannot answer that. I am Lady Adelicia Decontet, widow of Sir Rauf, merchant, money-lender, a man, Sir Walter, like you, with fingers in many, many pies." She threw a glance full of hatred at Castledene, whom she regarded as the origin of her present difficulties. "Two years ago last April, on the eve of the Feast of St Erconwald, I married Sir Rauf, we exchanged vows at the church door and my purgatory began."

"My lady," Corbett intervened, "what has this to do with the present case?"

"Oh, Sir Hugh, everything. I was married in the April of the year of Our Lord 1301. Now Sir Rauf, as Lechlade here," she clicked her fingers, "will bear witness, found it very difficult to sleep. He would often go back down to his chancery chamber to study his ledgers or count his silver. On the fifteenth of July of that same year, the Feast of St Swithun, my husband went downstairs. The night was hot. I too found it difficult to sleep. I rose and went to the casement window of my bedchamber, which overlooks the rear garden of Sweetmead Manor. I was about to retire when I heard the postern door at the back of the house open, and my husband emerged with a shuttered lantern. He went up the garden path, placed it on a turf seat and returned. A short while later he dragged out

112

what looked like a corpse, though it was bound in sacking and tied with cord. Earlier that day he had declared that he wished to do some gardening; I was surprised, for he rarely ventured out in the garden. He'd left it as a wilderness, as again Lechlade will bear witness. Anyway, he pulled the bundle of sacking along the path and disappeared behind some bushes. He must have been there for at least an hour before he came back wiping his hands, picked up the lantern and returned to the house. I could hear him going into the buttery to wash his hands. I retired to bed and fell asleep. The next morning I rose as usual and broke my fast. My husband retired to deal with business matters; Lechlade disappeared, so I went out into the garden. I walked behind those bushes where I'd seen my husband go, and noticed the freshly dug earth —"

"Lady Adelicia," Corbett interrupted, "what is the point of all this? You are accusing your dead husband of committing a murder and burying the corpse of his victim in the garden behind your house?"

Lady Adelicia, face now white as snow, nodded, her eyes pleading with Corbett, who realised what path she was about to take.

"I know," she stammered, "I know something of the law, Sir Hugh. I wish to turn King's Approver. I accuse Sir Rauf Decontet of homicide."

Corbett sat back in the chair and glanced quickly at Castledene, who shook his head.

"Two things." Corbett leaned forward, resting his elbows on the table. "First, everyone here must gather at Sweetmead Manor tomorrow between the hours of eleven and twelve. I wish to search the house as well as that garden to establish the truth of what you say, Lady Adelicia. Second, you may know the law, Lady Adelicia, but I regret to inform you that you are wrong in this matter. To turn King's Approver means that you accuse another person of a felony in the hope of receiving a royal pardon. The person you accuse has the right to answer; in this case, however, that is impossible. Your husband is dead. I do not think the royal justices will accept such a defence."

Lady Adelicia swayed slightly, hands clutching the table. She glanced at Berengaria and then over her shoulder at Wendover, who'd been standing near the door. During the interrogation Corbett had watched the captain of the city guard: he seemed nervous and agitated. Corbett suspected Wendover had a great deal to do with the proceedings before him, and wondered if he should challenge him directly, but decided against it. He was about to turn to Sir Walter Castledene when there was a loud knocking on the door and a liveried servant hurried in. He bowed to Corbett before hurrying across to whisper in Sir Walter's ear. The Mayor glanced up.

"Sir Hugh, Parson Warfeld is here. I thought he too should give evidence."

Corbett nodded. "He is a cleric," he declared, "a priest. I think it best if this room is cleared of everyone except you, Sir Walter," he nodded at Ranulf, "and my clerk." Corbett rose, pushing back his chair. "Lady Adelicia, Master Desroches, Lechlade and Berengaria, I thank you. Lady Adelicia, you must remain in your cell beneath the Guildhall, at least until tomorrow." He held up his hand to quell her protest. "Tomorrow we shall go out to Sweetmead Manor and see for ourselves. I thank you."

Corbett walked away and stared out of the window, waiting for the room to empty. Wendover looked as if he wanted to stay, but Ranulf jabbed his hand, indicating that the captain should leave. He did so just as Parson Warfeld came bustling into the chamber, mopping his face with the hem of his robe. Corbett made the priest comfortable on one of the chairs and personally served him a cup of posset, then sat down next to him.

"Parson Warfeld, I thank you for coming. You know the proceedings before me. I will be blunt and to the point. Lady Adelicia is accused of murdering her husband Sir Rauf sometime on the afternoon of the Feast of St Ambrose. Physician Desroches came to the house to meet his client, but unable to gain access sent a boy to fetch you from St Alphege's. Is that correct?"

Parson Warfeld gulped the mulled wine and nodded.

"And when you arrived?"

Parson Warfeld put the goblet down on the table; Corbett noticed his hand was shaking slightly. The room fell silent except for Castledene, who was drumming his fingers on the table, and the squeak of Ranulf's pen across the freshly scrubbed parchment.

"Well, well . . ." Warfeld gasped. He then proceeded to tell Corbett exactly what the clerk had already heard, starting from the moment he had been summoned to Sweetmead and finishing with Castledene's decision to arrest Lady Adelicia and bring her to the Guildhall.

115

The parson shrugged. "There was nothing more I could do. I have visited Lady Adelicia in prison and have lodged Master Lechlade and Berengaria in my own house. They are no real problem; there's always plenty of work to do in and around the church. The priest's house at St Alphege's is well furnished. 'In my Father's mansion there are many rooms'," Parson Warfeld quoted jokingly from the scriptures. "I really can't say any more, Sir Hugh."

"Did Sir Rauf, or Lady Adelicia, ever ask to be shriven by you?" Corbett asked.

The smile faded from Warfeld's face.

"I know, I know," Corbett conceded. "You can reveal nothing told to you under the seal of confession. I didn't ask for that. I asked whether you ever heard their confessions."

"I will not reply to that either, Sir Hugh. But I will tell you this: there were rumours, whispers about Lady Adelicia not being satisfied with Sir Rauf, and her trips into the city."

"Are you saying she was meeting someone else?" Corbett asked.

"I'm saying nothing, Sir Hugh. I merely report what I've heard."

Corbett thanked him and asked him also to be present on the morrow between eleven and noon at Sweetmead Manor. Parson Warfeld agreed, bowed to both of them and left.

"Ah well." Castledene walked towards the door, closed it and leaned against it. "Sir Hugh, what can be done here? Lady Adelicia must face the charges levelled against her, whilst this business at Maubisson ... I have," he added hastily, "despite the snow, sent couriers to all ports asking for harbourmasters and port-reeves to search for Servinus. He must be the assassin!"

Corbett shrugged. "I cannot comment on that, Sir Walter. I have my doubts. Why should Servinus wait to come to a foreign country to strike? At a closely guarded manor like Maubisson, in the depths of winter, in a strange city? How did he do it without resistance from his victims? How did he escape?" He shook his head. "All I know is that the matters before us are as dark and bleak as the weather outside. We stand on the edge of a tangled forest of evil deeds, full of danger; we must thread our way carefully through it."

CHAPTER
SIX

Dies irae et vindicatae.
A day of wrath and vengeance.

Columba

A short while later, Corbett and Ranulf mounted their horses, cloaks pulled tightly about them, and left the Guildhall. They made their way up the Mercery, turning right towards the corner leading to the Butter Cross, then along Burgate, which would take them to Queningate. Darkness was closing in. The air was still bitterly cold, the ground slippery as the ice hardened, yet the stalls and shops were very busy. The narrow, dirt-filled streets were illuminated by flaring torches, the light pouring through tavern and alehouse doors and windows. The shifting murk, the din, clamour and foul smells reminded Corbett of a wall painting in a church depicting the streets of hell. The rakers and scavengers were out with their dung and refuse carts. Pilgrims in their worsted cloaks, displaying pewter badges depicting the martyred head of Becket or the ampulae or miniature flasks representing the martyr's blood, battled to make their way to and from the cathedral. They screamed abuse at the apprentice boys who darted from the stalls like greyhounds to pluck at sleeves and cloaks, shouting their goods, inviting

118

passers-by to inspect "ninepins for sale all in a row", "boots of Cordovan leather", "candles white and pure as a virgin", "hot pies", "spiced sausages", "sharp knives".

Tavern hawkers and idlers were encouraging two drunken women to fight; each would hold a penny in her hand, and the first to drop it would be judged the loser and dipped in the freezing water of a nearby horse-trough. A city serjeant fighting to control a loose donkey tried to intervene, whilst bawling for the market bailiffs with their metal-tipped staves to assist him. A chanteur stood on a plinth at the corner of an alleyway off the Mercery; he was telling a group of gaping pilgrims to pray most urgently and earnestly before Becket's shrine: "Because," he declared, "the time of doom is fast approaching." The chanteur informed the pilgrims how he had recently returned from Paris, where a friend had invoked demons to advance him in his studies. On his deathbed, just in time, this friend had been persuaded to repent; as his fellow scholars assembled to sing the funeral psalms around his bier, the man fell into a deep sleep. He dreamed his soul plunged into a dark, sulphurous valley where a gang of fiends tossed his soul about, whilst others prodded him with claws which surpassed the sharpness of any earthly steel. When the man eventually woke up, he vowed to change his life, went on pilgrimage to Becket's shrine and received God's calling to enter the Benedictine order. So, the chanteur concluded, they too must pray most earnestly to save themselves from the traps and lures of Satan.

Corbett half listened to this man, clamorous as a sparrowhawk, as he waited for the street to clear before him. At last they moved on and reached the centre of Canterbury, with its great Buttery Cross soaring above the stalls and booths. On the top step a Crutched Friar was delivering the sentence of excommunication against a felon who had dared to rob his church.

"I curse him by the authority of the Court of Rome, within or without, sleeping or waking, going or sitting, standing and riding, lying above the earth and under earth, speaking, crying and drinking; in wood, water, field and town. I curse him by Father, Son and Holy Spirit. I curse him by the angels, archangels and all the nine orders of heaven. I curse him by the patriarchs, prophets and apostles . . ." On a lower step, totally ignoring the friar, a relic-seller pointed to his leather chest, claiming it contained the stone where Christ's blood was spilt, a splinter from the Lord's cradle, a certain crystal vessel bearing shards of the stone tablet on which God had inscribed the law for Moses, straps from Jesus's winding sheets and fragments from Aaron's robe. A gang of burly apprentice boys standing around him demanded that the miraculous chest be opened to show them such wonders. The relic-seller refused and a brawl ensued. Market bailiffs and beadles were busy at the stocks, locking in foists, roisterers and drunkards alongside breakers of the King's peace or the market regulations. A deafening clamour of noise dinned the ear. Corbett looked up at the great mass of Canterbury Cathedral rearing above him, black against the darkening sky. He cursed quietly, and Ranulf, riding slightly behind him, leaned forward.

"Master, what is it?"

"I still have the King's special task to do," Corbett murmured, his words almost lost beneath the noise of the market. "Perhaps tomorrow."

Eventually they had to dismount and lead their horses. The ground underfoot was thick and mushy, dung and mud mixing with the refuse thrown from the stalls and taverns. A moonman pushed his way through, wheeling a barrow with a small bear chained to it. Corbett wondered idly where he was going, only to be distracted by a loud-mouthed apothecary who plucked his sleeve, claiming he had an electuary distilled from silver which would cure all ills. Corbett shrugged him off as he glimpsed a goldsmith's sign. He told Ranulf to hold the horses and walked over. He wanted to divert himself for a while, and was resolved to buy something unique for Lady Maeve.

The merchant behind the stall quickly appraised Corbett from head to toe and immediately led him into the back room of his shop, where he took down an iron-bound coffer locked with three clasps. He opened this and showed Corbett an array of diamonds, pearls, emeralds and sapphires which he called by fancy names such as "Bon Homme", "The Dimple", "The Barley-corn", "The Distaff", "The Cloud", "The Quail", "The Chestnut", "The Ruby King". Corbett studied each one, promised the man he would return and left the shop.

Rejoining Ranulf, Corbett grasped the reins of his horse and they walked on. Ranulf realised that any attempt at conversation would be futile, whilst he himself was eager to drink in the various sights of the city, catch a pretty eye or win a smile from some lovely face. At last they were clear of the main trading area. The bells of the city began to clang out the tocsin, the sign for the market to close and all good citizens to return to their homes. They passed the churches of St Mary Magdalene and St Michael, then turned left, following the route they'd taken into the city, along the old boundary wall through Queningate and out into the countryside. Once mounted, Ranulf spurred alongside Corbett to question him about what happened at the Guildhall, but he received little satisfaction.

"I know nothing." Corbett reined in and stared up at the sky, where the clouds were breaking up. He murmured a prayer. "At least there'll be no more snow tonight." He sighed. "What I must do, Ranulf, is reflect and think." His horse skittered on the trackway. "And this is a lonely place. Come now, God knows who follows us."

On their return to St Augustine's, they found Chanson, much improved, sitting in the small refectory enjoying a dish of rabbit stew with onions and a pot of ale specially brewed at the abbey. Corbett and Ranulf took off their boots, changed, washed their hands and faces and came down to join him. The room was well lit by torches and candles on the table and heated by braziers in every corner. It was a pleasant refectory with paintings on the wall depicting Christ's Last Supper and his meeting with the disciples at Emmaus. A soothing and relaxing place. Ranulf insisted on telling a story about a stingy abbot and his grasping guest master. A visitor once sheltered in their abbey for the night. He was given only hard bread and water, and a thin straw mattress to sleep on. In the morning he protested to the guest master, who simply shrugged off his complaints. As he left the abbey, the visitor met the abbot and immediately thanked him for his lavish hospitality.

"Of course," Ranulf joked, "the abbot immediately disciplined the guest master for wasting his resources. And then there's the other story," he continued, "about a priest who'd been visiting his mistress. He arrived home late at night. Beside his church stood a haunted house, and as the priest passed, he heard a voice shout: 'Who are you?' The priest went over. 'I'm the parson of this church,' he declared, 'and who are you?' 'I speak from hell,' the voice replied. 'Are you sure you are a priest?' 'Why?' the parson replied. 'Well,' the voice declared, 'so many priests are in hell, I didn't think there were any more left on earth . . .'"

Ranulf stopped as the guest master bustled in to inform Corbett that Les Hommes Joyeuses would like to see him the next morning to thank him for his kindness towards them. Corbett agreed, then decided to join the good brothers in the choir to sing Vespers. Ranulf claimed he was tired and said he'd make his own oraisons.

Corbett went over to the darkening church. For a while he squatted at the foot of a pillar watching the monks file in as the bells marked the hour. He then respectfully approached the abbot, who indicated the stall next to him and gestured for a lay brother to bring a psalter. Corbett revelled in the atmosphere. For a while he could lose himself in this beautiful church with its curving arches and ornate pillars, the high altar bathed in light, the lamps and lanterns glowing and the massed voices of the brothers as they chanted the evening prayer. He glanced round. It was also a ghostly place. Shadows shifted amongst the monks, their faces half hidden in the light, tonsured heads lowered, yet all was redeemed by that melodious chant echoing through the church, reaching every darkening corner.

Corbett sang lustily with the rest, and later, as he sat listening to the lector, he thought of Griskin. The reader had chosen a text from the Second Book of Samuel, declaring in a clear, carrying voice David's lament over Saul and Jonathan: "'Alas, the glory of Israel has been slain on the heights! How did the heroes fall and the battle armour fail!'" Corbett wondered how Griskin had been trapped, but put such thoughts away as they rose to sing the psalm: "Lord of hosts, how long will you ignore your people's plea . . ."

Once Vespers was over, Corbett remained in his stall. He politely refused the abbot's invitation to join him in his parlour, smiling up as the other monks passed by, for he wanted to be alone. He turned in the stall and stared at the high altar. Its great candles still flamed vigorously. He looked down the church, where a night mist had curled in beneath the door, moving like a cloud up the nave. He glanced up at the top of the pillars; gargoyle faces smirked stonily back. The place was now empty. He suppressed a shiver, got up, genuflected towards the pyx cup hanging from its gold chain, and made his way out through the Galilee Porch.

The night was freezing cold. Corbett walked along the path into the deserted cloisters. Lanterns hung between the pillars. At one point he stopped and glanced around. He felt uneasy. The cloister garth was hidden under a deep frost. In the centre a lonely rose bush extended its stark arms upwards as if seeking solace from the bitter cold. Shadows danced in the moving light of the lanterns. Somewhere a bell clanged. A voice echoed, then all fell silent. Corbett walked briskly on. Once again he paused and turned round. He felt he was being watched, yet nothing but a deathly silence permeated these holy precincts.

He was halfway down one side of the cloisters when the crossbow bolt zipped through the air and smacked into the grey ragstone wall behind him. He immediately crouched down, protected by a rounded pillar, and glanced across the cloister garth. The other side was hidden by the dark; an army could lurk there and he would never see it. "*Pax et bonum,*" he shouted, hoping more to attract attention than discover who his assailant was. A voice echoed chillingly back.

"*Pax et bonum,* King's man, royal emissary." Another crossbow bolt sliced through the air.

Corbett realised that the archer, whoever he was, did not intend to kill but to frighten. There was no attempt to take aim, to mark his quarry. He half rose and glanced around the pillar. He could detect nothing. He stared up at the carving grinning back at him, a monkey's face shrouded in a cowl with glaring protuberant eyes, tongue sticking out between thick lips, a wicked grimace on an evil face. He edged his knife out of its scabbard. He was safe as long as he didn't move. He heard a movement on the far side of the cloister and quickly shifted into the shadows so as to confuse his attacker. Abruptly a door at the far end of his side of the cloister opened, and a voice shouted:

"Who's there? Is everything all right?"

"God save you, Brother," Corbett called out. "I'm Sir Hugh Corbett, King's emissary. I'm a little lost." He heard a sound from across the garth and realised his assailant was slipping away. The lay brother came lumbering forward. Corbett waited until he was almost upon him before he moved. "Thank you, Brother." He grasped the lay brother's hand and stared into his face. "I was a little bit overcome and confused. Which way is it to the guesthouse?"

The lay brother was full of questions, but Corbett walked as fast as he could towards the door and the pool of light shed by the lantern hanging from its hook. Once inside, he relaxed, his body sweat-drenched, his heart thudding. The lay brother stared at him curiously.

"Sir Hugh, is all well?"

"Yes, yes," Corbett gasped. "Just a phantom of the night, nothing much. I'd be grateful, Brother, if you would escort me to my companions."

Back at the guesthouse, Corbett found Desroches sitting at a table with Ranulf and Chanson, sharing a cup of wine. The physician rose as he entered.

126

"Sir Hugh, I have been waiting some time. I thought Vespers was long over?"

"It is," Corbett declared, sitting down and willing himself to relax. "But Master Desroches, why have you come at such a late hour in such inclement weather?"

"Parson Warfeld is also here. He has gone to see the prior on some business, but —"

"I asked what you wanted," Corbett insisted. He felt tired and exasperated. He wished to retire and compose his thoughts. He wanted to write to Maeve, meditate, allow his mind to float.

"Lady Adelicia," Desroches declared. "She is pregnant."

"What?" Corbett exclaimed.

"You know what that means," Desroches continued evenly. "She cannot face execution now. Once we had left the Guildhall chamber, she demanded to see me. She claims that her courses have stopped for the last two months. I believe, Sir Hugh, after a superficial examination, that she is indeed pregnant. I have consulted with Parson Warfeld." He paused as the priest bustled through the door, shaking the water from his robe.

"Sir Hugh," Warfeld declared. "Has Master Desroches told you the news?" The parson eased himself over the bench and sat down. Grasping the wine jug, he poured himself a generous goblet and slurped noisily from it. "Our good physician told me the news and thought you should know — whilst I had business with the prior over the supply of communion breads so I came with him. It's impossible!" he gasped.

"What do you mean?" Corbett asked.

"Well," Desroches sighed, "one important fact: Rauf Decontet may have married Lady Adelicia, but outside the seal of confession, Parson Warfeld and I can assure you, Sir Hugh, that he could no more have begotten a child than a eunuch in the seraglio of the great Cham of Tartary."

"Parson Warfeld?"

"Sir Rauf often talked about it," the priest replied. "How he would love to have a son. Sir Hugh, in a word what Master Desroches and I are saying is that Sir Rauf Decontet was impotent, incapable of begetting a son. Therefore, the Lady Adelicia must have had a lover. I suspect you know who —"

"Wendover!" Ranulf intervened. "It's Master Wendover, captain of the city guard."

"True, true," Desroches murmured.

"Who is Wendover?" Corbett asked. "What is his background?"

"He is Sir Walter Castledene's man, body and soul," Warfeld replied. "He served in his personal retinue, and when Sir Walter was elected mayor, Wendover was appointed captain of the city guard. He is a Canterbury man, a former soldier; he has seen service here and there. A blustery man but of good heart, with an eye for the ladies! More importantly, Sir Hugh, he was present when Adam Blackstock and *The Waxman* were brought to judgement. He witnessed the hanging."

"And he was also on guard at Maubisson," Corbett declared, "when Paulents and the others were killed." He filled his wine cup and sipped it gently. He was beginning to feel sleepy. He needed to withdraw, reflect and collect his thoughts. He recalled the lament of David over Jonathan and thought of poor Griskin, as well as something Les Hommes Joyeuses had said to him. "Is there anything else?" he asked.

Desroches got to his feet; Parson Warfeld also.

"We thought it only proper to tell you now," the physician explained. "I mean, before we met tomorrow morning."

"And Decontet's house is still under guard?" Corbett asked.

"Oh yes," Parson Warfeld replied. "I pass it many a time. It is securely guarded at every entrance. Sir Walter Castledene has insisted on that."

"And Maubisson?" Corbett asked.

Desroches shrugged. "I don't know, Sir Hugh. Perhaps you had best ask Sir Walter yourself."

When the two men had left, Corbett finished his wine whilst his comrades chattered amongst themselves. "I was attacked!" he intervened brusquely, immediately the conversation died. "On leaving Vespers," he continued. "An assassin, a bowman as in the forest. Two crossbow bolts were loosed. I do not think he intended to kill but to warn me." He smiled thinly and was about to get up when Ranulf put a hand over his.

"Sir Hugh, you should go nowhere by yourself. Next time I will be with you. Lady Maeve insists on that."

"And me," Chanson declared hotly. "My leg is well, the ulcer is healing."

"Who could it be?" Ranulf mused. "Desroches was with us before Vespers ended and never left."

"And Parson Warfeld?"

"He came but then went to see the prior; a lay brother took him there."

Corbett rose to his feet. "I shall retire to my chamber. I will close the shutters over my window, lock and bolt my door, then I shall think. Gentlemen, good night . . ."

Corbett flung down the quill in desperation and glared at the triptych on the wall celebrating the arrival of St Augustine in Kent and his meeting with the Saxon king. He noticed with amusement how the artist had depicted Augustine in all three panels as if suffused by a golden glow, whilst his adversaries, the Saxon king and his entourage, were hidden in a cloud of shadows. He rose and stretched, easing the soreness in his legs and arms. He ignored the goblet of mulled wine standing on the table and stared down at the document taken from Paulents' casket. In truth, he was unable to break the cipher. At first he had thought it would be easy. Now a faint suspicion pricked his mind: was it all a farrago of nonsense? But in that case why was Paulents carrying it? As far as he could see, the so-called Cloister Map made no more sense than the jabbering of an idiot. Or was it just that he was frustrated? He had used his own cipher book, moving the letters scrawled on that piece of vellum, but all to no avail. Only the occasional word made sense.

Eventually Corbett had diverted himself by writing to Maeve, sending love and affection to her and the children, and concentrating on the petty aspects of their life such as the use of the long meadow at Leighton, the manor's claims to the advowson of the local church, as well as his rights as manor lord over assart and purpresture. He left most of these things to Maeve, who loved the complex legal claims underpinning tenure. She thoroughly enjoyed arguing with her attorney, Master Osbert, their audacious serjeant at law, about payment in fee or the true meaning of assart. Once he'd sealed his missive to her, Corbett turned to the letters he'd received from Westminster. The first had been dispatched under the Secret Seal. The second was from the prior of the abbey there, William de Huntingdon. The King's missive, written hastily, probably by Edward himself, gave details about the Lady Adelicia's wardship. How it had been granted to Sir Rauf Decontet at the behest of Walter Castledene. How both men had been colleagues and comrades in the past and proved themselves to be loyal servants of the Crown. In other words, Corbett reflected cynically, they had loaned the Exchequer considerable amounts of money. Corbett had asked for such information before he left Westminster. He was surprised Sir Walter hadn't described his relationship with Decontet more accurately, and wondered whether Castledene should be the right man to sit as judge of oyer and terminer in the case. The King had had no difficulty in sharing such information. Corbett could imagine Edward, iron-grey hair framing that falcon face, his right eye drooping, lips puckered, as he stood in some chancery chamber, kicking at the rushes and dictating the letter. Afterwards, pushing the poor scribe aside, he'd added a sentence in his own hand, a postscript about his precious snow-white hawk, now ill at the royal mews, reminding Corbett to pray at Becket's tomb that the bird should recover.

"I wish to God you'd given me more information about Castledene and Decontet," Corbett murmured. He tapped the letter against the table. That was another question he hoped to ask Sir Walter when they met tomorrow morning. In fact, although Corbett had made no progress with the cipher, he had decided how he would manage these affairs. So far he'd simply blundered around, acting on what others said or what he observed: that must end. He unrolled the King's letter again and studied its hasty last line: "*Dieu vous bénoit, par la main du Roi.*" The Norman French letters were ill-formed, but the King wished Corbett well and assured his principal clerk that he still enjoyed his royal master's favour and love.

The second letter, from the Prior of Westminster, was brief and succinct. Brother Hubert of Canterbury had left their community early in the summer of 1293. Before his swift departure he had destroyed all records of himself and disappeared from view. He had never returned. Hubert's departure, the prior confided, was as abrupt and sudden as a summer storm. Until then he had been a veritable beacon of light: a great scholar with a flair for study, well liked by his brethren, an obedient monk who strictly observed the rule of St Benedict in every way. As to his description, he was slim, of medium height, with comely face and pleasant manner. The only thing the prior had discovered was that Brother Hubert had received a mysterious visitor around the time of Pentecost. Once he had left, Brother Hubert had retreated to his private cell claiming sickness; three days later he was gone. Rumours had seeped back that Hubert had forsaken not only his vows, but any love of God, becoming a *venator hominum* — a hunter of men — but the prior could not comment on this.

Corbett put both letters down as he heard a knock on the door and Ranulf calling his name. He unlocked and unbarred the door, and Ranulf came in bearing a fresh goblet of posset wrapped in a napkin. Uninvited, he sat down on a stool.

"Chanson is sleeping, master, and so you should be."

Corbett took the goblet, sat on the edge of his bed and sipped carefully. He was determined on a soul-fast sleep, no heart-shaking dreams, phantasms or nightmares fed by too much wine. He stared down at the cold grey stone floor and shivered at a nasty draught which seeped like a fiend beneath the door to prickle the skin.

"Master?"

Corbett glanced up.

"What sense do you make of this?"

"What sense?" Corbett laughed. "Why, Ranulf, none at all." He sipped once more from the wine, put the cup down between his buskined feet and leaned forward, hands together. "Ranulf, have you heard from Lady Constance?"

Ranulf blushed at the mention of the daughter of the Constable of Corfe Castle. He'd met her only a few weeks before when he and Corbett were on royal business in the West Country.

"Oh, not yet, Master, but this present business?"

"I mention this present business because you are determined on advancement in the royal service or, if you decide so, to enter the church as a priest, though one spurred by great ambition. Is that not true, Ranulf?"

His manservant shuffled his feet, wiping the palms of his hands on his hose, but he held Corbett's gaze. This was a matter he had often discussed with Master Long-Face. Ranulf was determined on his own advancement. He had studied every book Corbett had loaned him, and scrutinised his master's methods as carefully and avidly as any hungry cat would a mousehole.

"One thing I have taught you," Corbett held his hands up as if in prayer, "is never to make a judgement until you've collected all the facts, everything you can. What we are dealing with here, Ranulf, is murder, the killing of another human being by another, an unlawful slaying. Rest assured of this: murder is the fruit of a poisonous, hateful plant. Remember, however, it's always the fruit, the rotten blossom, not the root. Think of a bush thrusting up on the edge of black, weed-filled water full of rotting cones and dead leaves. On that bush is a ripening fungus, full and plump as a cushion. You don't like the countryside, Ranulf, yet you must have passed such scenes: that's what murder is like, some rotten bush fed by hate, anger and resentment. It's what we have here. On the one hand there's that

134

poor family massacred at Maubisson. Why? How? We also have Decontet, his skull shattered like a wine jug. We have seen some of murder's fruit: the corpses, the hatred, the division. But in this case the roots go much deeper: Blackstock the pirate waging war at sea, dying a violent death; his half-brother Hubert fleeing from his monastery to become a hunter of men . . . and still we haven't reached the roots. Why did Blackstock turn to piracy? What caused Hubert, a good monk, a follower of St Benedict, to renounce his vows and acquire a reputation as someone who feared neither God nor man? It's only when we dig deep that we find the source, and possibly the cure, of all this rottenness. Many questions have to be asked and their answers closely analysed. If God gives me life and health, that is what I shall begin to do tomorrow." He rose to his feet and stretched out his hand for Ranulf to clasp. "Say your prayers," he murmured. "And if the spirit takes you, join me in the stalls for the Lauds Mass. Let's sing, praise God and ask for his guidance . . ."

Corbett rose long before daybreak. He opened the shutters and peered out through an arrow-slit window. The moon was still distinct, though distant, like the brightness of a small coin. It hadn't snowed but it was bitterly cold. Corbett had to use a pair of small bellows to fan some heat back into the braziers before he stripped, washed, and dressed for the day. He took out woollen hose from the panniers, thick socks, a heavy worsted shirt and a quilted cote-hardie. Around his waist he wrapped his sword belt, even though he was attending Mass; once there he'd unbuckle it and place it in the porch. From the noise in the chamber next door he realised that either Ranulf or Chanson, or possibly both, was preparing to join him. He put the metal caps over the braziers, made sure the shutters were closed and left, locking the door behind him.

He waited in the refectory below, refusing the ministrations of a sleepy lay brother. Ranulf and Chanson, also dressed against the cold, soon joined him. Ranulf's face was fresh and cleanly shaven but Chanson looked as if he'd just tumbled out of bed. The three of them made their way through the cloisters and joined the monks as they filed like dark shadows into the candlelit church. Corbett and his companions sat in those stalls reserved for visitors. As so often, certain words from the Scriptures caught Corbett's attention and made him concentrate on the battle in hand. When the lector recited "For it is close, the day of their ruin, their doom come at speed", he half smiled, for the text neatly summarised what he'd said to Ranulf, though for a while that would have to wait.

Once Lauds was over, Corbett and his party stayed just within the rood screen as the Jesus Mass was celebrated. Afterwards they adjourned to the refectory in the guesthouse, where a lay brother served salted bacon, soft cheese and jugs of watered ale. When they had eaten, Corbett ordered Ranulf and Chanson to prepare for their journey into the city, whilst he excused himself, saying he wanted to ensure Les Hommes Joyeuses were settled; it was the least he could do for fellow travellers. Ranulf demanded to accompany him but Corbett refused. On the insistence of his comrades, Corbett took a small arbalest from their weapon store and left, following the trackway leading through the fields to the disused church of St Pancras and its old priest's house. The sky was lightening, though the darkness still clung, a sharp contrast to the white shroud of snow which covered everything, trees stark and black, bushes and undergrowth all weighed down by ice. Crows and ravens, defying the biting wind, walked stiff-legged across the snow, only to burst upwards in a flurry of black feathers at his approach. Corbett passed disused outhouses with their coarse grey stone and narrow slit windows. A fox slunk by, its coat all smeared with mud, belly close to the ground. Now and again he stopped to glance back, yet there was nothing but the path sneaking behind him. He rounded a bend and immediately paused. A figure, cowled and bent, was shuffling towards him. Corbett's free hand went to his dagger as the dark shape approached, but it was only a beggar man, grey-faced and shivering, who stared watery-eyed at him then whined for a coin, which Corbett spun in his direction. The clerk watched the beggar man pass him by, then continued on his way.

At last the grim tower of St Pancras loomed above the trees. Corbett relaxed as he smelt wood smoke and the tasty odours of food mixed with the acrid tang of horse and hay. He crossed a small footbridge, up a path and through a crumbling lychgate into God's acre. The church was nothing more than an old barn-like structure under a much-decayed sloping roof, with a squat ugly tower built on one side. Its lancet windows were boarded up, as was the old porch door. Corbett went round the church and heaved a sigh of relief. Les Hommes Joyeuses were already aroused, their gaudily covered carts lined up before the old priest's house. The fence around this had crumbled, its thatched roof sagged, whilst the door and shutters hung loose. Fires had been lit and women were preparing small cauldrons of oatmeal or laying strips of salted meat across makeshift grills. A man came from behind a wagon, an arrow notched to his bow. Corbett put his arbalest down and lifted both hands in a sign of peace; in this poor light he didn't want to make a mistake.

"Greetings," he called out. "Greetings to Les Hommes Joyeuses. I seek the Gleeman."

"Sir Hugh." The Gleeman, hood pushed back, came out of the priest's house shouting at the bowman not to be a fool, and beckoned Corbett forward.

CHAPTER
SEVEN

Hominum que contente mundique huius et cupido.
Man's struggle with man and the lust of the world.
Medieval poem

The clerk went into the small hall of the priest's house. This had been cleared, the floor scoured; a weak fire crackled in the hearth and the narrow windows were blocked with blackened straw. The Gleeman asked the woman tending the hearth and the children clinging to her robe to leave. He invited Corbett to sit on a stool by the fire whilst he squatted down next to him, his back to the inglenook, as if they were old comrades, which in truth they were. Corbett waited until the small hall was emptied, then extended his right hand. The wind-chapped face of Robert Ormesby, former clerk, now Gleeman of Les Hommes Joyeuses, broke into a smile. Neither Ranulf nor even the King knew that Ormesby was Corbett's spy. Corbett paid him directly from his own purse for the information he collected as he and his troupe wandered the wealthy towns and villages in the east and south of the kingdom.

"A mere coincidence," Ormesby whispered, "meeting you on Harbledown Hill." He forced a smile. "The minute I heard about three horsemen led by a king's clerk, I guessed who it was." He gestured round. "I thank you for our lodgings."

"You are well?" Corbett leaned closer to the fire.

"I still have dreams, nightmares," Ormesby muttered, not meeting Corbett's eyes.

"About Stirling?"

The Gleeman looked away, breathing quickly as he strove to clear his mind of that fatal battle six years earlier when the Scottish leader Wallace had trapped the English vanguard at Stirling Bridge.

"I still see them," he muttered, "the Scots, a mass of men bristling with steel tips like some huge, malevolent hedgehog advancing towards us, great horns blasting, war cries ringing out. Cressingham, that stupid bastard!"

Corbett just stared into the flames. He'd lost other friends, mailed clerks, at that disaster when Hugh de Cressingham, Knight of the Swan and Edward's treasurer in Scotland, had insisted on his hasty advance across Stirling Bridge, walking straight into Wallace's trap. For men like the Gleeman, the only consolation was that Cressingham himself had been dragged from his saddle and killed, his fat corpse skinned to make tokens for the Scots; Wallace had even made a belt out of the piece given to him. King Edward had hurried into Scotland and reversed the defeat by his victory at Falkirk, but Ormesby had seen enough. He left the royal service, moved to a village outside Glastonbury and married a local girl. She had died in childbirth, so Ormesby had used his little wealth to finance Les Hommes Joyeuses and assumed the role of the

140

Gleeman, their leader. Corbett had met him three years earlier during a commission of oyer and terminer in Essex, and promptly recruited him. Ormesby roamed the roads and collected all the gossip and tittle-tattle which Corbett could sift on behalf of his royal master.

"And your news?"

"I received your letter before the snows came," the Gleeman replied. "We moved into Suffolk, following the River Denham, making enquiries amongst the villagers, the wise women, the tavern-hunters, the wandering chapmen. It's true, Sir Hugh." The Gleeman's eyes glittered greedily. "There's gossip," he whispered, "about what they call the Haunt of Ghosts."

"The Haunt of Ghosts?"

"A lonely place, Sir Hugh, desolate moorland except for a dozen tumuli or grave-mounds, not far from the Denham. The gossip is that in ancient times a great king, with a treasure hoard beyond all expectation, was buried somewhere close. People have searched for it but nothing's been found. A local priest talks of maps and charts, but . . ." He shook his head.

"And recently?" Corbett asked.

"A bailiff near Denham said that about three or four years ago strangers came into the area asking about the local lore and legend, but he cannot remember their names or faces. Sir Hugh," Ormesby jabbed a finger in the air, "a great treasure does exist. There have been enquiries recently, nothing precise, just whispers, like the breeze on a summer's evening."

"But there has been no report of diggings, of anyone searching for the treasure?"

"As I said, local lore and legend, recent enquiries, strangers coming in and out with heads hooded and faces hidden. You must remember, Sir Hugh, it's a busy place, people passing to and fro from Ipswich and the other market towns. The legends are so ancient no one really pays much attention."

"And Blackstock, *The Waxman*?"

"Well known along the Colvasse peninsula. *The Waxman* often slipped into the coves and inlets around Orwell. Blackstock was respected and liked, regarded as a hero. He and his men never plundered or pillaged. They paid good prices to the local peasant farmers and kept the peace. Blackstock restocked and refurbished his ship, filled water barrels and slipped away like a sea mist."

"And his half-brother, Hubert the Monk?"

"Again, gossip, but no one ever saw him. People said that Blackstock would meet someone, probably Hubert, at a derelict hermitage on the River Orwell." He paused. "Ah yes, that's its name: St Simon of the Rocks. The locals also claim Blackstock was probably heading there when he was trapped by two war cogs against the coast in the October of 1300. The villagers still talk of the sea fight which took place. How afterwards Sir Walter Castledene's ship *The Caltrop* sailed into Orwell with Blackstock's corpse dangling by its neck from the poop. To be sure, Sir Hugh, the peasants did not like that." The Gleeman thrust a small log and some kindling into the charcoal now glowing strongly in the hearth. He turned, wiping his hands. "Do you want something to eat or drink?"

142

"No, no thank you."

The Gleeman got up and went into an adjoining room, probably the buttery, coming back with a tankard of ale and a hunk of bread. He drank and ate noisily.

"A bloody sea fight!" he said between mouthfuls.

"Were there any survivors?"

"Oh yes. According to the villagers, Castledene did the same as Blackstock had done to his crews. I believe he hanged his prisoners though he may have thrown some of them overboard. They could either drown or make their way to the shore; that's where Castledene made a mistake. You see, Sir Hugh, along most coastlines shipwrecked sailors are shown very little mercy, but Blackstock and his crew were liked. One man survived and he was helped. No one knew his name. He was sea-soaked, half dead; they gave him some hot oatmeal, dried his clothes and sent him on his way."

"And *The Waxman*, the ship itself?"

"Taken away, given to the merchants who'd helped Sir Walter."

"What happened to Blackstock's corpse?"

"Well, Sir Walter Castledene and Paulents were triumphant. They took their ships into Hamford Water, near Walton on the Naze. The crews feasted. Blackstock's corpse was dragged along the cobbles on a hurdle behind a horse before being hung from some gallows out on the mud flats. They put a guard about it, let it dangle there for the sea birds to have their fill, and then," the Gleeman shrugged, "according to popular rumour, it was flung into the sea, certainly not given honourable burial. I tell you, Sir Hugh, Castledene and Paulents made few friends that day."

"And Hubert the Monk?"

"Ask Sir Walter Castledene. Hubert rarely showed his face, and after his brother's death he disappeared completely. No one has seen him since."

Corbett stared into the flames, watching one of the logs crackling in the heat. Outside he could hear the chatter and noise of Les Hommes Joyeuses as they prepared for another day. Somewhere far off tambourines sounded. Corbett realised that the morning was moving on; he had to return to St Augustine's. He undid the purse on his belt, drew out some silver coins and pressed them into the Gleeman's hands.

"Sir Hugh, why do you ask me? Sir Walter will tell you all this."

"No, Master Gleeman." Corbett patted him on the shoulder. "He'll tell me what he wants me to know, whereas you will tell me what you saw and heard. Do you know what caused such hatred? Why did Blackstock take to the sea and Hubert leave his monastery to become a hunter of men?"

"Just rumours, Sir Hugh, legends about their childhood."

Corbett stared up at the rough carving above the hearth, then glanced around. A strange place, he mused; so comfortable just staring into the fire, yet he could also feel the cold, seeping draughts, and the Gleeman's impatience: there was a day's work ahead and he wished Corbett to be gone.

"And so we come to Griskin," Corbett said. "You knew who he really was? You referred to him at Harbledown."

"He spoke to me about his golden days, being a scholar in the schools. I recognised he was your man, Sir Hugh. He would come and go like the breeze. He rejoiced in acting the leper. He used to laugh at that, the way he could move so easily; not even outlaws or wolfsheads would approach him. He came into our camp and introduced himself. He carried a medallion like I do, the one you gave us to recognise each other. I'll be honest, I'd met Master Griskin before, though in different disguises. In fact," the Gleeman smiled, "if he'd wanted to, he could have joined our troupe. He was a true troubadour, a mime who rejoiced in his various roles. He reeked like a midden heap, and his face and hands were painted and roughened as if he'd suffered some grisly affliction. I met him outside the camp and asked him what he wanted. He replied that he'd come looking for Hubert the Monk. I couldn't help him but I told him what I told you. We met just after we'd crossed into Essex. We were staying near Thorpe-le-Soken, for we tend to lodge near the coast. Fishing communities are friendlier than villages deep in the countryside, especially in winter. I asked Griskin if fortune had favoured him. Now he'd drunk quite deeply on ale; you know he liked that?"

Corbett nodded.

"One of his great weaknesses," the Gleeman continued. "If he didn't drink, he didn't drink, but once he did, he rarely stopped. Anyway, Griskin said that he knew someone called Simon of the Rocks. I didn't know what he meant."

Corbett recalled how the Merchant of Souls had mentioned the same name.

"Have you ever heard of St Simon of the Rocks?" Corbett asked.

"Vaguely. Griskin talked about the hermitage on the Orwell. How Hubert the Monk may have disappeared, though he suspected where he was hiding. Then he mentioned Simon of the Rocks; I think that's the name of the hermitage chapel along the Orwell. Anyway, Griskin seemed keen to press on, so I let him go. He said that if he discovered anything of interest he would return. We stayed at Thorpe-le-Soken seven days. The following week, a chapman, a wandering tinker, came into our camp to warm himself by the fire. He talked about the gallows outside Thorpe-le-Soken; of a man hanging there completely naked. Those who'd seen the corpse thought it was a leper. Of course I became alarmed. Griskin hadn't returned, so I and some of the men went out. The gibbet is high and stark, overlooking ice-blasted wastelands. A harsh, dark place, Sir Hugh, where the clouds hang down like the wrath of God. The biting wind tugs at your clothes as if it was a fiend sent to plague you. We saw the gibbet from afar, the corpse swinging like a rag. I tell you this." The Gleeman leaned closer in a gust of ale and sweat-soaked clothes. "I knew something was wrong. That gibbet was rarely used except for the occasional cattle thief or a felon caught red-handed by the sheriff's comitatus. I drew closer.

146

One glance told me it was Griskin. He'd been stripped completely naked. The noose, tight around his neck, was looped through the hook on the arm of the scaffold: a monstrosity out of a nightmare. His belly was puffed out like a pig's bladder, tongue fastened between his teeth, eyes popping out. The crows and ravens had already been busy."

Corbett closed his eyes and muttered the Requiem.

"I knew Griskin. I couldn't leave him, so I cut him down. We buried him there and erected a makeshift cross. I looked at the corpse." The Gleeman tapped the side of his head. "There was a blow here. I believe Griskin was enticed out on to that lonely wasteland of hell, his head staved in, then he was hanged, half alive, his breath choked out."

"You think Hubert the Monk was responsible?"

"Who else, Sir Hugh? What would a leper have worth stealing? How could a leper threaten anyone? Even outlaws stay away from them. No, someone had discovered Griskin was not what he claimed to be, that he was searching for something or somebody. Of course it must be Hubert the Monk."

"You've heard what happened at Maubisson?"

"The news is all over the city," the Gleeman replied. "An entire family hanging by their necks in that lonely manor with no sign of violence: they are talking of ghosts and demons . . ."

"They can talk about that to their hearts' content," Corbett snapped, "as long as they call them Hubert. Ah well, Master Gleeman, so what have we discovered? That a treasure lies somewhere out in the wastelands of

Suffolk near the River Denham. That there are legends about it, and always have been; that people have searched for it but no one has found it. There has been a quickening of interest, and then what? We have Blackstock and his half-brother; did they know where the treasure was? Adam Blackstock was certainly sailing to meet his brother so they could unite and discover this king's ransom. However, Blackstock's ship was attacked, and Blackstock was killed and gibbeted. Only one of his crew apparently survived. I sent messages to you and Griskin to learn all you could about Hubert the Monk and the lost treasure. Nothing is truly discovered except rumours and stories, but then Griskin is murdered."

Corbett patted his thigh, got to his feet, opened his purse and slipped another coin into the Gleeman's hand. He stared around the old priest's house, the crumbling plaster, the cracked floor, the gaps in the windows, the sagging roof, the dirt and filth brushed into a corner. On reflection he didn't like this place, he wanted to be gone. The story the Gleeman had told him about poor Griskin's death was equally filthy, horrid and menacing. He thought of his walk back through the lonely woods to St Augustine's. He turned at the door.

"Master Gleeman, I would like an escort, maybe two of your men?"

"Sir Hugh, I can't spare any. I've sent some out to snare rabbits in the wasteland, but I can ask two of our boys." The Gleeman stood up, and went outside shouting. A short while later two lads, merry-faced, bright-eyed and clothed in rags, came leaping up. They introduced themselves as Jack o' the Lantern and David of the Mist. They danced around Corbett like sprites, asking him questions, chattering away in a patois he couldn't understand. He bade adieu to the Gleeman and moved away, the boys dancing in front of him, shoving and pushing, kicking up the snow, scaring the birds, flinging their arms out. Corbett smiled at the sheer exuberance of youth, a welcome relief from that dank cottage and the sombre news he'd received.

"Come here, lads," he called. "Come here."

Both boys fell silent and came running up. Corbett noticed they were barefoot.

"You have no shoes."

"It's not our turn to wear them, sir; it's our turn to collect sticks, so we are pleased to act as your guides."

"And very good guides you are. Where are you from?"

"We live in Birch Hall or Birch Manor," Jack o' the Lantern replied.

"We have lived there for years," David of the Mist teased as he chased his brother off.

Again Corbett called them back. "Birch Hall, Birch Manor, what do you mean?"

The two lads started laughing, pushing and shoving each other, and pointed to the trees on either side of the trackway.

"This is Birch Manor; this is Birch Hall: the trees, that's where we live." And chattering like squirrels on a branch, they ran ahead of Corbett, leading him back into the grounds of St Augustine's Abbey.

Corbett was well down the lane when he heard his name being called. He turned and watched the figure emerge from the mist. The Gleeman hurried limping towards him.

"Sir Hugh! Sir Hugh!"

Corbett walked back. The Gleeman paused, hands on his side, gasping for breath.

"What is it, man?"

"I forgot something about Griskin! When we cut him down from the scaffold and buried him . . ."

"Yes?"

"His left hand had been cut off, severed completely at the wrist. I never understood why. I've heard stories, but I thought I should tell you."

Corbett stared down the path; the mist was growing thicker. Behind him he could hear the boys shouting at him to come, how the abbey buildings were in sight, just a short walk, almost as if they could sense his apprehension.

"I thank you, Gleeman." He raised his hand and bowed. "I am grateful; as you say, God knows why anyone should do that."

He went back to join the boys, now skipping and leaping like hares in front of him. They passed through a gate into the abbey grounds. The boys, still dancing from foot to foot, asked him if he wanted anything else. Could they look around? Corbett called them closer and pressed a coin into each of their grubby hands.

"No, no," he declared, smiling down at them. "Go back. The Gleeman is waiting for you. I think he has other errands waiting."

The boys left as swift as lurchers, heading for the gate, jostling each other. Corbett watched them go. For a brief moment he felt a deep sense of envy at their innocence. They had no fear. To them this was not an icy, mist-strewn place where all sorts of demons and dangers lurked. He sighed and walked on across the snow-covered yards and gardens. Now and again a brother would pass him and whisper a salutation, Corbett would reply absent-mindedly; all he could really think of was poor Griskin, naked, bloated, and hanging from that lonely scaffold over those icy marshes. He had reached the small cloisters leading down to the guesthouse when he heard his name being called.

"Sir Hugh, Sir Hugh!"

He turned round. The guest master came hobbling up, one hand held out, the other containing a leather sack bound and sealed at the neck. The monk handed this over, saying it had been left for Corbett at the abbey lodge, but by whom he couldn't say. He then questioned Corbett about his lodgings. Were they warm and comfortable? Corbett nodded distractedly and the guest master, remembering other duties, hastened away.

Corbett walked into a shadowy alcove and lifted the bag up. It was of thick Spanish leather, the string pulled tight, the neck sealed with wax. He broke the seal and undid the knot, loosened the sack and put his hand in. He drew out a linen cloth containing something cold and hard. Even as he undid the folds, he felt a shiver of apprehension, then stared in horror at what he'd uncovered: a human hand, severed at the wrist, blackened like a piece of cured meat, and in between the forefinger and thumb, a blood-red tarot candle, its wick charred from burning. Corbett swallowed hard and tried to control the nausea in his stomach. Bile gathered at the back of his throat. He wanted to scream, to throw it away. He turned the hand over. The flesh had been smoke-dried, shrunk like a scrap of rotten pork. He placed it gently back in the linen folds and dropped the gruesome package back into the sack, tying the knot tightly. Then he sat down on a small bench in the alcove to control his breathing, the hot sweat on his back turning icy.

"Griskin's hand!" he whispered.

He stared across at a small fountain covered in ice, the garden bed around it frosted and dead, then closed his eyes and leaned back. He knew what he'd been sent. A talisman, a diabolic token, the Hand of Glory, the curse of a hanged man. He fought to control his anger. He didn't believe in such nonsense, but he recognised that Griskin's killer, possibly Hubert the Monk, had done this to frighten him.

He took a deep breath, rose to his feet and walked through the abbey buildings until he found the smithy in the main stable yard. A lay brother stood at the entrance hammering a piece of metal with a huge mallet. The crashing stilled as Corbett approached.

"What can I do for you, sir?" The brother looked Corbett over from head to toe, then glimpsed the ring on his left hand. "Ah, you must be our guest, the King's man."

"You have a fire," Corbett asked, "a forge?"

The man nodded. Corbett handed the sack over. "Do not look inside; burn it, burn it now!"

The smith shrugged, took the sack and walked inside. Corbett stood and watched the great door of the forge opened; the abomination was thrust in and the door closed.

"Push it deeper into the coals," he urged.

The smith shrugged, opened the forge, pushed the sack further into the coals with a poker, closed the door again, then walked back outside.

"Sir, what was in there?"

"Something devilish," Corbett replied, "but fire will cleanse it!"

He stood for a while in the smithy, relishing its warmth, the smell of horses, hay, and roasting iron. Then he went across to a makeshift lavarium and, pouring water over his hands, washed them carefully, drying them on a napkin. He thanked the smith, took directions to the guesthouse and returned there. He could hear Ranulf and Chanson as soon as he entered the small downstairs refectory; they were singing, and Ranulf was teasing his comrade. Corbett stamped up the stairs. Ranulf and Chanson came out of their room to meet him, took one look at Corbett's face and hastily retreated.

Corbett went into his chamber, slamming the door behind him. He slung down the small arbalest from his shoulder, took off his war belt and lay down on the bed. He found it difficult to concentrate. He tried to recall a Goliard song he loved to sing to Maeve: "*Iam dulcis*

153

amica — now my sweet friend . . ." but the words and tune were difficult to recall. He swung his legs off the bed. Ranulf and Chanson knocked on the door and came in.

"Master, we are sorry."

Corbett brushed aside their apology. He could not tell them about where he'd been or his meeting with the Gleeman, so he fended off their questions in a flurry of preparations.

Ranulf leaned against the aumbry and narrowed his eyes. Master Long-Face was certainly agitated, but about what? Edward the King often took Ranulf aside and, leaning close, his right eye almost closed, would grasp the clerk's arm until Ranulf winced with pain. The King would then instruct Ranulf to keep a vigilant watch on Sir Hugh. Ranulf had long realised this was not solely due to affection. In a word, Edward of England did not trust Corbett fully.

"Too soft," he'd whisper. "Corbett has a heart and a soul, Ranulf." Then the King would add, "Which is more than he can say about us! Eh, Master Ranulf?"

The Senior Clerk in the Chancery of the Green Wax had never truly answered that question, either to himself or to the King. Ranulf had not decided what choices he would make. All he concentrated on was the road sweeping in front of him, the path to honour, power, glory and wealth. In truth, Corbett was that path, and so he had to keep Master Long-Face safe, not just for Maeve, little Edward and Eleanor, but more importantly for himself.

154

"You are ready?" Corbett, booted and spurred, his cloak tied about him, was ready to leave. Ranulf hastened to follow. They went down to the courtyard, where Chanson had prepared the horses. A short while later they left the abbey precincts. Corbett, slouched low in the saddle, allowed Ranulf and Chanson to lead as they wound their way up past St Queningate church and into the city. He felt strange. He had still to recover from the shock of that gruesome hand. He wanted to concentrate, yet the scenes around him came like images in a dream or wall paintings glimpsed in a church. A row of crows cawed on the side of a cart. Traders and tinkers hurried by, their trays full of trinkets, scent boxes, St Christopher medals, Becket badges, inkwells and quills. A relic-seller, his skin burnt dark by the sun, bearded, with fierce glaring eyes, was bawling how he was prepared to auction the Virgin Mary's wedding ring, one of Christ's shoe latchets, and a piece of the door from the church Simon Magus had built in Rome. A master of the drains and ditches, preceded by two ruffians carrying a tawdry banner displaying the city arms, proclaimed to all and sundry how "the flushing of the drains and sewers as well as the houses of easement on this side of the River Stour will be carried out before the eve of Christmas". A group of nuns clattered by in their black soutanes, woollen pelisses, white linen caps and rounded boots. Nearby a beggar had frozen to death in the stocks and the officials were arguing about who should remove the corpse and bury it. Children in rags, feet bare, jumped over frozen yellow pools. Householders pulled sledges across the ice heaped with Yule logs and greenery to decorate their homes for the great feast. Stall-owners shouted prices above the clatter of the carts. Pedlars and pilgrims, merchants and moon people, rich and poor, cleric and lay, all jostled like a shoal of fish along the narrow streets, made even more crowded by the stalls and shops. Somewhere an Angelus bell tolled to remind the faithful to recite one Pater, one Ave and one Gloria. However, most of the faithful seemed more intent on following the delicious odours trailing from the alehouses, taverns and pastry shops where the makers were drawing out fresh batches of gold-encrusted pies full of hot minced beef, highly spiced to hide its age.

Corbett and Ranulf dismounted on the corner of an alleyway outside the piscina of the cathedral church of the Holy Trinity. A lay brother allowed them into the monks' cemetery, though this was no haven of peace as it also served as sanctuary for wolfsheads, outlaws and other fugitives from justice. A gang of wild men in their ragged hoods and animal-skin hats, they were dressed in garish rags, though all were well armed as they squatted around roaring campfires eating, drinking and arguing with the drabs and whores who'd come looking for custom. They glanced greedily at Corbett and his two companions, but the clatter of weapons and Ranulf's hard stare persuaded them from any mischief.

"Where are we going?" Chanson whispered.

"To Becket's shrine," Ranulf replied. "I've explained before. His Grace the King, well, you've seen his menagerie at the Tower: dromedaries, camels, lions, huge cats, apes and monkeys; he likes his animals but he truly loves his hawks. On one occasion he almost beat to death a falconer who made a mistake and harmed one of them. Anyway, two of the precious birds at the royal mews near Eleanor's Cross are ill. The King had two golden coins blessed over their heads and has asked Corbett to bring them here as an offering." He nudged Chanson playfully. "Better than taking a wax image. I heard about one poor nuncius who carried one of those to Walsingham. By the time he arrived, the image had melted."

"And?"

"Made little difference," Ranulf whispered. "The bird was already dead."

They hobbled their horses in the monks' cemetery, leaving Chanson on guard, while Corbett and Ranulf went round through the deep snow under the brooding cathedral, a splendid mass of stone buttresses, soaring walls, elaborate cornices, grinning masks and stone-eyed faces. They slipped through a side door and entered a mystical world of arches, lofty vaults hidden in the darkness with shafts of grey and coloured light pouring through the windows; some of these were stained and painted, others opaque. They passed a glorious pageant of painted walls and squat round pillars, their cornices gilded at top and bottom, across floors tiled and decorated with phoenixes, turtle doves and sprouting lilies. Plumes of warm, sweet candle smoke wafted through the icy air in a vain attempt to fend off the cold and the stench of pilgrims.

The cathedral was fairly empty, only the most ardent visiting the shrine in the depth of winter. Corbett and Ranulf went singly along the choir aisle, turning right at the presbytery and up a long, worn flight of stone steps into Trinity Chapel, which housed the great table tomb of Becket. Above this the glorious shrine, its protective screens pulled up, shimmered like a vision from heaven. Ranulf gasped in amazement. Notwithstanding its great size, the shrine was entirely covered with plates of pure gold, yet that was hardly visible due to the precious stones which studded it: sapphires, diamonds, rubies, balas rubies and emeralds. Corbett and Ranulf walked around to study this magnificence more closely. On all sides the gold was carved and engraved with beautiful designs and studded with agate, jaspers and cornelians, some of these precious stones being as large as pigeon's eggs. The tomb seemed to glow as if it housed some mysterious fire, and Ranulf easily understood why so many flocked here from all parts of Europe to pray before the blessed bones of Thomas à Becket.

Corbett approached the monkish guardian of the shrine, using his seal and signet ring to gain immediate access to the small cushioned alcoves in the altar tomb. There he knelt, pressing his lips against the cold marble. He closed his eyes and whispered a prayer, not so much for the King or his blessed falcons, but for himself, Ranulf, Chanson, and above all Maeve and their two children. He paused, crossed himself, then rose and gave the offering of two gold coins to the hovering sacristan. He went down the steps, lit a taper before the lady altar and left.

158

Ranulf was determined to tell Chanson everything he had seen, but Corbett was insistent. The hour was passing. They must meet Castledene and the rest of them at Sweetmead Manor. They collected their horses and led them out of the cathedral precincts, down narrow, stinking, ice-cold runnels haunted by dark shifting shapes, over a wooden bridge spanning the Stour, past St Thomas's church and across the wastelands, following the frozen beaten track leading to Sweetmead Manor.

CHAPTER
EIGHT

Desunt sermones, dolor sensum abtulit.
Words fail and sorrow numbs the senses.

Paulinus of Aquilea

Hidden behind a line of trees, Sweetmead proved to be a splendid square three-storey building of shiny black timber and pink plaster which stood on a ragstone base behind its own red-brick curtain wall. The double gate to this had been flung open, and even though all the noonday bells were yet to ring, Castledene, Wendover, Parson Warfeld, Physician Desroches, Lady Adelicia, Berengaria and Lechlade were already gathered on the small pebble-strewn forecourt before the steps to the main door. Corbett noticed how the windows of the house were firmly shuttered. City guards stood everywhere, and had been there for some time judging from the rubbish strewn around the blackened circles in the snow where they'd built their campfires. Hasty introductions and salutations were exchanged. Corbett asked Castledene if Servinus had been seen. The Mayor shrugged.

"No sign whatsoever, Sir Hugh. The roads are clogged; even so, I've sent more couriers to the nearest ports." He shook his head. "He must still be hiding in the city, though a foreigner would find it difficult to

160

find any sanctuary here. I have given my men his description; sooner or later he'll be seen."

Corbett chewed on the corner of his lip and stared around.

"Lady Adelicia." He beckoned her away from the sharp-eyed Berengaria.

"Sir Hugh?" Lady Adelicia drew close.

"Madame, you are enceinte?"

Her cold blue eyes held his.

"The father?" Corbett asked. "Sir Rauf?"

"My secret, Sir Hugh. More importantly, I cannot hang or burn, and why should I? I hated him but I did not kill him!" Adelicia's voice was quiet but she spat the words out, the curl of her lips turning that beautiful face ugly. Corbett turned away, his patience exhausted; he had decided on his course of action. He strode to the foot of the steps.

"Open the door."

He was weary of this Hodman's bluff, of blundering around, of being poked and pushed like some blindfolded fool. Time was passing. He had questions to ask and they had to be answered. Wendover and the guards hurried to obey. Castledene came over to speak, but Corbett held up a gauntleted hand.

"Sir Walter, I have decided on what I must do." He let his hand drop gently on the Mayor's shoulder. "You must send two of your men back to your clerks in the Guildhall. I want," he squeezed Castledene's shoulder, "every record, every scrap of parchment your chancery holds about the pirate Blackstock and his half-brother Hubert. They have to be brought here, now!" He brushed aside Castledene's protests and went up the steps. "And you." He grabbed Wendover by the arm. "Light all candles, lamps and lantern horns, refill braziers, every hearth must have a fire. Light the ovens, and then check the stores and the buttery. Send one of your men to the tavern we passed as we crossed the wasteland; it has a red sign."

"The Antlered Stag," Parson Warfeld intervened. "That's it."

"Buy food, a cask of ale."

"And the money?" Wendover was still impudent.

Corbett pointed at Castledene, then strode into that house of death.

Sweetmead was truly ill named. It was a forbidding place. Its entrance parlour was well furnished, but the dark cloths against the walls and the matching turkey rugs were all sombre-hued, whilst the central staircase of heavy oak swept up into the gloom. It smelt sour despite the pots of freshly pressed flowers and herbs standing in the corners. To his right, through a half-open door, Corbett glimpsed a small hall with a mantled hearth, long trestle tables, painted arras and table screen. To the left lay Sir Rauf's chamber; its door, snapped clean off the leather hinges, leaned against the wall, the bolts and clasps at both top and bottom twisted or broken. Corbett crouched down and inspected the heavy inside lock. He recognised the subtle, intricate work of a truly skilled craftsman, probably a locksmith from one of the London guilds.

He walked into the chancery room and waited whilst others hastened to pull back shutters, light lamps and

162

tend to the hearth. The chamber was low-ceilinged, its white plaster ribbed by black-painted rafters. The walls, a faint lilac, were draped with heavy cloths interspersed with a crucifix and funereal scenes from the Scriptures. A close, soulless chamber, its shelves were crammed with tagged rolls of vellum. Against the walls stood iron-bound chests and coffers, all secured by chains and locks. A heavy oaken desk, covered in sheets of vellum, quills, parchment knives and inkwells, dominated the room. Corbett crouched down, lifted the cream-coloured turkey rug from the floor and scrutinised the dried bloodstain. Castledene came over to explain how the corpse had lain. Corbett nodded, then left and went up the stairs.

The house was freezing cold, even more so here. Castledene and Lechlade clattered up behind him. Corbett asked for Lady Adelicia's chamber, and Lechlade pushed past and led him down a small gallery, throwing open a door. Once again Corbett inspected the lock; it was very similar to the one to Sir Rauf's chamber. He pushed the door open and entered a comfortable bedchamber. Its walls were painted a restful green, and the furniture was unlike that in the rest of the house; its table, chairs and quilted stools were fashioned out of gleaming polished elm. To his right stood a four-poster bed draped with gold-fringed blue curtains; next to that was a large aumbry for clothes. Brightly coloured drapes and vividly painted triptychs gave the room a light, elegant look. Castledene explained where the bloody napkins had been found. Corbett simply nodded, left and clattered back down the stairs and through the door leading to the buttery, scullery and kitchens. The rear door, already unlocked, led out into a derelict wasteland. Once this must have had the makings of a fine garden; despite the snow, ice and blustering bitter-cold breeze, Corbett could still make out the outlines of lawns, tunnelled arbours, turf seats, a broken fountain, a shabby pavilion and broken-down trellises. He heard a sound behind him and smelt Lady Adelicia's perfume.

"When you saw Sir Rauf with what you think was a corpse that evening, where did he go?"

Corbett turned. Lady Adelicia stood just within the doorway, her face shrouded against the cold. She pointed to a clump of old cider-apple trees. Corbett led everyone across. The trees clustered together, but a narrow space stretched between them and the wall; it was choked with tangled undergrowth, but Corbett noticed one area, about a yard long and the same across, which was thinned as if recently weeded. He ordered the guards, who'd brought picks and mattocks, to dig in that spot, rejecting Castledene's protest that the ground would be iron-hard.

"It may well be," Corbett smiled thinly, "but this would be a shallow grave. Sir Rauf was an old man; he would not have dug deep. He would never have realised that anyone would come into his garden specifically looking for what he had hidden. Moreover," he gestured round, "this part of the garden is shrouded by trees and undergrowth; the soil may not be so difficult to break." He beckoned the guards forward. "Half a mark between you," he offered, "if we can have what's buried here within the hour."

There was no further protest. Corbett walked back into the house, ordering Lady Adelicia to be detained in her own chamber. He asked Ranulf to make a quick search from garret to cellar, and excused Parson Warfeld and Desroches from further attendance but warned them that they must return before sunset.

As they left, the guards arrived from The Antlered Stag with pastries, ale and two covered dishes of diced vegetables. Chanson saw to their distribution while Corbett walked back into Sir Rauf's chamber, now warmer and better lit. He sat down in the high-backed leather chair in front of the desk and felt the weals in the wood beneath the leather-topped arms. Curbing his own angry frustration, he began to sift through Decontet's ledgers for the last four years, insisting that the shuffling, ale-reeking Lechlade assist him. Once he'd started, Corbett discovered this to be an easy task. Decontet may have been a merchant, but he was also a clerk to the bone. The ledger entries were all neatly written up for each quarter, both income and expenditure. Corbett quickly learnt of the vast array of Sir Rauf's wealth: sheep, wool, skins and parchment, wine from Gascony, cereal, timber and furs from the Baltic, as well as loans to various individuals and groups including the King and leading courtiers. Nevertheless, despite such wealth, Decontet was extremely parsimonious, even with his own wife, who was only given meagre amounts. One set of expenditure entries, money sent through trusted merchants to unnamed individuals in the ports of Hainault, Flanders and Brabant, caught Corbett's eye. No reason was given, nor was the generous income — "a *certis navibus*, from certain ships" — explained. Corbett smiled to himself. He had worked for many months in the Exchequer of Receipt at Westminster under the eagle eye of Walter Langton, Bishop of Coventry and Lichfield, Treasurer to Edward I: in various ledger accounts seized by the Crown, he had come across similar entries. In truth, Decontet, like other leading merchants in London and Bristol, had engaged in more than a little piracy, secretly funding fighting ships in return for a percentage of their profits, with the Crown turning a blind eye. Was Castledene correct? Had *The Waxman* been one of Decontet's investments? After all, Sir Rauf was a Canterbury man, like Blackstock and his half-brother.

"Sir Hugh?" Castledene stood stamping his feet in the doorway. "Sir Hugh, they have found it."

Corbett and the others gathered in the kitchen, where the decaying sacks had been laid on the square-paved floor. Corbett paid the half mark to the guards, dismissed them, then undid the folds. The skeleton they concealed was complete, all flesh had long rotted, nor was there any trace of clothing, belt or boots.

"He, and I think it was a man, must have been buried naked," Corbett observed. "Flesh rots quickly, leather not so." He picked up the skull, still hard but yellowing, turned it and pointed at the shattered bone. "Killed by a fierce blow to the back of his head, but who was he and why was he murdered?" Corbett's questions, of course, weren't answered, and he recalled those mysterious entries in the ledger. He had no proof, no evidence, yet he was certain that this unfortunate victim was related to *The Waxman* or some other nefarious dealings of Sir Rauf. Indeed, he was convinced that all these grisly murders were connected to the capture of Blackstock's ship.

Corbett returned to the chancery chamber, where Lechlade was carefully filing everything back. The servant mumbled something under his breath, but Corbett was tired of conversation in hushed tones. He must act and do so determinedly. He instructed Lechlade to tell the guards to take the remains found in the garden to Parson Warfeld's church for burial, whilst he turned to the sheaf of documents sent from the Guildhall relating to Adam Blackstock and Hubert the Monk. Slouched in Decontet's chair, he sifted through these, finding nothing much but listing the important relevant facts.

Corbett now decided to take more public action. Chanson was sent across to St Alphege's to borrow a Book of the Gospels, then returned to prepare the hall for Corbett's summary court. Outside, the wintry evening gathered in, but the fires and braziers were now crackling merrily. Corbett dispatched exchequer notes to levy more purveyance from shops and nearby alehouses. Ranulf, who always surprised his master with his culinary skills, busied himself in the kitchen, assisted by a pink-cheeked Berengaria and a sweaty-faced Chanson. They prepared manchelet, a veal stew in white wine, honey, parsley, ginger and coriander. Shortly before it was ready, the savoury odours trailing through the house, Ranulf searched out his master.

"Sir Hugh?"

Corbett, reflecting in front of the hearth, turned sleepily. "Is the meal ready, Ranulf?"

"Soon." Ranulf smiled. "It's just that . . ." He walked over, put his hand on the back of the chair and leaned down to whisper into Corbett's ear. "Master, I have been through this house as you told me, from cellar to attic. I have searched for food, pots . . ."

"And?" Corbett asked.

"Everywhere I go, master, I have the feeling it has already been inspected very cleverly, thoroughly scrutinised for something."

"You are sure?" Corbett turned in the chair.

"Certain, master. Not just an ordinary search, but something else. Now whether it took place before Sir Rauf was killed or afterwards . . ." He shook his head. "I don't know."

Under Ranulf's direction, the meal was hastily served to all who wanted it in the hall, a long, gloomy chamber warmed by the fire roaring in the hearth. Desroches and Parson Warfeld returned, but Corbett kept his own counsel. The meal continued quietly; even the guards, sitting at tables or on the floor with their backs to the wall, whispered amongst themselves, aware of the oppressive atmosphere. Afterwards Corbett had the hall swiftly prepared. A high-backed chair was placed at the centre of the high table on the dais, a similar chair on the other side, with stools at either end for Ranulf and

Parson Warfeld. Corbett ignored protests from Castledene and others at being kept waiting so long. Ranulf undid the chancery bags, taking out a replica of the privy seal, a crucifix, and Corbett's commission with its huge purple seals. This was unrolled in the centre of the table, kept flat by weights placed at each corner. The crucifix on its stand was moved to the right of this, the royal seal to the left. Corbett called for his war belt, drew his sword and laid it across the commission. Ranulf busied himself with his own chancery tray, aware of the deepening silence amongst the others gathered further down the hall. They knew what was about to happen. Corbett had the candelabra lit and brought closer. He grasped the sword in one hand, the seal in the other, then held them up.

"Edward, by the grace of God," he intoned, "King of England, Lord of Ireland and Duke of Aquitaine, to all sheriffs, bailiffs, officers of the crown and all faithful subjects, know you by these letters patent I have appointed Sir Hugh Corbett, Keeper of the Secret Seal, to investigate all matters affecting our Crown and Person in our royal city of Canterbury. All subjects on their loyalty to the Crown . . ." The solemn words rolled out, Corbett's powerful voice echoing through the hall as he laid a duty on each and every one to tell the truth, which they would swear on the Book of the Gospels, adding that anyone who told a lie was guilty of perjury and would suffer the dire consequences. Corbett knew the commission word for word, and he emphasised the power and the strength of the royal warrant. At the end, having given the place and date of its issuing, he put the seal back on the table, his sword across the commission, and gestured at the others to approach the dais.

"You have heard what the King has ordered," he declared, his voice still carrying. His gaze moved from face to face. "These are important matters. Master Ranulf here will keep a fair summary of what is said. Parson Warfeld will swear each person on oath that they tell the truth. I shall call you one by one. You shall answer my questions!"

The hall was cleared. Corbett declared he would have no need for the city watch; Chanson would guard the door. Ranulf bowed his head to hide his smile, then gazed cheekily across at the Clerk of the Royal Stables. Chanson was full of his own importance as he took up position, war belt strapped about him, an arbalest already primed on a bench beside him. Ranulf knew the truth. There were two things you never asked Chanson to do: the first was to sing, and the second was to touch any weapon, as Chanson would do more harm to friend than foe.

Corbett coughed, and Ranulf's smile faded. With the hall empty except for a highly nervous Parson Warfeld, Corbett took his chair, snapped his fingers and beckoned Warfeld on to the dais. The parson sat on the high stool and placed his hand on the Book of the Gospels, repeating the words Corbett said, promising to tell the truth or face the full penalties of statute and canon law, under which anyone guilty of gross perjury would face the hideous sentence of being crushed to death.

170

"Very well." Corbett relaxed in the chair and stared hard at the cleric. "Parson Warfeld, you are a priest at St Alphege?"

"I am, Sir Hugh."

"For how many years?"

"Two."

"Did you know Adam Blackstock, Hubert the Monk or Blackstock's ship *The Waxman*? Is there any connection between you and that ship, its captain or his half-brother?"

Warfeld opened his mouth, then glanced quickly at the Book of the Gospels, its leather covering etched with a brilliant cross of gold.

"I . . ."

"The truth!" Corbett insisted.

Warfeld lifted his face. "I had a cousin," he declared, "a sprightly young man. He lived near Gravesend."

"He was a sailor?"

"Yes. He worked the cogs between London and Dordrecht; sometimes he joined the wine fleet."

"And?" Corbett asked. "Parson Warfeld, you are on oath. Be brief and succinct."

"His ship was attacked by *The Waxman*. My kinsman was his widowed mother's only son. Blackstock took no prisoners; the ship and all its crew simply disappeared off the face of the earth."

"And revenge?" Corbett asked.

"What revenge, Sir Hugh? Blackstock is dead. Hubert has disappeared. My cousin's death was one of those tragedies; there are many in the city of Canterbury who have suffered similar."

"And there is no other link or connection between you and *The Waxman?*"

Warfeld pulled a face and shook his head.

"Though you didn't tell me that at the beginning?"

"Sir Hugh, you didn't ask."

Corbett half smiled. "Very well, very well." He tapped the table. "Were Sir Rauf and Lady Adelicia ever shriven by you?"

"Yes," Warfeld replied. "At Easter or thereabouts, as canon law dictates. Sir Hugh, I cannot break the seal of confession."

"I'm not asking you to. Their marriage was sterile, loveless?"

Warfeld nodded. "From the little I know."

"Was Sir Rauf impotent?"

"Sir Hugh, Desroches and I have spoken on that. I was his priest, not his physician." Corbett sensed the good parson knew more, but decided not to press the matter.

"Did you know Lady Adelicia had a lover?"

Warfeld's eyes slid away. Corbett studied this priest, fresh-faced, plump, well fed, with a glib tongue for ready answers. Warfeld stared down at the tabletop. Corbett realised how they were both circled by pools of light from the candelabra, and beyond that was the darkness, threatening, quiet, concealing the truth about what had happened in this dreadful house.

"Parson Warfeld, I asked you a question. You are on oath. Did the Lady Adelicia have a lover?"

"I've told you the rumours," the priest replied grudgingly. "She was seen at The Chequer of Hope, as

172

was Wendover, captain of the city guard." Warfeld joined his hands as if in prayer. "Sir Hugh, I can join with Desroches and speculate about Sir Rauf and Lady Adelicia, but I cannot tell you facts. Canon law very clearly states a confessor must be prudent —"

"Very good," Corbett interrupted, "but there were rumours that Lady Adelicia had a lover, and Wendover was the man named?"

"Yes, but no one dared speak about it. Sir Rauf could be a vicious man. He may only have had Lechlade as a servant, but if he wanted to, he could whistle up bully boys from the city."

"Did you know anything about Decontet's past?"

"No, only that he was born in Canterbury. He prospered, he used the riches of this life to buy the world and so lose his immortal soul." The priest shrugged.

"And on the day he died, that Thursday, where were you?"

"I have told you, I was in my church. A boy burst in; he said he'd been sent by Physician Desroches and that there was something very wrong at Sir Rauf's house so I must come swiftly. I gathered my cloak, put on some boots — the weather was cold as I remember — and hurried over."

"And when you arrived?"

"Desroches and Lechlade were inside the house — standing in the porch. Sir Rauf's chamber was locked. Desroches hammered on it but there was no answer. We made the decision to break down the door. Desroches told us to concentrate on the hinges. Lechlade had informed us about the lock, how it was special and its key held only by Sir Rauf. We snapped the hinges, forced the door and entered the chamber. It was confusing. The door itself had slipped out of the lock so it had to be held, then leaned against the wall. Candles were burning, though some had guttered out. Sir Rauf lay on the floor, face towards his desk. The base of his skull," Parson Warfeld tapped the back of his own head, "was smashed, the blood forming like a puddle around him. I did what I could. I whispered the words of absolution, the rite of the dead, then we waited. Oh yes, we did search the house, but we discovered no further disturbance. We tried Lady Adelicia's chamber and found it locked, then she returned and came into Sir Rauf's chancery chamber. By then Desroches had sent for Castledene, who also arrived."

"Tell me precisely," Corbett demanded, "what happened."

"Well, Lady Adelicia and her maid were riding palfries. They came through the main gate and on to the forecourt. Lechlade went out to help them dismount and brought them in. Desroches told her the news. Lady Adelicia did not seem very upset. She viewed the corpse and answered the Mayor's questions — or tried to. Sir Walter examined her cloak —"

"Why?"

"He said that was the procedure to be followed."

"And where was the cloak?"

"In Sir Rauf's chancery chamber."

"And?"

"Bloodstains were found. Sir Walter asked Lady Adelicia where the blood might have come from. She replied that perhaps she may have passed a flesher's stall or brushed a wall in the shambles and stained it. Sir Walter insisted that we visit her chamber."

"And who had keys to that?"

"Ah yes, I remember that well." Warfeld's fingers fluttered to his lips. "When we found Sir Rauf, we also found a keyring on his belt. Lechlade recognised that. Three keys in all: one to his coffer, one to his own chamber held only by him, and the third to his wife's, but we didn't force that door. We thought it would be improper until Lady Adelicia returned."

"And Lady Adelicia had her own key?"

"Yes, Sir Walter insisted that we go to her chamber and search it. By then she was under suspicion. We went up. Lady Adelicia unlocked the door and we entered. We found a napkin stained with dried blood lying on the floor, as if dropped in a hurry. Lady Adelicia proclaimed her innocence and denied any knowledge of it. Castledene ordered the room to be searched, and more bloodstained napkins were found behind the bolsters on her bed. Sir Walter immediately took her into his care as his prisoner, saying she would have to return with him to the Guildhall. After that," Warfeld shrugged, "the rest you know."

"And why did Desroches go to the house?"

"Sir Hugh, I don't know. He was Sir Rauf's physician."

"Specially hired by him?"

"I think so, but you'd best ask him. Sir Rauf spoke highly of him. That was one thing Sir Rauf cared about: his own health. No physician dislikes gold, Sir Hugh, and Sir Rauf could be generous when he wanted, or when it suited him."

"Was Desroches a constant visitor?"

Warfeld pursed his lips and shook his head. "Not that I know of. He was simply his physician. I think he visited both Sir Rauf and Lady Adelicia. I know little more except one thing . . ."

"What?" Corbett asked.

Ranulf's quill squeaked as it raced across the parchment.

"Lady Adelicia's journeys to Canterbury were fairly common, at least once a week. Now, Sir Hugh, I am parson of St Alphege, and one of our problems is mice." He smiled. "I have more mice than I have parishioners. I wage constant war against them. Now and again I go out for a walk to get away from their squeaking, the dirt between the benches. God's fresh air can be so soothing. I walk across the wasteland. Sometimes I'd see Lady Adelicia leave, but on occasion I would glimpse her young maid, Berengaria, come hurrying back."

"On foot?" Corbett asked.

"Oh yes. I mean, the journey into Canterbury is not far. Lady Adelicia liked to ride there. From what I gather, they would both stable their horses in a nearby tavern and go on to The Chequer of Hope. Lady Adelicia acted foolishly. She thought she was in disguise but people could see through that. If you go back to the same place regularly, it's only a matter of time before tongues begin to clack."

"But you sometimes glimpsed Berengaria hurrying back?"

"Oh, certainly, and she did do so furtively." He coughed. "Berengaria now lodges with me, but I have not asked her myself. I dare not intrude. I tell you this," the parson stammered, "because others may have seen her. I only saw her return on two or three occasions. I thought that confirmed the rumours. I mean, when a lady goes to the market, her maid always accompanies her, so it's a matter of logic, isn't it? What was Lady Adelicia doing so as to dismiss her maid, to let her go where she wished? But," Warfeld shrugged, "you'd best ask them yourselves."

Corbett felt uneasy at Parson Warfeld's glib answers. Was the man just nervous or was he hiding something, simply unwilling to become involved?

"Are you finished with me, Sir Hugh?"

"No, Parson Warfeld, I'm certainly not, and I want you to stay until I am. You are to administer the oath to each witness on the Book of the Gospels. When you have done this, you may leave and I will quickly question each person. So, you'd best bring in Wendover."

A short while later the captain of the city guard swaggered insolently in, sword slapping against the top of his boot. Corbett glanced quickly at Ranulf and winked. The Senior Clerk in the Chancery of the Green Wax sprang to his feet, roaring at Wendover to show more decorum. How dare he come into the presence of the King's justice bearing arms? Did he not know the law on treason? The sword belt was immediately unbuckled and handed to Chanson and a more humble captain took his seat to mumble the oath. Corbett waited until Parson Warfeld had left.

"Master Wendover," he leaned across the table, "you are on oath so I'll come quickly to the point. You are Lady Adelicia's lover, the possible father of her child."

Wendover glanced nervously about.

"Yes or no!" Ranulf bawled.

"Yes!" Wendover replied.

"For how long?" Corbett asked.

"About a year in all."

"And you met at The Chequer of Hope tavern?"

"Lady Adelicia was most insistent; you see, I have a chamber there. She came disguised, though I knew others saw us. I heard the tittle-tattle myself. Lady Adelicia didn't seem to care, almost as if she wanted Sir Rauf to discover her indiscretions. Perhaps she was more in love with loving than with me." Wendover blinked and Corbett glimpsed the anxiety in the man's face. His eyes were bloodshot, lower lip quivering. Wendover was highly nervous or else he'd been drinking, possibly both.

"And that Thursday afternoon when Sir Rauf was murdered?"

"It was as usual; she came with her maid, Berengaria —"

"Ah yes," Corbett interrupted. "What happened to the maid when Lady Adelicia was closeted with you?"

"She was left to her own devices. She was often sent on shopping errands so that when Lady Adelicia returned to Sir Rauf she could show what she'd been doing."

"And that was what happened on that particular day?"

"Yes, yes. What Berengaria did and where she went . . ." Wendover shook his head. "I don't know."

"And you, Captain Wendover, what did you do? I mean you dallied with your lady of plaisaunce, and afterwards . . . Did she leave first or you?"

"I left first."

"Why?"

"I had to go back to the Guildhall. I was becoming nervous."

"Or tired of Lady Adelicia? She was so importunate?"

"I was becoming nervous, Sir Hugh. I left the chamber, she was sleeping."

"And you went back to the Guildhall?"

"Yes, yes, I did."

"You have witnesses to that?" Corbett asked.

Wendover shrugged and looked away.

"But you could have gone to Sir Rauf's house. I mean, he was a wealthy man."

"How could I!" Wendover almost shouted. "I never went there. Adelicia had told me enough about Sir Rauf and his iron-bound coffers, his special locks, his chamber fortified like a strongroom. Why should I go there?"

"To rob him?"

179

"But he was never robbed. When Sir Walter went across later, I accompanied him. Sir Rauf was killed, but nothing was missing."

"Did you search?"

"Yes, yes, we did, but nothing was disturbed."

Corbett leaned back in his chair, resting his elbows on its arms. He stroked the pommel of his sword on the table before him.

"And before all this, Wendover? Before Sir Rauf and Lady Adelicia? Were you born in Canterbury?"

"Yes, Sir Hugh, baptised at the font of St Mildred's church. I was a foundling. I'm now past my thirty-fifth summer. I've been a soldier most of my life."

"You have been Castledene's man?"

"Oh yes, Sir Hugh, always his faithful retainer."

"You were with him on board ship when *The Segreant* and *The Caltrop* trapped *The Waxman* and its crew?"

"Oh yes."

"What happened?"

"As you say, we trapped that pirate against the Essex coast, Sir Walter and the Hanse ship. How, I don't know, but I heard the chatter. How Paulents had suborned Blackstock's lieutenant, a man called Stonecrop. He gave Sir Walter the times and seasons . . . but you'd best ask him."

"And when the ship was captured?"

"Blackstock refused to surrender. We had royal archers aboard, Welsh longbowmen; they shot him down. Sir Walter later had Blackstock's corpse stripped and hung by the neck from the poop."

"And Stonecrop?"

"Sir Walter showed him little mercy. He may have been a traitor but he was still a pirate. Sir Walter had him thrown overboard. Most reckoned he'd die in the freezing, turbulent seas. I later heard rumours that he may have reached land, but he never reappeared in Canterbury." He shrugged. "At least to my knowledge."

"Sir Walter trapped *The Waxman* for a reason, didn't he? He was searching for a particular document."

Wendover pulled a face, slouching on the stool, shoulders hunched. "I don't know, Sir Hugh. There was chatter about a manuscript kept in a coffer. After the ship was taken, Sir Walter and Paulents were beside themselves when they could not find it. They scoured that ship from prow to stern. It was all in vain. Sir Walter was very angry."

"And afterwards?"

"We rounded the Colvasse peninsula and sailed up the River Orwell, where we berthed for a while. Sir Walter was searching for Blackstock's half-brother Hubert, but there was no sign of him; never has been either."

Corbett let his hands fall away from his face and leaned across the table. "And Maubisson? You were in charge of the city guard. Your instructions were to guard that manor carefully, and yet four people, visitors to this kingdom, indeed the King's own guests, were brutally murdered. No, no, don't gossip about suicide." Corbett half laughed. "They were killed, hanged! How, Wendover?"

"I don't know," the captain replied wearily. "I've thought about it time and time again. We knew Sir Walter's visitors were coming. Maubisson was prepared, stores laid in. I searched every chamber. We ringed that manor house. The foreigners arrived, looking tired. I had a few words with them. They went into the manor house, and locked and barred the doors and shutters. I circled the house with my men; the rest you know. Until we knocked at that door and demanded entrance, we saw, we heard, we glimpsed nothing untoward. Sir Hugh, I truly don't know what happened."

"And Servinus?"

Wendover sighed. "A tall man, no hair, I remember that, dressed in black leather like . . ." he flicked his fingers towards Ranulf, "a professional swordsman, a former mercenary. He had a harsh face, with heavy-lidded eyes."

"He was well armed?"

"Oh yes, he had a war belt. When I saw him enter the house, he also carried an arbalest. I would reckon he'd be a difficult man to kill."

"But he has now disappeared?"

"Sir Hugh," Wendover leaned over pleadingly, joining his hands together, "nobody left Maubisson that night, I assure you!"

"Yet afterwards?" Corbett declared. "I mean, when the doors were forced and the corpses found, surely there was chaos and commotion; someone could have escaped?"

"I don't think so," Wendover replied. "We were vigilant yet nobody noticed anything. Sir Hugh, I know you've been round Maubisson. Did you see any footprints, any sign of a shutter being prised or a door being forced?"

Corbett didn't reply, but stared at a point behind Wendover's head.

"Thank you, Captain," he said eventually.

Wendover remained seated.

"I said thank you," Corbett repeated.

"Sir Hugh," Wendover begged, "the Lady Adelicia . . ."

"I don't know," Corbett replied. "That is a matter for you and her to talk about. For the moment she is still the King's prisoner, as you too could well be, Master Wendover."

CHAPTER
NINE

Aspice quam breve sit quod vivimus.
How short a while we live.

Marbord of Rennes

Berengaria was next to be sworn. She seemed unabashed by the proceedings and quickly mouthed the words of the oath administered by a still nervous Parson Warfeld. She sat all demure, hands in her lap, eyes bright with excitement, as if she'd been invited to some Yuletide mummery. She quickly explained how she was a parish child, placed in service, and about eighteen months previously had entered into the service of Lady Adelicia, who had been a most gracious mistress. How on the day Sir Rauf had been killed she and Lady Adelicia had visited the stalls in Canterbury. As she chattered on, Corbett let his hand fall with a crash against the table. Berengaria jumped, startled, then forced a sweet smile, hunching her shoulders, fingers pushing tendrils of hair from her face.

"How old are you?"

"Oh, seventeen, eighteen summers, Sir Hugh," came the gushing reply.

Corbett turned to Ranulf. "Do you think she'll hang?"

"Oh undoubtedly, she has reached the age."

"Hang?" Berengaria's voice turned to a screech; her smile had now faded. "Hanged? Sir Hugh, I've done —"

"You've committed perjury." Corbett leaned across the table, pushing the candelabra closer as if to examine her face more carefully. "You're a liar, Berengaria. I can see that in your eyes. You're certainly a perjurer. We know that Lady Adelicia visited Captain Wendover in his chamber at The Chequer of Hope. I believe," Corbett laughed, "half of Canterbury knows that! And you, little Berengaria, sent hither and thither to buy this and buy that? I don't think so. According to a witness, on those afternoons Lady Adelicia visited Canterbury and was closeted with her lover, you sometimes went back to Sir Rauf's house. Why? Did you go back that afternoon?" Again Corbett's hand fell with a crash. "You're on oath, wench, this is not some parlour game. You either tell the truth, hang or be pressed to death!"

Berengaria, face all pale, would have jumped off the stool, but Ranulf half rose so she settled herself quickly, staring bleakly at Corbett, who suppressed any pity at the terror he'd caused. This young woman knew more than she'd confessed. They were not here in this gloomy hall to listen to her lies. He had been attacked and threatened, his friend Griskin had been killed; why should he show compassion to her?

"Very good, Berengaria. On the afternoon Sir Rauf was killed, did you go back to Sweetmead Manor? Did you come here?"

Berengaria nodded.

"Why? Tell me the truth."

Berengaria closed her eyes and put her head down. "I knew matters between Sir Rauf and Lady Adelicia were not good, but Sir Rauf had his needs. One day I met him in the garden beyond. He told me what he wanted the Lady Adelicia to do in his bedchamber and how she had refused. He offered me a piece of silver, and later that day I visited him in his chancery chamber."

"And what happened?" Corbett asked, hiding his surprise that this young, comely maid could make such a confession.

Berengaria raised her head. "You are not poor, Sir Hugh. You don't know what it's like to be a beggar, to be sent hither and thither. Sir Rauf was kind — at least to me. I would kneel before him and render his need."

"And the Lady Adelicia didn't know?"

"Oh no! Not her! Not the lady of the manor!" Berengaria's voice was rich with malice.

"Did Sir Rauf know what Lady Adelicia was doing? He did, didn't he? You told him."

"Yes, he did." Now Berengaria sounded calm and calculating. "He once told me that he would go to the church courts and have his marriage annulled. He said he had talked about that to Parson Warfeld. How it hadn't been properly consummated. Sir Rauf promised that if I bore witness and told the court exactly what Lady Adelicia had done, who knows who might be his next wife? So when Lady Adelicia went into Canterbury, she thought I would go amongst the stalls, visit this merchant shop or that, or dawdle in a church. Sometimes I didn't. I'd immediately hasten back to Sir

Rauf and tell him exactly what had happened and administer to his needs. He'd pay me a coin, stroke my hair and tell me to wait, to be patient."

"And Lady Adelicia knew nothing of your betrayal?"

"Betrayal, Sir Hugh? What did I owe her? Sir Rauf paid me. He had put a roof over my head. He looked after me and promised he would do so in the future."

"So Sir Rauf was going to apply to the archbishop's court for an annulment?"

"Yes, Sir Hugh. The marriage had not been properly consummated. Lady Adelicia refused Sir Rauf's advances."

Corbett stared in astonishment at this young woman, marble-hard eyes in a set, determined face. He realised the mistake he had made. Berengaria was highly intelligent, a born intriguer, a plotter.

"And the afternoon Sir Rauf was murdered?"

"I went back," Berengaria replied. "I came through the main gate and up the path, slipping through the trees. Sir Rauf often arranged to leave the front door open, off the latch, unlocked and unbarred. We were never disturbed. Lechlade was always drunk. We would hear him singing or shouting to himself. That day, though, both the front door and the one at the rear were locked and secured. I knocked but there was no reply. I realised something was wrong but I couldn't stay too long so I hastened back. I visited a stall in the Mercery and bought some ribbons and a little thread my mistress had asked for. I later met her, as planned, at the Butter Cross. When we arrived back at Sweetmead, we found . . ." For the first time ever

Berengaria showed some genuine emotion. "We found Sir Rauf had been murdered."

"Do you think," Ranulf asked, "Lady Adelicia could have also secretly returned home and done such a mischief?"

Berengaria narrowed her eyes. "I thought of that," she replied in a half-whisper. "She wanted him dead, but no, I don't think she had the time, the strength or the will. She's squeamish. If she'd wanted someone killed, she would have hired that oaf of a lover, Wendover, to do it for her."

"As you came and went to Sweetmead," Corbett asked, "did you see anybody else?"

Berengaria shook her head. "No, sir, it was a cold winter's day. Packmen, carts clattering along the road, but no one I recognised."

"Surely," Corbett asked, "if Sir Rauf had agreed to keep the door open, and on that particular day it was locked, you must have become suspicious?"

"I realised something was wrong," Berengaria was flustered, "but not that! I said Sir Rauf would often leave the latch off, but not always. If the door was locked that was a sign he could not, or would not, receive me." She forced a smile. "He had other business."

"A wasted journey?" Ranulf asked.

"Not really." Berengaria pouted. "Sir Rauf would still give me a coin. You see, sirs," Berengaria breathed in deeply, "he enjoined me to be prudent, and I was very, very careful."

"So the door had been locked before?"

"Of course." Berengaria turned to Ranulf. "Sir Rauf had visitors, or Lechlade would be staggering to and from that tavern."

"You've heard," Corbett asked, "about the skeleton found in the garden?"

Berengaria shook her head. "I know nothing of that. My mistress never told me. Sir Rauf did have visitors late at night, people coming and going. I asked him once but he said that was his business and I was not to worry about it."

Corbett stared down the darkening hall. A sconce light fluttered, the cresset torches were burning low. He felt tired, and his back ached; he wished to be away from here.

"Do you think, Berengaria, as your mistress is now pregnant, that she knew Sir Rauf planned to claim their marriage wasn't consummated, and intended by her pregnancy to show this to be a lie?"

"It's possible, Sir Hugh. She had no love for Sir Rauf, but sometimes she'd talk about what she'd do when he was dead and all his wealth came to her."

"And now?" Corbett asked. "You'll not return to your mistress's service. Sooner or later what you have told me will become public knowledge."

"Ah, Sir Hugh, I listen very carefully to the Scriptures. How one should save against the evil day. Sir Rauf was generous to me. I have money put aside, and once this is over, I will leave Lady Adelicia's service. She must give me a good recommendation. After all, if she knows about me, I certainly know about her."

"Blackmail?" Ranulf asked. "You'd blackmail your mistress?"

"Master Ranulf," came the quick reply, "if you had sat in a corner of an alleyway stinking of urine and dung, shivering in rags, blackmail is nothing compared to that! Are you finished with me, Sir Hugh?"

"Yes, yes, I am for the time being."

Berengaria got off the stool, gave Sir Hugh a mocking bow, waggled her fingers at Ranulf and walked saucily from the chamber. Corbett stared in disbelief at the door closing behind her.

"Don't be surprised, master." Ranulf didn't even lift his head. "I could find girls in London half her age who'd do the same for a penny. What she said is true. When you're poor you'll do anything!"

Corbett shook his head. He still felt uneasy. Berengaria hadn't told him the full truth. She was concealing something, or had she decided to peddle a farrago of half-truths? What was wrong? He sighed and shouted at Chanson to bring Castledene in.

Sir Walter entered, face pinched and pale. He'd lost some of his haughtiness, though Corbett could tell by the way he was gnawing his lower lip that the mayor was finding great difficulty in accepting royal jurisdiction being imposed on him. Corbett did not wish to alienate the man. He rose in deference but showed no partiality. Once Castledene had taken the oath and Parson Warfeld had been dismissed, Sir Hugh reassured the mayor that he did not wish to interfere in the liberties, customs, rights and privileges of the King's City of Canterbury but that the matters before

190

them were pressing and urgent and he needed satisfactory answers to certain questions. Castledene was astute and skilled enough to realise that Corbett was simply going through the usual diplomatic phrases and protocols, so he sat on the stool half nodding as Corbett delivered his formal speech.

"Sir Hugh," Castledene pushed his hands up the voluminous sleeves of his gown, "you are a busy man and so am I. This is one matter amongst many. I am here to answer your questions. I am on oath. I will do so honestly."

"Very well." Corbett asked for a brazier to be brought closer and one of the candelabra from further down the hall to be placed on the table.

"The parents of Adam Blackstock and Hubert the Monk, our two outlaws?" Corbett began. "I know something about their deaths. Sir Walter, you are a Canterbury man, I would like to hear it from you. This time add as much detail as you can provide." He indicated the pouch at his feet. "I have been through the documents sent from the Guildhall, but there is very little; perhaps you can fill the gaps?"

"Sir Hugh, you must remember we are talking about events which occurred thirty years ago, when I was young, sprightly and slim as a willow wand. Merchants like myself and Decontet were just starting out; we were petty traders in this city. We had very little to do with such matters, or what happened afterwards."

"You talk of 'we'?" Corbett asked.

"At one time, Sir Hugh," Castledene sighed, "Decontet and I were very close, almost like brothers.

But life is like a knife: it sinks deeper and it turns. Decontet became Decontet and I followed my own path."

"And the beginning of this tragedy?" Corbett asked.

"Well, Sir Hugh, if you need a lesson in history . . ."

"No I don't, Sir Walter."

"What I am about to tell you," Castledene spread his hands out, "is well known. In 1272 the old King died at Westminster. Now, as you know, when he died, Edward, his heir, was in Outremer on crusade. There was a breakdown in the king's peace; armed gangs carried out raids throughout the kingdom. Merchants were afraid of being attacked; the same happened here in the Weald of Kent. Canterbury was fairly quiet but there were attacks; a gang of rifflers — we don't know their identities because they went masked, hooded and visored — attacked farms. In the main they simply stole moveables: cattle, stock, treasure, anything they could lay their hands on. However, on that night, the Year of Our Lord 1272, the Feast of Finding the True Cross, they attacked Blackstock's manor near Maison Dieu. To be brief, Sir Hugh, the place was looted and razed to the ground. Blackstock's father and his second wife — I forget the woman's name; it may have been Isabella — were killed together with their servants. Adam, their younger son, escaped unscathed, as did his half-brother Hubert, who was a scholar at St Augustine's Abbey."

"St Augustine's?" Corbett asked, "You are sure?"

"Oh yes, St Augustine's. Of course, the Royal Justices moved into the shire on a commission of oyer and terminer. Special assize courts were set up, but no one ever discovered who was responsible for that murderous attack. Adam was placed as an apprentice to a trade in the city; his master is long dead. Hubert, as you know, continued his studies and moved to the Black Monks' house at Westminster, which he left abruptly to become a *venator hominum*. Of one thing I am certain: he never returned to Canterbury. Adam, on the other hand, like many apprentices, became disillusioned and drifted away. The next we heard of him was that he was in Brabant and Hainault consorting with privateers and pirates, later becoming one of their principal captains."

"He attacked your ships?" Corbett asked. "Did he single you out?"

"Yes and no," Castledene replied with a sigh. "You see, Sir Hugh, I am one of the few merchants in Canterbury who actually owns ships. Others, like Decontet," he allowed himself a half-smile, "would advance monies for this voyage or that."

"But you were different?"

"Yes, I was different. I owned ships; I still do. Blackstock preyed on my craft, not because of any personal hatred towards me — I hardly knew him — but out of hatred towards the city of Canterbury. Perhaps he held it responsible for the tragedy."

"Was it?"

"Of course not! And in the end I had to plot Blackstock's destruction." Castledene waved a hand. "You know the rest of the story."

"And afterwards?" Corbett asked.

"After that, Sir Hugh, I heard nothing about Hubert the Monk or anyone or anything connected with *The Waxman*."

Corbett drummed his fingers on the table.

"And so we come to Maubisson, Sir Walter. I understand that Paulents' family landed at Dover on Monday. What happened next?"

"I'd been preparing Maubisson, making sure all was safe and well. I ordered Wendover to bring in stores and goods."

"When did Wendover join your household?" Corbett asked. "He has served at sea, hasn't he?"

"He has," Castledene agreed. "He's a Canterbury man, a good soldier who has seen many years' service both on the King's ships and abroad. I cannot fault him."

"Except that he allowed four people to die at Maubisson and the bodyguard Servinus to escape."

Castledene shrugged. "I cannot answer that, Sir Hugh, not at the moment."

"Let's go back to Dover," Corbett continued remorselessly. "Paulents landed there; what happened next?"

"He sent a message to me that he and his family were ill, so I told him I would meet him at Maubisson with a physician. I did so: Desroches accompanied me. He thought there was nothing wrong. He provided them with a little camomile to quieten the stomach and the other humours. Paulents' wife was much taken with Desroches and begged him to stay with her, but he

194

declined. After that, well, we left the manor, the guards were mounted, the rest you know."

"And Decontet's murder?" Corbett asked. "The afternoon when the messenger came to see you?"

"I was in the Guildhall," Castledene replied. "I immediately went out with some of the city guards. I saw what you've heard; well, most of it. Sir Rauf lying in his chamber, the back of his head staved in, nearby a set of fire tongs coated in blood. His lady wife's cloak was smeared with blood, napkins soaked in blood were found in her chamber. I had no choice, Sir Hugh. I had to arrest her."

"And did you investigate, Sir Walter, the question of the keys? How a man had had his brains smashed out in a locked chamber, the key being still upon his person? Or how bloody napkins were found in the chamber of the dead man's wife? Again locked; only she and her dead husband had the keys?"

"Sir Hugh, Sir Hugh." Castledene waved a hand before his face. "My mind was plagued by other worries. I was expecting Paulents. There was little love lost between Lady Adelicia and Sir Rauf, but that was their concern. What I have told you is the truth."

Corbett did not believe that; he had more questions, but not for now. Sir Walter was exhausted, his face grey, his eyes red-rimmed. Once he'd been dismissed, Lady Adelicia swept in. Despite her haughty mien and arrogant air, she proved remarkably cooperative. She admitted that her husband had been impotent, at least when it came to normal intercourse. She referred to his "filthy" practices, to which she had refused to consent, and talked openly of Wendover as her lover to take or leave at her whim. She spoke coldly, dispassionately, lip curling whenever she mentioned her husband's name, those beautiful cornflower-blue eyes diamond hard. Corbett sensed this young woman's hatred for her dead husband. At the same time he felt a deep sorrow for the rough manner in which her girlish illusions and dreams had been so abruptly and cruelly shattered. She admitted to knowing nothing about her husband's mercantile interests or his secret business. Nor could she elaborate on what she had already said about seeing Sir Rauf on that summer's evening dragging what she suspected was a corpse wrapped in sacking from the house into the garden. She shrugged prettily, conceding that her dead husband was a secretive man who'd kept close counsel, admitted visitors at all hours and taken them immediately to his chamber.

Listening to her carefully, Corbett concluded that Sir Rauf was not so much an honourable citizen but a merchant who meddled and dealt in matters of the dark, best hidden from anyone's eyes, including his wife's. As to Lechlade, Lady Adelicia was equally disparaging, dismissing him as an ale-sodden oaf, sottish in his behaviour and manner, who seemed totally unaware of what was happening around him. Lechlade was her husband's serf, sent on this errand or that, with no life of his own. Perhaps she sensed Corbett's sorrow at her situation, for she became more coy and flirtatious, so Corbett decided to change tack.

"Did you murder your husband, Lady Adelicia?"

"No, I did not. I could not. He was found with his skull smashed in a locked room; only he had a key and that was found on him."

"But the bloodstained napkins in your chamber? Only you and your husband had keys to that room. Did yours remain with you when you were closeted with Wendover at The Chequer of Hope? Your maid, Berengaria, could she have taken it?"

"Sir Hugh, I am not as stupid as you think, or, indeed, as Berengaria might. I grew suspicious of what she did when I was with Wendover. I heard rumours that she would return to Sweetmead Manor, and saw marks of affection between her and Sir Rauf, but what did I care? What did it matter to me? Berengaria is a veritable minx; she lives on her wits and, given her life, I can hardly blame her. What's more important is that she did not interfere with me or what I was doing. She did not take my key."

"Lady Adelicia, does the ship *The Waxman* mean anything to you?"

"I have heard of it, Sir Hugh, and learnt what happened to its master, Blackstock, but no."

"And the bloody business at Maubisson?" Corbett asked.

"Again only what I've heard."

"And you claim total innocence of your husband's death?"

"Of course, Sir Hugh. I should be free. I object to being locked in a cell beneath the Guildhall. Surely that must not continue?"

Corbett clicked his tongue. "Lady Adelicia, you are enceinte. You were once a king's ward. I'll put you on oath. Providing you remain within this house under the custody of the city guards, you may stay here."

The relief in the young woman's eyes was obvious. Her lower lip quivered, tears brimmed, and she bowed her head, shoulders shaking slightly.

"I am innocent, Sir Hugh. I hated my husband but so do many wives. I did not kill him, I swear to that."

Lechlade came next. He was so drunk he could hardly repeat the words Parson Warfeld uttered and kept slipping off the stool. Ranulf found it amusing, and his shoulders began to shake until Corbett glared at him. Chanson came over and forced the man to sit properly. Lechlade leaned against the table, spittle drooling down his unshaven chin, and glared blearily at Corbett.

"What do you want with poor Lechlade?" he slurred. "I've done nothing wrong! I wasn't always a servant, you know. I was a clerk myself once; I had prospects, but . . ." He shrugged. "I worked for a while for Sir Walter Castledene. I was dismissed for being drunk and Sir Rauf hired me. He paid me little, gave me a garret to sleep in and sent me here and there. Sir Hugh, I spend most of my days staring at the bottom of a tankard wishing it was full again."

"Do you know anything about *The Waxman*, Hubert the Monk or his half-brother Adam?"

Lechlade licked his lips and looked longingly over his shoulder at the door as if expecting Chanson to produce a tankard of frothing ale.

"Master Lechlade, I asked you a question."

Lechlade leaned across the table, his breath reeking of the herbs and veal Ranulf had cooked. "Sir Hugh," he slurred, eyes heavy, "of course I've heard of Blackstock and Hubert, but they really mean nothing to me, just chatter in the market square, feathers on a breeze, here today, gone tomorrow."

"But your master, Sir Rauf Decontet, did he not subsidise *The Waxman*?"

"Perhaps he did, perhaps he didn't, I don't know. He never discussed his business dealings with me."

"And the people who came at the dark of night, slipping across the wasteland, knocking furtively at the door?"

"Sir Hugh, again I was Sir Rauf's manservant. I cleaned the tables, I swept the floor, but once my hours were finished —"

"I know!" Corbett broke in angrily. "It was another tankard of ale. So you know nothing about that skeleton buried in the garden?"

"Nothing, Sir Hugh. It was as much a surprise to me as to anybody else."

"And your mistress's doings with Wendover?"

"Lady Adelicia does not like me, Sir Hugh, though I've tried to help her when I can. Where possible she kept away from me, so I kept my distance from her! Where she went, what she did meant nothing to me. True, there was bad blood between the master and her, anyone could see that, even a drunk like myself. I know my wits may be sottish, my brain dulled, but they sat at table and hardly conversed. She kept to her chamber, he kept to his. She was more interested in her powders and dresses, or chattering to that insolent maid of hers, than anything else."

"And on the afternoon Sir Rauf was killed?"

"Oh, I remember that. Lady Adelicia and Berengaria left, mounted on their palfreys. I watched them go. I'll be honest, Sir Hugh, I'd heard the rumours, but," he shrugged, "I have nowhere else to go. I kept my lips closed. I did not wish to be dismissed from Decontet's service. Well, I always seize opportunities to drown my sorrows. You see, when Lady Adelicia was out of the house, Sir Rauf would lock himself up in his chancery chamber. Only the good Lord knows," he slurred, "what he did."

"Did he keep monies in the house?"

"Very little, Sir Hugh. Most of it went to the goldsmiths, both here and in London."

"And that particular afternoon?"

"As I've said, I bought a jug of ale, went up to my garret, drank and slept. I only knew something was wrong when I heard that pounding on the door and Desroches shouting!"

"What do you think of Desroches?"

"Well, he's been in Canterbury for over three years, I believe, and, like all physicians, loves gold and silver. He is skilled enough. He brought himself to the attention of the council, and purchased a house in Ottemele Lane. It's no great mansion house but he lives within his means. Sir Rauf tolerated him."

"Did he treat Sir Rauf?"

"For a number of minor ailments. Sir Rauf was as strong as an ox. Anyway, on that day I went down and opened the door for Desroches, and the rest you know."

"Did you ever discover," Corbett asked, "that Berengaria sometimes returned to be closeted with Sir Rauf?"

Surprise flared in Lechlade's eyes.

"Impossible!" he slurred.

"No, it's true."

Lechlade wiped his mouth on the back of his hand and suppressed a belch. "Before Sir Rauf married he would sometimes go out at night. He visited the mopsies and the doxies of the city, or so I suspect. Berengaria has a pert eye. She is the sort of girl who would catch Sir Rauf's attention. If there was no bed-twisting with Lady Adelicia, Berengaria, I suppose, in return for money and favour, might be more obliging." Lechlade was now mumbling his words, eyes drooping in sleepiness.

"You're mawmsy," Ranulf barked. "For the love of God sleep, clear your wits, empty your head of ale fumes."

Lechlade shuffled to his feet. He gestured at Ranulf, bowed mockingly at Corbett and slouched towards the door.

Desroches came as a welcome relief, clear and precise, gaze moving from Ranulf back to Corbett. He answered the clerk's questions bluntly, declaring that he'd been a physician in Canterbury for over three years. He'd been brought to the attention of Sir Walter Castledene and Sir Rauf and openly admitted that the prospect of profit was one of the attractions of being in Sir Rauf's service. He also confirmed that the dead miser had had an iron-hard constitution and suffered very few ailments. Desroches had certainly heard about *The Waxman*, Hubert Fitzurse and his half-brother Adam, but nothing tangible or significant. He freely admitted that Sir Rauf, on at least one occasion, had talked about his impotence with the Lady Adelicia, though he conceded that Sir Rauf was not a gelding.

"You see, Sir Hugh, with such conditions it may not be the man's fault."

"You mean the Lady Adelicia?"

"In a word, yes, Sir Hugh. I believe Sir Rauf, despite the fact that he held the purse strings and held them very fast, was rather frightened of Lady Adelicia, her beauty, her comeliness. To other men this would be a spur, but to Decontet it was a rein. I suspect he found satisfaction elsewhere, but how and with whom," he shook his head, "I do not know. The Lady Adelicia acts very cold and distant. I'll be blunt. I'd also heard the rumours about her. Canterbury may be a city, but it's no different from a village: people watch, people listen; sooner or later Sir Rauf would have discovered the truth."

"And the afternoon he was murdered?"

"Sir Rauf had asked me to visit him. He'd sent me a letter the previous Sunday. I had not replied. Anyway, on that particular day I walked over to his house about mid-afternoon. You already know the rest."

"Tell me again," Corbett asked.

"I knocked and knocked. At last Lechlade came down. We then tried to rouse Sir Rauf, but there was no answer. You know," he waggled his shoulders, "I had an ominous feeling something was very wrong. I decided not to do anything, not with just Lechlade present. So, as I've said, I went out and found a farmer's boy and sent a message asking Parson Warfeld to join us. We then broke the door down. Sir Rauf lay face down; the blood had gushed out of the back of his head. Apparently he'd been dead for some time. Parson Warfeld tended to him. I sent another messenger to Castledene and waited for him. Lady Adelicia returned; she was questioned, the blood was seen on her cloak and her room was searched."

"Do you think she killed her husband?" Corbett asked.

"No, I don't," Desroches retorted.

"Why do you think that?"

"She certainly hated Sir Rauf; that was well known. She had little to do with him, but," he spread his hands, "she is not the killing sort. She is too much a lady, too delicate, and of course there's that great mystery: how could anyone get into that chamber, commit murder, then escape through a locked door?"

"The windows?" Ranulf asked.

"Impossible." Desroches moved in his chair. "You've seen them, Sir Hugh: too small. The casement door is narrow whilst the shutters were clasped and barred. Lechlade and Warfeld will tell you that." He shook his head. "It's impossible," he repeated. "A true mystery."

"Very much like Maubisson," Corbett observed. "And what happened there?"

"Sir Hugh, again from what I gather, Paulents landed at Dover, he and his family fell ill and sent a message to Castledene. Castledene met them at Maubisson on the Dover Road. He asked me to join him."

"Why?" Corbett asked. "Why you?"

"I'm indentured to the city council, Sir Hugh. Castledene was about to receive important visitors. I was part of his care for them." He smiled. "Perhaps I'm a little more amenable than other physicians."

"And Castledene's guests?"

"I didn't think they were suffering from any contagion; only from seasickness. They certainly felt better when I met them. I know little, Sir Hugh, about the secrets and mysteries which existed between Paulents and Castledene. What I do know is that the visitors were in good health. I also learnt that Sir Walter and his guest had been threatened, but little else. Paulents' wife asked me to stay with them at Maubisson but I refused. I had to return to Canterbury."

"You gave them some physic?"

"I mixed a little camomile in a jug of wine when we met." Desroches smiled. "Both Castledene and I drank cups from the same jug."

"And the bodyguard Servinus?" Corbett continued.

Desroches lifted his hands. "What can I tell you, Sir Hugh? He was dressed in black leather, slightly fastidious, a professional soldier, harsh-faced with a balding head. Very much like Wendover; a man who gloried in the camp and the clash of armour. Paulents' wife seemed rather sweet on him. He certainly acted the part of the valorous warrior."

"So you think he was a fighter?" Corbett asked.

"He would certainly have given a good account of himself in any attack."

"Do you think he could be guilty of murder?"

"Sir Hugh, I cannot answer that. I mean —" Desroches was about to continue when suddenly a raucous shouting broke out. The door was flung open and Castledene burst into the chamber.

"Sir Hugh, you must come! A man has been killed!"

CHAPTER
TEN

Inferno tristi tibi quis fatetur.
Sad in your hell, who will confess to you?

Sedulius Scottus

Corbett ordered Ranulf to stay while he and Chanson, followed by Desroches, went out into the icy passageway. Castledene led them through the back of the house and outside. It was bitingly cold and a ring of torches glowed at the far end of the garden. Wendover came hurrying up.

"Sir Hugh, one of our city guards has been killed."

Desroches hastened ahead. Corbett followed and reached the group of men gathered round the corpse sprawled face down in the snow. Desroches glanced up, shaking his head.

"Dead!" He pointed to the heavy crossbow quarrel embedded deep between the man's shoulder blades. "A fatal wound." He turned the corpse over.

As Corbett stared down at the victim — a young man, sandy-haired, his eyes staring unseeingly, his face slightly unshaven and pockmarked — he noticed something amiss: the guard wasn't wearing the ordinary liveried cloak, but a light blue one usually worn by Wendover.

"What happened?" Corbett asked.

"Oseric, that's his name." One of the men spoke up. "He'd been with us only a few months."

"What happened?" Corbett insisted.

"He went out to relieve himself," the man replied. "He was in a hurry so he took Wendover's cloak. He was gone for some time. We were all in the buttery, drinking and chatting. I became concerned."

Corbett snapped his fingers, ordering the torchbearers to move closer to the speaker. The man, small and squat, glared angrily at him.

"Why should someone kill one of us?" he asked.

Corbett shook his head and stared round the snow-covered garden, the bushes and trees, the high curtain wall. Once again the Angel of Death had swept in, soft and silent, invisible yet menacing, like some formidable hawk floating over the fields of this world, keen to grasp a living soul in its greedy claws. But why now? How? Who had guided it in, selected its prey? He walked back towards the rear door and noticed the shuttered windows on either side; he tried both of these but they held fast.

"Sir Hugh, what is happening here?" Castledene came hurrying up.

Corbett turned. "Sir Walter, I do not know. What I suspect is that the assassin thought he was killing Wendover; instead poor Oseric met his death, but how?" He gestured at the back of the house. "I can't say."

"Is it true?"

Corbett turned. Wendover stood dancing from foot to foot, his blue cloak now draped over one arm.

"I am not sure," Corbett replied. "He was wearing your cloak and he was killed. You know as much as I do, Master Wendover." He took a step forward. "Or do you know something more?"

Wendover, crestfallen, shook his head.

"Then I suggest you and your companions look to Oseric's corpse."

Wendover glared at Corbett, swung the torn cloak round his shoulders and stamped off.

"Sir Hugh?"

"Yes, Sir Walter."

"The manuscript you took from Paulents' coffer: have you broken the cipher?"

Corbett walked over to him. "No, Sir Walter, I have not. Indeed, I deeply suspect it is a farrago of nonsense." He rubbed his arms, increasingly aware of how raw and biting the night had turned, then led Castledene back into the house and summoned Desroches to join them. Once inside the chancery chamber, Corbett warmed his hands in front of the fire.

"I have questioned enough. We shall return to Maubisson. I know," he straightened up, "the hour is late, but you, Sir Walter, and you, Master Desroches, must accompany me. We'll walk that manor house again. Wendover will accompany us. We'll see if there is anything we have missed."

Corbett issued instructions for the city guard to be placed around Sweetmead. He informed Lady Adelicia, who received him icily, that she would not be returning to the Guildhall, but that she would remain under house arrest and not leave without his written permission. She agreed coolly. He also added that Berengaria and Lechlade could stay with her if they wished. He then thanked Parson Warfeld, and a short while later, hooded and cowled, cloaks wrapped firmly about them, they led their horses out of Sweetmead and took the road back into the city. It was bone-chillingly cold, black as a malkin. The bells of the city were calling for evening Vespers, booming like a death knell through the darkness.

Once out of Sweetmead, Ranulf rode in front. Castledene urged his horse forward, its hooves slithering on the freezing ground, and tugged at Corbett's cloak.

"We'll not go through the city," he advised, "but take the road to the postern gate and down Warslock Lane. It will be easier."

Corbett agreed. In the end it was a strange journey. The horses were nervous and slithered on the ice. A piercing breeze blew under a cloud-free sky. Dark shapes came and went: tinkers and chapmen, carters travelling back into the countryside. The occasional torch shuddered in the dark. Here and there a lantern glowed, casting its reflection on banks of snow or pools of frozen water. They had to pull aside to quieten their horses as a group of Crutched Friars, led by a crucifer, processed by with two biers on their shoulders carrying the corpses of beggars found frozen near Schepescotes mill. The air became strangely sweet with the fragrance of incense. The awesome words of the funeral dirge, "My soul is longing for the Lord, more than the watchman for daybreak", rolled through the air like a sombre tambour beat and caught an echo in Corbett's mind. He longed for daybreak; not just for a fresh new day, but for an end to this frozen darkness around him, the sense of menace and the spine-chilling dread and fear which cloaked the mysteries now gripping him fast in their vice-like grip. He wanted to be home, to be with Maeve. He took a deep breath and blinked his watering eyes.

"Sufficient for the day is the evil thereof," he muttered, and forced himself to hum the tune of a Goliard song, *"Fas et nefas ambulant"*. He waited until the funeral cortege had disappeared into the gloom, then, much to the surprise of his companions, burst into song. Ranulf decided to accompany him. The Latin words of the merry chant rang out like a challenge to the darkness about them. When they had finished, Corbett felt more settled and calm. They were now following a secure path, cleared by the constant traffic around the city walls. Castledene pointed out certain buildings: St Mary Northgate to their right, and in the far distance to their left, the dark mass of St Gregory's priory.

At last, after an hour's ride, they reached Maubisson. Its gates, walls and grounds were still patrolled by the city guard. Doors and window shutters had been sealed with the insignia of the city. These were now broken and opened. Castledene ordered Wendover to go into the house to light torches, lamps and candles as well as rekindle fires in the hearth. Inside it was winter-cold and dank. Corbett walked into the ill-lit hall. He still found it a harrowing place. Even though the corpses had been removed to a nearby church, his eyes were drawn to those grim iron brackets fastened to the wall, those terrible branches which had sprouted such gruesome fruit. He shook himself from the hideous reverie and ordered his companions to search the manor. Accompanied by Chanson, he carried out his own search, whilst Ranulf followed the others, vigilant for anything untoward. They found nothing.

Corbett was glad to leave, to be free of a place which seemed to reek of evil. He went down the steps, mounted his horse and, gathering his reins, stared down at Castledene and Desroches.

"We have finished for the day," he declared. "I need to reflect."

"Sir Hugh?"

"Yes, Master Desroches."

"May I accompany you?"

"Why, Physician," Corbett joked, leaning forward and stroking his horse's neck, "are you not tired of our company?"

Desroches stepped closer, grasping the bridle of Corbett's horse. He forced a smile, but then quickly winked as if communicating a secret.

"I could do with some company." He let the bridle go and stepped back.

Corbett shrugged. "We are returning to St Augustine's Abbey; you can be our guest at supper."

Desroches agreed and clambered gingerly on to his own palfrey. Corbett could see he was a poor horseman. They said farewell to Castledene and the others and made their way out on to the main thoroughfare. Desroches pushed his horse alongside Corbett's. "Sir Hugh, I am glad of the company. I must tell you two things. First, when poor Oseric was killed, Wendover was not in the buttery." He noticed Corbett's surprise. "Lechlade told me that."

"And second?"

"From the little I gather, Lady Adelicia knew more of her husband's dealings than she pretends."

"How so?"

"Sir Hugh, she saw her hated husband bury that corpse and did not use it against him."

"Master Physician," Corbett edged his horse closer, "you've earned your supper."

Once back at the abbey, Corbett went to his own chamber, leaving Ranulf, Chanson and Desroches to wait in the refectory below for the guest master to serve some food. On the table outside his chamber a lay brother had left two jugs of wine, red and white, covered with a napkin. Corbett opened his door and went in. He took a tinder, lit the candle on its stand in the centre of the table and then the other capped candles. As he rekindled the brazier, warming his hands over it, he heard a soft footfall on the gallery outside and whirled around, hand going to his dagger. There was a knock on the half-opened door.

"Come in!" Corbett shouted.

The guest master stepped in, his face all concerned.

"Sir Hugh, I learnt you were back," he gabbled. "I came up to see if all was well. I mean, I told your companions —"

"Yes, yes," Corbett interrupted. "If some supper could be served we'd be grateful. Perhaps more braziers? The night is chillingly cold."

The guest master nodded. He was about to turn away when he paused, peering at the wine jugs Corbett had placed on the table beside the candle.

"Sir Hugh?"

"Yes, Brother?"

"You brought your own jugs?"

Corbett felt a tingle of fear curdle his stomach. "Brother, what are you talking about?"

The guest master walked across and picked up the napkin. He held this up and peered at the stitching along its hem, then crouched down and moved the jugs.

"I know every jug and cup in this guesthouse." He straightened up. "That napkin was not fashioned by us, whilst the jugs certainly do not come from our kitchen." He picked up one of the jugs and went to sip from it.

"Don't!" Corbett urged. He walked across, took the jug from the surprised monk's hand, sniffed and caught a rather faint bitter smell, as if some herb had been crushed and mingled with the red wine. He picked up the white and detected a similar odour.

"Brother, do you have rats?"

"Does a cat have fleas?" the guest master replied. "Of course we do, we are plagued by them."

"Then give them a feast," Corbett urged. "Take some fresh bread and cheese, mingle them together, soak the mix in this wine, and put it in the cellars where no one else will see it. Tomorrow morning, or maybe even later tonight, come back and tell me what you found, but I urge you, Brother, do not drink this wine. I believe it is tainted."

"Tainted?" The guest master's wrinkled face became all fearful. "Sir Hugh, someone wishes to do you evil."

"Yes, Brother, they do. I'm the King's messenger in Canterbury and perhaps not everyone welcomes me as they should. I ask you to keep this matter close, even from your own abbot, as well as from my companions downstairs. Brother, how easy would it be for a stranger to enter this guesthouse?"

The monk stepped away from the table, wiping his hands on his robe, gazing suspiciously at the jugs. "Why, Sir Hugh, it's very easy to enter the guesthouse itself. But as for your chamber, they would have to hold either your key or mine."

"So it's quite possible," Corbett asked, "for someone to have brought those two jugs in and left them outside my chamber?"

"Oh yes, Sir Hugh. I mean, people are going to and fro all the time, very rarely is any mischief caused."

Corbett thanked him. The guest master gingerly picked up both jugs and napkin and left the room, shaking his head and muttering under his breath. Corbett waited until he'd gone, then slumped down on the edge of the bed. He unbuckled his sword belt and cloak, letting them fall around him, pulled off his boots and put on his buskins. Then he went to the top of the stairs and shouted for Ranulf. When his manservant came, Corbett met him halfway down the stairs.

"Ranulf," he patted his companion on the shoulder, "I'm tired and worn out. I have eaten and drunk enough. Give my apologies to Master Desroches. You and Chanson entertain him; I intend to sleep."

He went back to the chamber and checked it most carefully. Nothing had been disturbed. He doused the candles, except those glowing under their bronze caps, and climbed into bed, wrapping the blankets around him. Then he pushed his head hard against the bolster, closed his eyes and fell into a deep sleep.

He woke early, long before dawn, and left the guesthouse. He crossed the frozen yard, braving the winter darkness, until he reached the prior's kitchen, which served visitors to the abbey. He knocked hard on the door. A sleepy-faced servant opened it and ushered him in into the warm, fragrant bakehouse. Corbett told him what he wanted, and a short while later he left carrying a pannier of hot water from the pot dangling on a tripod above the hearth.

Once back in his own chamber, he stripped, washed and shaved. He put on fresh linen undergarments, choosing dark brown hose, a white cambric shirt and a thick fleece jerkin for protection against the cold. He built the braziers up, then drank a cup of water and went across to the writing desk. Once ready, he opened the leather pannier resting beside the leg of the table, pulled out a sheaf of parchment and sharpened a quill pen.

"Now I will impose order," he murmured. "Now I will establish a pattern."

Corbett steeled himself to ignore the growing sounds from the abbey as the monks rose and prepared for the first office of the day. He was tempted to go down and stand in the great oaken stalls and join them in their chanting of Matins, but that would have to wait. He dipped his pen into the green ink and wrote: *Primo: The Brothers*.

Corbett tried to marshal everything he'd learnt about Adam Blackstock and his half-brother Hubert the Monk, or Hubert son of Fitzurse, "The Man with the Far-Seeing Gaze". His pen raced across the parchment. Blackstock, according to the documents in the Guildhall, had been the pirate's family name, so why did Hubert use the "son of Fitzurse", his mother's maiden name? Was he just emphasising that two sons had survived that dreadful massacre? And why did he proclaim himself "The Man with the Far-Seeing Gaze"? Was that a reference to his planning and plotting these murders? Had he waited and bided his time? But where did this all begin? Corbett wrote the date 1272, then glanced up and stared at the crucifix on the wall. He remembered how the old King had died gasping at Westminster and the London mob had taken to rioting in the streets. There had been a breakdown in law and order, the king's peace being openly violated in the shires. The same thing had happened in Kent. According to what he'd learnt, Adam and Hubert's parents had been wealthy farmers; their manor house had probably been a fine building with vegetable gardens, herb plots, flowerbeds, stables, fertile fields for corn and lush pasture for sheep. Attacks by armed gangs on such manors became commonplace. Usually the rifflers plundered the house and drove away cattle and other livestock, but this attack had been different. Had people from the city of Canterbury been involved? Royal justices had investigated, but no culprits had been produced. Fortune had then turned her wheel again. Adam was put to trade as an apprentice, while Hubert had continued his schooling here in St Augustine's Abbey. Corbett made a note on a scrap of parchment beside him. He must look out for the *magister scholorum*, Brother Fulbert, and ask him what he knew.

Apparently Adam had been an industrious worker, and if he'd followed the usual path, he would have finished his apprenticeship, becoming a tradesman and eventually a merchant, a member of the Guild. Instead he had left Canterbury, finding his true calling as a sailor, working in the various ports along the east and south coasts of the kingdom before moving to the more exciting fleshpots in the coastal ports of Hainault, Flanders and Brabant. There he consorted with pirates and privateers, eventually becoming one himself, and securing swift promotion to command a redoubtable pirate cog, *The Waxman*, a veritable plague on shipping along the Narrow Seas and the wine routes to Bordeaux.

Corbett paused. His own childhood had been warm and loving, but he'd met others, at court and camp, brutalised by barbaric events in their early lives. Was this true of Adam Blackstock? Could he not forget the images he'd seen that hideous night, the screams of his mother, the futile attempts to resist by his father and others? Blackstock had later waged war against English ships, in particular those of Sir Walter Castledene. Was that because the mayor was a prominent merchant of Canterbury, or were there more secret reasons? Corbett had searched the official documents scrupulously, but now he quietly promised himself that he would return to the Guildhall manuscripts and study them more closely.

Hubert the Monk had acted in a similar fashion. Highly intelligent, he might well have graduated to becoming a *magister* in the schools. He finished his education at St Augustine's and in the Halls of Cambridge, took the solemn vows of a Benedictine monk, entered the community at Westminster under Abbot Wenlock, then he too had changed, swiftly and abruptly. According to the prior at Westminster, a mysterious visitor had visited Hubert and imparted certain information which had radically changed that young man's life. He had fled his monastery, renounced his vows and become a *venator hominum*, tracking down outlaws and wolfsheads, and handing them over to sheriffs, port reeves or town bailiffs in return for a reward. Hubert had certainly kept his distance from Canterbury. Why? Because he hated the city, or was there some other reason? He had plied his bloody trade in the south-eastern shires of the kingdom, keeping himself visored and hooded, a careful enough precaution by a man who did not wish his face to be known to the thieves and villains he pursued along the byways and country lanes of various shires.

Apparently the two brothers had lived separate lives until their paths had crossed, possibly about four years ago. Again it was the city of Canterbury which proved to be the cause and catalyst. Blackstock had intercepted a Hanseatic ship carrying the precious manuscript from Paulents which described in great detail an ancient, very rich treasure buried somewhere in Suffolk. Corbett had heard stories of such buried treasure up and down the kingdom. On one occasion he had even been commissioned by Edward himself to search for the lost hoard of King John allegedly engulfed in the Wash towards the end of that king's reign. Tales of the Suffolk treasure were common in the folklore of that shire, but Paulents had managed to establish its exact location and hoped to find the treasure along with his business colleague and fellow trader Castledene. However, Blackstock had seized the ship, stolen the manuscript and planned to meet with his brother to discover this ancient precious trove himself. In turn, Castledene and Paulents, with the help of the Crown, had decided to trap Blackstock.

The story of the ambush of *The Waxman* and Blackstock's death was familiar now to Corbett, but what of Hubert? Undoubtedly he had sworn revenge and disappeared from the world of men, but where was he now? The Cloister Map had also disappeared. Had Stonecrop stolen it from Blackstock's cabin? Corbett could imagine a ship preparing for battle. Had Stonecrop used the confusion to take the map, hoping to use it to negotiate with Sir Walter Castledene and Paulents? Instead, with the fury of battle still upon him,

Castledene had meted out rough justice and thrown Stonecrop overboard. Had that treacherous lieutenant managed to reach the shore, hide and make his way to Canterbury, that would certainly fit with the tally of dates. Then what? Corbett paused in his writing. "Yes, yes," he murmured. Sir Rauf Decontet had been a powerful merchant. Evidence that he had secretly subsidised *The Waxman* was not hard to find. Had Stonecrop arrived in Canterbury to threaten, to blackmail, to wheedle support? Had he brought that precious map? And had Sir Rauf Decontet, a man of few scruples, decided to keep the map and deal with any threats by crushing Stonecrop's skull in the dead of night and burying his corpse in that lonely, overgrown garden?

Corbett took a sip of water and returned to his writing: *Secondo: The Present Time*. Hubert the Monk had disappeared. Were he and Servinus one and the same? Had Hubert decided to travel to Germany and negotiate himself into Paulents' household? It was a possibility. Mercenaries wandered the face of Europe being hired by this merchant or that princely household. Hubert was a highly intelligent man, possibly with a command of languages and knowledge of the world. There was no description of him, so he could travel undetected. Moreover, why should Paulents refuse such an addition to his household, especially when he might live in fear of revenge attacks by Adam Blackstock's half-brother? Whatever, Hubert the Monk had disappeared, as had the map and Stonecrop. However, Paulents had not given up trying to find that lost treasure. He'd discovered fresh evidence but this time decided to bring it to England himself. He had travelled across Europe, taken ship to Dover and landed there with his wife, his son, their maid and the bodyguard. Paulents and his family had apparently fallen ill, though whether this was due to some contagion or a cruel sea passage could not be established. What was certain was that on the same day they landed at Dover, they received a threatening note, as did Castledene in Canterbury. But how could that have been organised? Corbett paused. If Hubert was hunting both men, it would be possible to arrange through a trader, chapman or tinker for the same message to be delivered to two different individuals in two different towns.

Paulents, undeterred, had travelled on to Canterbury, where he'd been met by Castledene and Desroches, who'd pronounced their sickness caused by the hardships and rigour of their journey. Paulents had then taken up residence at Maubisson with its secure gates and walls, its doors and shutters locked and barred, a ring of guards circling it. Corbett was satisfied from the evidence he'd seen that Wendover had carried out his task faithfully. He closed his eyes for a while and tried to imagine that hideous hall, only this time the fire was burning merrily, candlelight gleaming, Paulents and his family, together with Servinus, relaxing over their evening meal. They would feel comfortable and secure. They were in Canterbury, in a fortified manor house; they had little to fear. Corbett opened his eyes and continued writing. So what had happened that night? How had four able-bodied people been hanged from those iron brackets on the wall? Just left there dangling, strangled, eyes popping, swaying slightly in the jumping shadows? Neither he nor Desroches had found any trace of an opiate or powder, no other mark of violence to their bodies. It was impossible to conclude that all four, at the same time, had decided to take their own lives. Was Servinus responsible? Had he killed them? But how? And how could he have escaped undetected, a foreigner in a snow-bound city? What was the motive behind the murders? Revenge? Or the theft of that secret map?

Corbett rose, went over to the coffer and took out the map he'd so carefully studied. He tapped it against his hand. He had no proof, just a suspicion, but he truly believed that this was not the genuine map. He had studied every secret cipher used in Europe, be it by the Papal Chancery or that of Philip Le Bel of France. Sooner or later he could prove that old adage of the schools, that if a problem exists, so must a solution; it is only a matter of time. Yet with this one . . . He placed the document back in the coffer and returned to his chancery desk.

Corbett heard the faint singing of the monastic choir as they chanted the first psalms of Lauds. One verse caught his attention: "It is He who will free you from the snare of the fowler who seeks to destroy you. He will conceal you beneath his pinions and under His wings you will find refuge. You will not fear the terror of the night nor the arrow which flies by day, nor the

222

plague that haunts the darkness, nor the scourge which devastates the noon-tide."

"I hope so," Corbett murmured. "I pray so."

He was tempted to go down and share in the comfort of that holy place. Instead he promised himself that when the bells rang for the Jesus Mass he would join the good brothers; until then he must confront the evils which beset him.

Tertio: Decontet. Sir Rauf was undoubtedly a miser, a secret supporter of pirates and privateers, an unscrupulous man with no thought for the morrow except for how much money he might make. Lady Adelicia, his young bride, certainly hated him and he had replied in kind. Little wonder she had found comfort with Wendover. Decontet may have also been a killer, responsible for Stonecrop's death and his hasty burial in that desolate garden. However, did such matters have any bearing on the events of that fateful Thursday afternoon? Lady Adelicia had left for the city with Berengaria. Once her mistress had been ensconced in Wendover's chamber, Berengaria had hastened back for her own meeting with Sir Rauf, who paid her good silver for certain sexual favours. Did Lady Adelicia know about that? She had indicated that perhaps she did, calling Berengaria a minx. Corbett recalled arrangements mentioned as he left Sweetmead the previous evening. How Lechlade would stay with Lady Adelicia, but that Berengaria had murmured something about remaining with her possessions at Parson Warfeld's house for the time being. Undoubtedly Berengaria was a sharp-witted, ruthless young woman, but on that particular day she had failed to meet Sir Rauf and so returned to Canterbury. Physician Desroches had then arrived; unable to arouse Sir Rauf, he'd waited until Lechlade had come down, roughly wakened from his drunken stupor. Desroches had sent for Parson Warfeld and the chancery door had been forced. Lady Adelicia had arrived, followed by Castledene. Questions were asked about the blood on her cloak and those gore-soaked napkins found in her bedchamber. She was arrested as the perpetrator yet the mystery still remained. How had someone entered a locked chamber, shattered Sir Rauf's skull and then escaped? Why wasn't there any sign of a struggle? How did the assassin, if it was not Lady Adelicia, go up to her chamber, drop the bloodstained napkin on the floor and hide more behind the bolsters? How could anyone do that without a key to her chamber? There were only two keys, one definitely held by Lady Adelicia and the other by Sir Rauf. Nevertheless, Warfeld and Desroches had been quite explicit: when the doors to both chambers had been either forced or opened, that precious keyring was still on Sir Rauf's belt. Had another key been fashioned? Corbett shook his head. Such locks were unique, the work of a craftsman, and any attempt to replicate their keys would arouse deep suspicion.

Quatro: Les Hommes Joyeuses and Griskin. Now Corbett wrote more slowly. Griskin had been a good spy, an able man who took careful precautions to protect himself. He'd disguised himself as a leper and travelled up into Suffolk, searching out those legends

224

about the lost treasure. He had reported to the Gleeman that he had discovered scraps of information, and made a mysterious reference to St Simon of the Rocks, but what did he mean? Griskin had later been trapped, murdered and gibbeted, probably by Hubert the Monk, which in turn meant that he had discovered something about that elusive hunter of men. What was it? Yet this begged another question. How had Hubert discovered the truth about Griskin? Was it through his own sharp wits, or had Griskin been betrayed? Had he been seen in the company of Les Hommes Joyeuses and someone reported this to Hubert? If that was the case, there was a traitor amongst Les Hommes Joyeuses. Could it be the Gleeman?

Quinto: The Waxman *and Hubert the Monk*. Who was Hubert? Where was he? Were he and Servinus one and the same? How could he move so quickly? Delivering warnings in both Canterbury and Dover? Following them through the woods when Corbett had returned with Desroches and Ranulf from Maubisson to St Augustine's? Who had attacked Corbett in the cloisters? Desroches had been in the refectory downstairs, but Parson Warfeld? And the others? Who had come to St Augustine's yesterday with that poisoned wine?

Everything pointed to *The Waxman*, the Suffolk treasure, the Cloister Map and Hubert's desire for vengeance as the hideous roots of this murderous affair. Yet was all this a false lure? Indeed, was Hubert even still alive? Was someone else using the past to conceal their own devious plot? Virtually everyone had some connection with *The Waxman*, including Warfeld. And what about Berengaria? And the Lady Adelicia, who could so innocently flutter her eyelids and deny any knowledge of her husband's doings? And Castledene? What was the truth there?

CHAPTER
ELEVEN

In domo frigus patior nivale.
Even in this house I am freezing cold.

Walafrid Strabo

Corbett sat reflecting. The chanting had now stopped and a bell boomed out announcing that the Jesus or Morrow Mass was about to begin. He hastily finished dressing, took his war belt and clasped it on, then threw a cloak over his shoulders, pulling up its hood to protect his head. He left and locked his chamber and went downstairs. The light was greying now. Here and there lay brothers were busy in the yard, opening stores; one was sawing wood, another drawing water. Corbett hurried into the tangled labyrinth of abbey buildings, down chilly, stone-hollow passageways, across frozen-carpeted gardens and eventually in by the Galilee Porch to the abbey church. The monks were now leaving their stalls. Corbett decided to attend Mass not at the high altar but in one of the chantry chapels along the transept, a comfortable place, its floor covered with turkey rugs, whilst chafing dishes in each corner spluttered warmth. He knelt on the prie-dieu and nodded at the old monk who came shuffling in to celebrate his Mass. Corbett leaned against the hard rest and watched the celebrant begin the mysteries, trying to school himself by concentrating on the crucifix above the altar. Once the Mass was finished and Corbett had made his thanks, he went into the Lady Chapel and lit three tapers for Maeve and his two children. He was about to leave through the main porch when he heard his name called. The guest master came hurrying down the church, the sleeves of his gown flapping like the wings of a bird, sandalled feet slapping against the paved floor.

"Sir Hugh," he gasped, "Sir Hugh, thank goodness I have found you! I have something to show you, the rats!" And before Corbett could ask him any questions, the guest master hurried from the church, leading him from the sacred precincts into a small cobbled yard. There he opened the door to an outhouse which reeked of rotting hay. On a broken stool stretched a piece of sacking bearing the bloated corpses of four rats, bellies distended, paws rigid, jaws open to display sharp protuberant teeth.

"Found them this morning," the guest master declared, "dead as nails. I put down the bread and cheese as you asked, soaked in that wine." He sighed dramatically. "Sir Hugh, someone meant to do you a great mischief."

"Well they didn't!" Corbett took a silver piece from his purse and, grasping the old man's hand, pushed it into his palm. "It's our secret, Brother. You mustn't tell anyone until we've gone. I also ask you to be most prudent in what food and drinks are served."

"Are you sure?" The old monk's eyes wrinkled in puzzlement. "Sir Hugh, you are in great danger, here in our abbey. It is a scandal! Father Abbot would be horrified."

"Father Abbot won't be," Corbett smiled, "because Father Abbot won't be told. Now, Brother, I have another favour to ask, a great favour. A *magister* once taught here, Master of the Scholars, Brother Fulbert? Is he still here? Can I talk to him?"

"Brother Fulbert, of course, he's an Ancient One. Come, I'll take you to him. He is an early riser, always has been." And he led Corbett off again down a maze of stone galleries, past brothers busy about their daily tasks. The abbey was now preparing for Christmas; wheelbarrows full of greenery stood around, berries blood red against the green holly. Yule logs were being hewed, Christmas candles placed in window embrasures, and the air was full of the swirling odours and fragrances of the various rooms and chambers of the abbey. Cooking smells from the kitchens mingled with those of dry leather and parchment from the scriptorium. Incense swirled the smell of oil lamps, whilst the perfumed gusts from the bathhouse mixed with the tang of compost some lay brothers were piling around the rose bushes, their roots recently cleared of snow. Here and there groups of monks stood gossiping, overlooked by stone-faced statues.

At last they reached a two-storey house enclosed by its own garden. The guest master gestured Corbett in, the raised door latch jarring noisily in such a quiet place. He led Corbett up some wooden stairs, along a polished gallery, and knocked on a door.

"Come in," a voice shouted. "You are always welcome, you know that."

Inside Brother Fulbert was seated at a table, shoulders shaking with laughter as he read a manuscript, peering closely at it, moving his finger slowly along the line of words. He did not look up as Corbett and the guest master entered, but continued chuckling to himself, intent on the manuscript. The cell was comfortable, well heated by the charcoal dish, whilst warm-coloured cloths against the wall and thick floor rugs fended off the chill from the freezing flagstones. The chamber was littered with manuscripts, spilling out from opened coffers. There was a book on a lectern, another opened on the half-made bed.

"Brother Fulbert?" The guest master leaned over the table.

The old monk glanced up. He had lank white hair which framed a pointed face, deeply lined and furrowed, though the eyes were bright as those of a robin redbreast. He nodded at his fellow monk and looked questioningly at Corbett. The guest master hastily made the introductions, and Brother Fulbert told Corbett to fetch a stool from the corner and sit opposite him as if he were a scholar from the schools. The guest master hastily retreated, closing the door firmly behind him.

"Well, well, well." Fulbert rested his elbow on the table. "So you are the King's man, the clerk? I heard about your arrival." He examined the ring on Corbett's left hand. "Senior Clerk in the Chancery of the Secret Seal. I was a royal clerk once, until I found my calling

230

after I entered the halls of Oxford. I met people who'd witnessed the Great Revolt there, when the black banners were raised and scholars fought running battles with the townspeople. I'd love to go back to Oxford, Sir Hugh." He sighed. "It has changed, but there again, I suspect the hidden flame still glows. Do you remember the old saying of the schools? 'If that which was there has not left, it must, therefore, still be there.'"

Corbett smiled in agreement.

Fulbert looked down once more at the manuscript, sighed again and pushed it away. He leaned across the table as if he was a conspirator. "Sir Hugh, don't tell anybody, but I am reading a copy of Abelard's *Sic et Non*. You know it?"

Corbett nodded.

"What does it say?" Fulbert's head darted forward.

"About two hundred years ago Abelard took the teachings of theologians and showed how they contradicted each other. His thesis was not well received by the Church, particularly by Bernard of Clairvaux, and led to fierce debate between scholars . . ."

"So it did, so it did," Brother Fulbert agreed. "And the papacy condemned it," he smiled mischievously, "which is why I like to read it. But you haven't come to hear an old hoary-head chatter on."

Corbett asked about Hubert. Fulbert immediately remembered him, nodding in agreement as Corbett described that young man's life.

"I am sad to hear the news. Hubert Fitzurse . . ." Fulbert gathered his thoughts. "He was a born scholar, a very pleasant young man. He was mature beyond his years, objective, dispassionate, hungry for knowledge as a cat for cream. Oh yes, I remember him well. When he concentrated, be it on a subtle treatise of mathematics or the intricacies of construing a Latin passage, he would give it his full attention." Fulbert held up a bony finger. "Hubert had the skill to become absorbed in whatever he was doing. He would move from one extreme to another in the blink of an eye. He was well disciplined but also an excellent mimic. He would watch and ape people's gestures and mannerisms: the way they walked, talked, how they held their heads, how they ate or sat. He was often a great source of amusement for his comrades, but not in an unpleasant way, Sir Hugh. He enjoyed a penchant for making others laugh, but never cruelly, whilst he was always ready to poke fun at himself. More than that," Brother Fulbert's gaze strayed back to the manuscript on the table before him, "I cannot say. If you ever meet him, Sir Hugh, give him my good wishes and prayers."

Corbett thanked the old man and went down the stairs into the yard. The guest master had left, so he stood for a while peering up at the sky, hoping the sun might appear. The air was not so cold; it had lost that stinging, sharp, knife-edged cut to it. Corbett stared around. He must remember to be careful; parts of this abbey were lonely and deserted, the ideal place for an assassin to prowl. Was Hubert, that hunter of men, now pursuing him? Did he wish to kill Corbett as an act of revenge against the King, who'd played his own part in the destruction of Adam Blackstock and *The Waxman*?

Or did he only mean to distract and frighten Corbett until this business was finished?

Corbett clenched his fist. Perhaps that was it. Hubert realised time was short, the opportunity to wreak his revenge brief. The clerk walked slowly across the yard. If he could only discover what had truly happened at Maubisson, bring it under the rigour of his logic. He paused, recalling what Brother Fulbert had said: *If that which was there has not left, it must, therefore, still be there.* Servinus! Corbett punched his thigh. Of course, no one had seen Servinus leave! The prospect of him escaping undetected was virtually impossible. Moreover, he was a foreigner, a mercenary; even in a city like Canterbury, visited by pilgrims, people would notice him. Castledene had his spies out, so why had they not found him?

"Because he never left Maubisson!" Corbett murmured. He quickened his pace, certain that the dark shadows and recesses of that forbidding mansion still held the secret of Servinus.

He intended to go back to the guesthouse, rouse Ranulf and Chanson and ride straight to Maubisson; then he thought of poor Griskin, his naked cadaver hanging from the gallows above those deserted mudflats. No, first he'd visit Les Hommes Joyeuses. He pulled up his hood, took directions from one of the brothers and found himself on the same path he'd taken the day before, leading past ice-bound fields towards St Pancras's church and its old priest's house. By the time he arrived there the entire company were busy. Having broken their fast, they had now laid out

233

the stage with its backdrop, ready to exploit a dry day to rehearse their play. People milled about. Corbett studied the scenery and marvelled at its skill to evoke the imagination. One painting, crudely done, showed the Gaderene demoniac in green satin being led on a gilt chain by his father dressed in yellow taffeta. Next to this were further scenes from the life of Christ: a blind man and his servant garbed in red and grey satin; beside them a paralytic in orange; the Apostles climbing the Mount of Humility towards Jesus, who stood resplendent in robes of velvet, crimson satin, damask and taffeta. At the far end of the backdrop was a vivid vision of hell, depicted as a soaring rock crowned with an ever-burning tower belching globules of black smoke from which Lucifer's head and body projected. The demon vomited flames of fire whilst holding in his hands writhing serpents and vipers. Corbett studied this then moved over to where the troupe was gathered around the Gleeman, who was standing on an upturned barrel, a piece of parchment in his hand.

"Today," the Gleeman shouted, "we shall start early, as darkness will soon be upon us. We must prepare our play for the twelve days of Christmas. The good burgesses of Canterbury, in their markets and outside their churches, will demand to see a play they've never seen before. So we must get all our items correct. We must have a palm for Gabriel to bring from Paradise to Mary. There must be a thunderclap. We need a white cloud to come and fetch St John preaching on Patmos and bring him before the door of the Virgin Mary's house at Ephesus. We must have another cloud to bring up the Apostles from the various countries; a cloth of gold robe for Mary's Assumption, together with a small truckle bed and several torches of white wax which the attendant virgins must hold. Jesus Christ must come down from Paradise to greet His Mother, accompanied by a great multitude of angels. So we must have fragrances as well as a crown circled with twelve stars. He will use these to anoint and crown her in Paradise." The Gleeman glimpsed Corbett and paused. "All these items must be ready. So come on," he clapped his hands, "the rehearsals must be underway before the Angelus bell." He climbed down from the barrel, shooing the troupe away.

"Well, sir, what can I do for you?" The Gleeman walked over to Corbett, smiling and winking. Corbett led him away from the rest.

"Tell me," he said, "when you met Griskin in Suffolk, he pretended to be a leper?"

"That's right, Sir Hugh," the Gleeman murmured. "He would come into our camp once darkness fell and seek me out. We would gossip, then he would leave. Why do you ask?"

"I believe," Corbett decided to be blunt, "that Griskin was betrayed."

"Sir Hugh, not by me!" The Gleeman stood back, hands to his chest. "I promise you, Griskin was safe with me and my company. No one would betray him."

"Tell me," Corbett moved closer, "Griskin was murdered when? At the end of November? Is there anybody, Master Gleeman, who's joined your company recently, mysteriously? Someone skilled, someone you

235

need, but nevertheless a stranger. You do hire men, don't you?"

The Gleeman nodded, eyes narrowing. He was about to open his mouth to reply when he coughed, turned away and spat. "We have such a man. He joined us around the Feast of All Souls, or All Saints, I can't remember which. He calls himself the Pilgrim. At first he acted suspiciously, but he was skilled in fashioning joists and other woodwork. He also proved to be a marvellous devil."

"A what?" Corbett asked.

"One of the mummers," the Gleeman explained. "Certain people possess that skill of mind to conjure up an appearance and act a part. The Pilgrim is certainly one of these. He played the role of a demon to perfection. I put it to the vote and we accepted him. Come." The Gleeman took Corbett by the elbow, pushing him gently towards the old priest's house. He ushered him inside the deserted kitchen, told him to sit on the stool before the fire and went out. A short while later he returned. Corbett looked over his shoulder, but all he could see was a dark outline in the doorway. He immediately sensed that this man, whoever he may be, was very fearful.

"Come in!" Corbett ordered, getting to his feet. "Master Gleeman, I prefer to be by myself." The Gleeman nodded and hastily withdrew.

Corbett took the stranger closer to the window. Lean and lithe, he reminded Corbett of a cat, with his slanting eyes, a face like the very devil, cheeks and jaw bare of any hair, all cleanly shaven. Corbett stepped back. The man had a thin, narrow face. He was dressed in yellow hose and a tattered scarlet jerkin. In his left hand he held a cither and in his right a crude form of bow. He made no sound, no comment, his mouth slack, lips open, only those eyes in that lean, vicious-looking face watching Corbett intently.

"What do you want?" The voice was guttural. "Sir, I asked you what you want with me. Master Gleeman said I had to talk to you."

"What is your name?" Corbett asked, stepping closer.

"Pilgrim."

Corbett drew his dagger and dug its point into the side of the Pilgrim's neck. "I am the King's clerk, his commissioner in these parts," he whispered, "and you, sir, when I ask a question, will answer truthfully. You proclaim yourself the Pilgrim, but I doubt you were called so at the baptismal font. What is your true name?"

"Edmund Groscote."

"Ah, well, Edmund Groscote," Corbett continued, digging the tip a little deeper until a small bead of blood appeared. Groscote winced but did not flinch; his eyes held Corbett's. "Just keep holding the bow and cither," Corbett warned. "Don't drop them; don't even think of looking for that knife hidden somewhere about you. Let me tell you a little about your life, Master Groscote. You're a cunning man, a conjuror, a foist, a nap, someone who lives on their wits. You have been pursued the length and breadth of the kingdom for this crime or that. I wager in some town in Suffolk or

Norfolk there are rewards on your head for all sorts of trickery, am I correct? Please answer the truth. You have nothing to fear from me except a pardon."

Groscote sighed. "The blade," he murmured. "I beg you . . ."

Corbett withdrew the dagger.

Groscote's body went slack. He backed away until he reached the door, then slid down, arms across his stomach, knees up. He glanced fearfully at Corbett.

"My name is Edmund Groscote," he repeated. "I am wanted by various sheriffs, port reeves and town bailiffs. I have a list of crimes any man would be fearful of. I was a clerk once, Sir Hugh — that is your name, is it not? Ah well," he continued, not waiting for a reply, "I was a clerk. On two occasions I've taken sanctuary, on three occasions pleaded benefit of clergy. So, Master Royal Clerk, if I am taken up again, I'll be hanged. I was born in Norfolk of good family, sent to school, studied hard at my horn book, but I took to devilry as a fish does to swimming or a bird to flying."

"And?" Corbett asked.

"I became the quarry of a *venator hominum*."

"Hubert Fitzurse?" Corbett asked.

"The devil's own," the Pilgrim retorted. "He was terrifying, Sir Hugh. You don't know what it's like to be hunted day and night by one man, a shadow, whose face you never see. So every tavern you enter, every alehouse you frequent, every marketplace you cross, you never know if he is there waiting for you. He had a fearful reputation. You'd be seized, bound and handed over to be hanged."

238

Corbett knelt down beside this frightened man. "But Hubert the Monk disappeared," he declared. "You joined Les Hommes Joyeuses on the Feast of All Souls last. For many a year the *venator hominum* had been quiet. He suddenly reappeared, didn't he?"

"I wasn't hiding from him," Groscote replied wearily, "but from others, members of a gang; we'd taken some silver and I had divided it, according to them, rather unfairly. Anyway, I decided to give up my nefarious ways and join the Gleeman's company. I was happy to do so. One night I was in the tavern. I was drunk, full of ale, my belly fit to bursting. I went out to relieve myself. I felt a dagger, like yours, Sir Hugh, nipping at my neck. I was pushed against the wall, my face scarred against the brickwork, and a hoarse voice whispered in my ear, asking me many questions. Was I not Edmund Groscote? Was I not a member of Les Hommes Joyeuses? Was I not wanted in this town or that for this crime or that? Of course, I had to agree. 'Do you know who I am?' the voice asked. I was too terrified to reply. 'I am Hubert Fitzurse,' the voice continued, 'the Man with the Far-Seeing Gaze, the *venator hominum*. You, Master Groscote, are my prisoner. Within a week you'll hang.' I begged for mercy, I spluttered for my life." The Pilgrim spread his hands, eyes fearful. "'No real need for you to hang, Master Groscote,' that voice whispered. 'I just want information about Les Hommes Joyeuses and the Gleeman. Has a leper visited your camp?' Of course I had seen one and confessed as much. Fitzurse told me to return to the same tavern at the same hour the following evening and tell him all I knew. I did that."

"What *did* you know?"

"Sir Hugh, many strangers enter the camp. I thought this man was a mummer, a travelling player, a moon person, a counterfeit man pretending to be a leper begging for alms. He had been noticed. I tried to find out a little more. How he and the Gleeman had been closeted together. I went back and told Fitzurse this. I met him in the shadows. He gave me a coin, and since then I've heard no more from him."

"And he has not approached you here?" Corbett asked.

"No, Sir Hugh."

Corbett rose to his feet, took a coin from his own purse and spun it at the Pilgrim, who caught it.

"Sir Hugh, what am I to do?"

"If you want to live," Corbett declared, "I would flee Les Hommes Joyeuses. Run as fast as you can, despite the snow; try and reach London. Take sanctuary in the Church of St Michael's, Cornhill. Tell the sheriff and his bailiffs that you do so at the behest of Sir Hugh Corbett, Keeper of the Secret Seal. If you stay there, Master Pilgrim, you may receive a pardon. If you do not, I would wager a tun of wine that the Man with the Far-Seeing Gaze will catch up with you, if not to kill you, then certainly to ask you more questions . . ."

Berengaria stood in the south transept of St Alphege's, her cloak pulled tight about her, warming her hands over the cresset candles lit before the statue of the martyred Saxon archbishop, who gazed sorrowfully down at her. Nevertheless, Berengaria felt comfortable.

240

Parson Warfeld was like any other man with his needs. He had given her comfortable lodgings in his finely furnished house, so why should she be in a hurry to return to Lady Adelicia? Berengaria had made her decision. She had enough silver salted away to bid Lady Adelicia adieu, perhaps obtain a few coins from her and seek her fortune elsewhere, and what better place than a priest's house? Parson Warfeld might be a cleric, but he had the same hungers and appetites as any man, the way he'd first looked at her, slyly, out of the corner of his eye, his tongue wetting his lips, how he would place his hand on her shoulder or arm. Sure enough Berengaria, with her winsome ways, had fluttered her eyelids and enmeshed Warfeld in her silken net. Of course there was the other matter. Warfeld had confessed to her about informing that snooping royal clerk about Berengaria's secret visits back to Sweetmead to meet Sir Rauf. How he'd often glimpsed her cloaked and cowled. Berengaria had masked her fury behind a smile, accepting the parson's protestations that he had to tell Corbett, he'd been on oath. Well, she thought, preening herself, sometime in the future she might have to tell someone about the good parson!

Berengaria had been with Warfeld when the morning Mass had been celebrated. They were about to leave the church to break their fast when Desroches arrived to see the priest on certain matters. Parson Warfeld had promised her a visit to a splendid cookshop closer into the city, and though she'd pouted prettily, the priest had decided to meet with Desroches and asked her to stay here until his return. Berengaria stared up at the tortured face of the saint and then walked along the walls, studying the paintings. The artist had conjured up a vividly cruel scene of hell, depicting a plain filled with men and women of all ages, lying naked, fixed with iron nails into the earth, writhing in torment. Demons moved amongst them beating them with whips. In another part of the fresco, victims sprawled on their backs whilst dragons, serpents and fiery toads thrust glowing needles into their bodies before devouring them. Some of the hell-bound corpses hung by hot chains fastened to one of their limbs; others were being tortured in red-hot frying skillets or pierced on spits roasting over fires. In a further scene, a house smoked horribly; nearby human beings were being lowered into vats full of molten metal, naked men and women being thrown back up into the air as if they were sparks of fire. Fascinated, Berengaria moved along. She felt no guilt at her own sin as she studied the wretches who, no longer able to endure the excessive heat, leapt into biting-cold rivers. In the centre of the fresco yawned the mouth of hell, a vast pit spitting out globes of black flames towards which a horde of evil spirits were dragging legions of lamenting souls, urging them on with scaly whips and burning tongs.

Berengaria shivered and moved back to the candle flame. This was an old church; Parson Warfeld had explained how it had been here before the Normans arrived. Berengaria didn't know who the Normans were; instead she now concentrated on her fingers. Parson Warfeld called them long and slender, elegant and beautiful, and that flattered her. She studied her hands as she thought about the future. She definitely had plans. She knew more than that clever-eyed clerk with his snooping ways and prying questions. She could wait, so why shouldn't the others, particularly her next victims? They would all have to wait for a while, though she'd hinted at what she knew. Oh yes, when they had all gathered at Sweetmead the previous evening, she'd shown her true mettle! She recalled a proverb a soldier had once taught her: "Sometimes it is best to half-draw your sword, let your enemy see the gleam of metal." Well she'd done that!

"Berengaria, Berengaria?"

She turned quickly. Apart from the candle glow, the church was mantled in darkness.

"Berengaria?"

"Who is it?" She moved from the transept into the nave. "Who called my name?"

She heard a sound behind her and turned. As the cloaked figure walked quickly forward, Berengaria's smile faded. She turned to flee, opened her mouth to scream, but the noose whipped fast around her neck, cutting off her breath, the blood rushing to her ears. The grip tightened and Berengaria choked swiftly to death.

Corbett and his two companions reached Maubisson around mid-morning; the city bells were still calling the faithful to the last Mass of the day. Wendover and a group of guards sat camped before the main steps of the manor. Corbett ordered them to open the doors and wait outside until he summoned them. Wendover tried to draw the new arrivals into conversation, but Corbett curtly waved him away, urging Ranulf and Chanson up into the gloomy hallway. Once inside, he slammed the door behind him and leaned against it.

Ranulf took off his cloak and slung it over a bench. Then he tightened his sword belt, easing the sword and dagger in the scabbard, nervous gestures because Master Long-Face had been in such a hurry. He had swept into the guesthouse, dragging himself and Chanson away from a platter of bread and honey, dried bacon and tankards of the most delicious-tasting ale, and urged them to bring the horses out. They had saddled them and galloped as swiftly as the snow and ice would permit back to this dire place.

"Sir Hugh," Ranulf forced a smile, "we have searched this house: there are no secret entrances, no recesses where someone could hide, no hidden tunnels or passageways."

Corbett took a feebly flickering torchlight from its sconce; then he fired one already primed and held it downwards, waiting until the flame caught. He thrust this into Ranulf's hand, telling Chanson to fetch another.

"My fellow scholars," he began, "I apologise for the swift summons and the hasty ride, but I have been thinking and reflecting."

Ranulf groaned quietly. Corbett was a great watcher, a patient man. Sometimes he would sit for hours just staring at a piece of manuscript, then suddenly he'd become more busy than a lurcher eager for the hunt.

"Ranulf, have you ever been asked to look at the clouds and search out a certain shape: a head, a horse, a shield?"

Ranulf thought of lying with Maeve's maid in a cornfield on a beautiful summer's day, but decided to hold his tongue.

"At first you cannot see what you are searching for, but when you do, it is so obvious."

"And what are we searching for here?"

"A body," Corbett declared, "a corpse. Master Servinus, to be precise."

"Paulents' bodyguard?" Chanson asked.

"Oh yes." Corbett clapped the Clerk of the Stables on the shoulder. "Well perceived, Master Chanson. We've been searching for how he could have escaped, not where his corpse might be hidden. If you, Ranulf, or I had killed someone here and wished to conceal the corpse, where would we choose?"

"Well, not here." Ranulf gestured around the hall. "Whilst the bedchambers are undisturbed."

"Where then?" Corbett repeated.

"The cellars?"

"Precisely!" Corbett led them out into the kitchen and towards the door built into the far wall. He opened this, more torches were brought, and he led them down the steps into the numbing-cold darkness. "These," Corbett's voice echoed sombrely as he held up the flaming cresset, "are a series of caverns, small rooms one leading into the other, possibly built to keep wine cool or as a strongroom for money. What we are looking for is a corpse."

They began their searches. All three had visited these cellars before, but now they moved carefully along the musty dark passageway, going from one chamber to the next. Most were filled with rubbish: broken chairs, benches, disused implements, cracked jugs, and cups, piles of sacking, barrels, broken coffers and chests. Corbett was sifting amongst some of these when he heard Chanson shout. The groom had started in the furthest cavern and was moving back towards them. He now held up his torch, waving excitedly at Corbett and Ranulf. They hurried in his direction. Chanson lowered the torch. Corbett saw how wet the floor was. Chanson turned to a huge barrel or vat with a spigot at the bottom, standing in a recess.

"That's been turned on and emptied, master, and it's big enough to contain a corpse."

Corbett ordered one of the broken chests to be brought. Standing on this, he drew his dagger and prised the massive lid loose. As he felt further in, his fingers brushed cold, marble-hard flesh. He hastily withdrew his hand and stepped down.

"Chanson, Ranulf, tip this vat over."

They squeezed between the vat and the brickwork and began to rock the barrel. Eventually it teetered over and fell with a crash; more liquid gushed out, but also the ale-drenched corpse. In the poor light Corbett glimpsed a peaked white face, black leather, and what looked like bloodied bandages across the man's stomach. Slopping through the ale, he told Ranulf and Chanson to lift the body. They went back along the cellar and up the steps, and laid the corpse out in the porchway. Corbett wiped his hands on his cloak and stared down at it.

"Always ugly in death," he murmured.

Ranulf agreed. Servinus had a thin, lean face; his eyes were stark open, staring in glassy fear; his head was completely shaved, cheeks slightly sunken, his mouth blood-splattered. In the man's chest was a hideous black and red wound in which a crossbow bolt still lay embedded. Wrinkling his nose at the smell, Corbett crouched down and removed the pieces of cloth from the man's stomach. Chanson began to retch and hurry for the door, hand to his mouth.

"Killed by a crossbow bolt," Corbett declared, "but then his assassin ripped open his stomach, God knows the reason why. The assassin staunched the wound with those cloths; that is why we found no trace of blood. Servinus was dragged, probably under the armpits, wounds to the front, from the hall down the cellar and thrust into that barrel. It would be easy enough. I am sure if that cavern was better lit we'd have glimpsed the occasional bloodstains. The ale was run off, the lid placed back on . . ."

"Why?" Ranulf asked.

"To distract us," Corbett declared. "To make us think, at least for a while, that Servinus might even be the assassin, Hubert the Monk in disguise. Now here is an interesting question, Ranulf." Corbett got to his feet. "If the other four were mysteriously murdered by hanging, why did our assassin use a crossbow bolt against Servinus?" He paused as the door opened and

Chanson returned wiping his mouth on the back of his hand.

"Sorry, master."

Wendover followed.

"I told you to wait outside!" Corbett snapped.

Wendover gasped in horror at the gruesome corpse sprawled on the hall floor, clothes soaked in ale, the ghastly face, the awful wounds to the chest and stomach.

"Sir Hugh." The captain's hand went to his mouth. "A messenger has arrived for you. He went first to St Augustine's Abbey. He is from Sir Walter Castledene, who asks you to come to St Alphege's. There has been a murder, Berengaria. What shall we . . .?" Wendover looked once more at the corpse, then turned, hand to his mouth, and ran outside.

"Master Ranulf, come with me," Corbett ordered. "Chanson, stay here, examine that corpse. Go back to the vat; was there anything else put in there with him? Tell Wendover I want this house searched one more time, then he is to join me at St Alphege's. Tell him to fetch a cart and bring the corpse over. Parson Warfeld has another Requiem to sing. Servinus can be buried in the poor man's plot in God's acre; the city will bear the expense."

Once outside, Corbett repeated his orders to Wendover, who stood by a tree, still retching and clearing his mouth. The captain nodded quickly.

"I'll do what I can," he gasped.

"You'll do what I order!" Corbett declared, patting him on the shoulder. "Come, Master Ranulf."

248

CHAPTER
TWELVE

Conserva requiem mitis ab hoste mem.
Guard my sleep against the enemy.

Arator

They left Maubisson, taking one of the city guards with them to show them the swiftest route around the city walls and in through the lychgate of St Alphege's. Castledene and members of his comitatus were already there. They'd dismounted, and their horses were being hobbled. Corbett called Castledene's name and the mayor hurried over. Corbett dismounted and quickly told him what he had discovered at Maubisson, ignoring the mayor's gasps, exclamations and litany of questions.

"No, no, Sir Walter." Corbett shook his head. "This is the heart of the problem. Four people were murdered by hanging in that dreadful manor; Servinus was killed by a crossbow bolt. Why?"

Sir Walter rubbed his hands and pointed back towards the church door. "Sir Hugh, there's other business."

"Yes, there is other business, but I must ask you to concentrate on this. Is there anything you knew about Servinus which might be useful? Why he was murdered in one way, the others differently? Please?" Corbett patted Sir Walter on the shoulder and hurried up the steps into the church.

Desroches was leaning against a pillar, staring down at Parson Warfeld, who was busy anointing the corpse with holy oil. Berengaria had lost all her prettiness, the noose fast around her throat, eyes glaring, face mottled, tongue protruding. She sprawled haphazardly. Corbett, listening to the priest's murmured prayers, knelt down and, using his dagger, cut the cord, loosened it and handed it to Ranulf. The body jerked strangely in death. Corbett straightened the legs and arms even as Parson Warfeld raised his hand in the final blessing and absolution. The priest looked haggard, eyes red-rimmed.

"She's gone!" he murmured. "Such a sweet girl. May the Lord Christ forgive her many sins and mine."

Corbett felt tempted to ask Warfeld to explain, but decided it would wait. He rose to his feet, beckoning the others to join him further up the nave near the rood screen before the sanctuary.

"Well?" he asked, turning abruptly. "What happened here?"

Parson Warfeld explained how Berengaria had felt comfortable in the lodgings he had provided. This morning he had come down and celebrated his morning Mass and they were planning to break their fast in a city cookshop when Physician Desroches had arrived and demanded to see him. He had told Berengaria to wait in the church and taken Desroches into the priest's house. When they'd finished, they walked back into the church thinking that Berengaria would be still waiting there.

"What you've seen, Sir Hugh," the priest added mournfully, "is what we discovered."

Corbett glanced at Desroches.

"The flesh is slightly warm," Desroches said. "She was hale and hearty when we left. The assassin must have slipped into the church and killed her. God knows why a poor maid should be murdered."

"I don't think she was as poor as you think," Corbett declared. "Berengaria had keener eyes and sharper wits than perhaps many of us presumed. I do wonder why she was murdered." He took a deep breath. "Master Desroches?"

The physician glanced up. "Sir Hugh?"

"We have found the corpse of Servinus, Paulents' bodyguard. He was killed by a crossbow bolt to his chest, his belly slit open, and hidden in an ale vat deep in the cellar. I asked Sir Walter a question. I also ask it of you. Four people were murdered in that hall, killed by hanging, very similar to poor Berengaria's death. Why should Servinus die differently?"

Desroches pulled a face. "Sir Hugh, I hardly knew the man. We exchanged a few words of greeting and that is all."

"And why did you come here this morning?" Ranulf asked.

"To see Parson Warfeld. Sir Hugh, I have told you, and Parson Warfeld will agree. I was not born in Canterbury, but my parents are buried here in God's acre. If you check the *Liber Mortuorum* — *The Book of the Dead* — you will find their names listed there. They both died sometime before Christmas, so this is their anniversary. I came to ask Parson Warfeld to sing the Requiem Mass for their souls."

"That is true," Parson Warfeld bleated. "Sir Hugh, we were not gone for long. The church is cold. Berengaria said she would warm her hands over the candle flames." He pointed at the transept, where candles glowed in the darkness beneath the shrouded statue of the saint. "I didn't think anything; I . . ." He faltered and walked away, shoulders shaking.

Corbett followed him. "Parson Warfeld," he whispered. The priest turned. "What was Berengaria to you?"

"Sir Hugh, I'm in God's house." He walked on, beckoning Corbett to join him. "Sir Hugh . . ." He paused, then whispered, "I must have my sins shriven; on this I'll tell the truth. Berengaria was skilled in the ways of men. I gave her good housing; she gave me some comfort." He glanced away. "You know what I mean?"

"Did she tell you she rendered the same for Sir Rauf?"

Warfeld stared down at the paved stone floor.

"Was there anything she said," Corbett insisted, "which could explain her own brutal death?"

"Sir Hugh," Warfeld whispered, "you described Berengaria accurately. She had sharp wits. You know she kept her own secret counsel."

Corbett nodded. "May I visit her room?"

"Certainly. Gentlemen," Parson Warfeld called out, "I beg you to stay here for a while. I have business with Sir Hugh."

He led Corbett out through a side door, and crossed the frozen ground to his comfortable two-storey house. They climbed the wooden stairs built on the outside; these led into a stairwell in the recess of which stood a narrow door. Warfeld pressed the latch and opened it. Corbett stepped into the room. It was neatly kept. In the corner was a comfortable truckle bed shrouded by drapes; warming pans and chafing dishes stood on a table, and next to this were a stool and a high-backed chair. There were shelves and pegs on the wall for clothes and robes.

"A tidy girl," Corbett observed.

He opened a coffer on the small table beside the bed; it was full of trinkets, gee-gaws, rings, bracelets, and a piece of brocade. Next to the bed lay a pair of soft buskined slippers. On the wall pegs hung a cloak, shifts and petticoats, linen underwear and a dress. Beneath these was a small box containing face paints and a phial of cheap perfume. Corbett pulled back the curtains of the bed, ignoring Warfeld's protests about "the possessions of a poor wench recently murdered". There was nothing. The bed had been neatly made, the faded gold coverlet pulled up over the bolsters. He was about to turn away when he glimpsed blurred marks on the whitewashed wall beneath the narrow window and leaned over. The scrawl had been done with a piece of charcoal. Corbett made out the word "Nazareth".

"Nazareth?" He turned to Warfeld, pointing to the scrawl. "That is fresh, is it not?"

Warfeld came across. "It was certainly not there before." He leaned over and brushed the wall, then took his finger away and stared at the charcoal dust on the tip. "Berengaria must have written it. That's right, yesterday evening when we returned, she asked for the name of the town where Jesus had been born. I said Bethlehem. She laughed and shook her head and said, 'No, the other place,' so I wrote 'Nazareth' out on a piece of parchment; she must have copied it from there. She said she knew her horn book, that she could read and write most letters."

"Why?" Corbett asked. "Why did she want to know that? More importantly, why did she write it?"

"Sir Hugh, as God is my witness, I don't know. I found Berengaria engaging; she was, as you say, sharp-witted. I am sorry she has gone."

Corbett finished his search but found nothing except a few more tawdry possessions. He followed the priest down the stairs and back across into the church. Castledene had ordered in some of the guards. Berengaria's corpse, already shrouded in a cloak, was being lifted on to a makeshift bier to be taken to the mortuary house in God's acre. Corbett stared across at the candle flames, wishing that statue could speak. Who had crept into this church and killed that hapless maid? Parson Warfeld and the physician Desroches were closeted together . . .

"Sir Hugh," Castledene came over and plucked at his sleeve, "I must have words with you."

They walked towards the door of the church.

"Servinus," Castledene whispered. "One thing I did learn, he never drank wine or ale. I remember him saying that. We were talking about how Paulents and his family felt. Servinus was also queasy, but declared that it could not be the ale or wine because he had taken an oath on some pilgrimage or other that he would never touch strong drink. Sir Hugh, that is all I know."

Corbett thanked him, then went across and informed Parson Warfeld about Servinus's corpse being brought to the church, and requested that Requiem Masses be sung for both his soul and that of Berengaria. Then he pointed towards the high altar.

"Lay them out there tonight," he said. "Ring their corpses with purple wax candles, sing the Masses tomorrow and have them buried before dark."

Warfeld hastily agreed. He was now embarrassed, eager to be rid of this prying clerk. Corbett and Ranulf left the church, collected their horses and led them down under the lychgate. Corbett turned and stared back. Castledene, Desroches and Parson Warfeld were huddled together on the steps, discussing some matter or other.

"We will never find the truth from them," Corbett declared.

"What truth, master?"

"Precisely, Ranulf, what truth?" He gathered the reins of his horse and moved away from the lychgate. "In this matter, Ranulf, it is time rather than evidence which is important. Think of myself and our adversary as two lurchers, two coursers, running either side of a fence. If my adversary runs faster he'll escape; if I run faster I'll catch him! Our killer wants to be swift. He wishes to wreak his revenge, discover the true whereabouts of the treasure and escape." Corbett gazed up; the sky was cloud free. "The weather is breaking," he declared. "It is freezing cold but I don't think there'll be more snow." He pointed across the wasteland. "We must visit the Lady Adelicia to enquire about her safety and security, and above all," he winked at Ranulf, "to discover whether she left the house this morning."

They made their way across the frost-encrusted common, the breeze biting at their faces, nipping their noses, cheeks and ears. Corbett pulled his cloak up. When they reached Sweetmead, the guards lounging around in the porches and recesses rose to greet them. They assured Corbett that no one had left the manor, though he was not too certain about how strict their watch had become. Lady Adelicia certainly looked as if she had not left the house. A furred nightrobe around her shoulders, bare feet pushed into buskins, her hair undressed, she met them in the small parlour and rose to greet them coldly. She apologised for the weak fire and complained bitterly about Berengaria, how she was supposed to be here to tend to her.

"Madam," Corbett caught her sleeve, "I bring you sad news." He told her exactly what had happened at St Alphege's, how Berengaria had been garrotted. Lady Adelicia heard him out coldly, nodding now and again, lifting her hand, fluttering her fingers, the only sign of any emotion.

"Lady Adelicia," Corbett continued, "I must be blunt with you. We have discovered that when you met Wendover in The Chequer of Hope, Berengaria did not go to the stalls or shops but hurried back to

Sweetmead. I believe she — how can I put it — did certain services for your husband."

Lady Adelicia sat propped in the chair, her face towards the weak fire. "Berengaria was like a cat in an alleyway." She didn't even turn her head, but talked as if whispering to herself. "She lived on her wits, with a keen eye for mischief. I realised Sir Rauf knew about myself and Wendover but that he didn't really care! I guessed it must be Berengaria: when we did go to the markets, she seemed to have more money than she should. Now she's dead. Why, Sir Hugh?"

Corbett shrugged. "Mistress, before I continue, do you know the whereabouts of Lechlade?"

She pointed to the ceiling. "Sprawled upstairs drunk, I suppose, as he always is."

Corbett excused himself, told Ranulf to stay with Lady Adelicia and walked out into the passageway and up the stairs. He passed the gallery where Lady Adelicia and Sir Rauf's chambers stood, and went up further into a small stairwell. The door to the facing room was off the latch; he pushed it open. Lechlade's garret was nothing more than a sty, dirty and dishevelled, with hardly any furniture. Lechlade sprawled on a pallet bed in the far corner, snoring like a pig, one hand grasping a tankard. Corbett looked distastefully round: dirty clothes were piled in the corner, a broken knife, a pair of tattered boots, some crusted pots and a cracked jug littered the floor. He walked quietly towards the bed and stared down. The bolster was stained, the sheets dirty and grimy, the blanket Lechlade had wrapped

257

about himself holed and moth-eaten. He left and rejoined Lady Adelicia and Ranulf in the parlour.

"Lady Adelicia," Corbett declared, "I must warn you, your life too may be in danger."

She looked up, startled. "Me?" she said. "Why should anyone wish to kill me?"

"Perhaps they have already tried," Corbett replied, pulling the stool closer, staring into the hard eyes of this young woman. "Lady Adelicia, you did not kill your husband, and yet somebody stained your cloak with blood either at The Chequer of Hope or when you arrived home. Somebody else put those bloody napkins in your chamber. How? I don't know. For what reason?" He watched the colour drain from her face. "Oh yes, somebody wanted to dispatch you to either the stake or the noose. They certainly wanted you out of this house. Why is that, Lady Adelicia? To search for something?" Now he had her attention. Corbett stretched out his hand and brushed hers; it felt cold as ice. "Lady Adelicia, you must realise your life is in great danger, not because of Wendover or anything else but because of what you know, or might know, or might have found. You told me about seeing your husband at the dead of night, dragging what you thought was a corpse from this house, to bury in the garden beyond?"

She nodded.

"But there again, I've been in that garden; it is all tangled and overgrown. And it would have been dark when your husband brought that corpse out. How did you know what he was dragging? And if your husband, whom you hated so much, had committed such a foul

258

act, I wager, Lady Adelicia, you would have certainly used that against him. Surely you must have been curious? You could have gone out to that part of the garden when your husband was distracted, and discovered what was truly buried there. Instead, you tell me some fable that by mere chance you are standing by your window in the dead of night and you see your husband dragging out a corpse. You even know where he buried it. Lady Adelicia," Corbett's voice rose sharply, "I am no fool. This mummery must stop! I want the truth."

Ranulf, leaning against the doorpost, arms folded, smiled falsely at her. "We could, master, take Lady Adelicia to London. A stay in a Tower dungeon, the Fleet or Newgate might loosen her tongue."

"Don't threaten me!" she snapped. "Neither of you knows what it's like to be a woman alone in a world of men."

"Then tell us," Ranulf said. "Otherwise, mistress, you will be depicted as a murderess, or who knows, whoever killed Berengaria might creep in here. They are searching for something. What?"

Lady Adelicia drew herself up, hitching her robe closer about her shoulders. "About eighteen months ago, on the Feast of St John the Baptist, I was here in the parlour. Sir Rauf, as usual, was locked in his chancery chamber, counting his wealth. There was a knock on the door. Lechlade had done his duties, but the sun was setting. You've seen Lechlade? Like a pig in its sty or a dog returning to his vomit, he was in some ale-drenched sleep. I went out and opened the door. A man stood there. I didn't like him. He was cloaked, though I could glimpse the stained jerkin beneath, and his boots were scuffed. He had a lean face, a slight cast in one eye. I was about to drive him away as one of those noisome beggars when he demanded to see Sir Rauf. 'Tell him Stonecrop is here.' I did so. My husband came quickly enough when I told him the reason. He swiftly ushered Stonecrop into his chamber. I was intrigued, curious. My husband had had visitors before in the dead of night, but there was something about Stonecrop and the way Sir Rauf was so eager to see him, so I decided to eavesdrop, as I often did. I put on a pair of soft buskins and listened very carefully. Sometimes Sir Rauf could not be heard, but this time voices were raised. To get to the point, Sir Hugh: Stonecrop was a sailor; he'd apparently been on *The Waxman* when it had been captured. He had been flung overboard, swum ashore and taken refuge. Afterwards, he was forced to tramp the roads. He claimed he'd been burnt by the summer sun, drenched by spring rains, frozen on winter mornings. He explained how he was weary of slogging through mushy leaves in autumn woods, tired of the poor fare at country alehouses and hedge taverns. Sir Rauf asked what that had to do with him. Stonecrop replied that Sir Rauf was a wealthy man who lived high on the hog. Did the authorities in Canterbury know his true calling? How he had paid good silver to Adam Blackstock and *The Waxman*? Sir Rauf scoffed at this. Stonecrop demanded money. Sir Rauf again jeered and refused. Stonecrop turned towards the door. He then declared how, just before *The Segreant* and *The Caltrop* had closed for combat, he'd slipped down to Blackstock's cabin and taken from a coffer a certain map which revealed the whereabouts of a great treasure in Suffolk. He'd kept it safe in a leather wallet. If Sir Rauf was willing they could share such a hoard.

"I didn't hear what happened next, but Sir Rauf called him back. They haggled over this map, Stonecrop eventually declaring he'd go to Sir Walter Castledene, who would give him more for it; he'd also tell the mayor about the secret doings of Sir Rauf Decontet. My husband grew abusive, but Stonecrop laughed and came back towards the door. I heard a crack, like a whip being lashed, and someone fall; even through the doorway I could hear my husband breathing heavily. I don't truly know why I did it, but I knocked at the door, pressed the latch and it opened. My husband was standing there. He had a wooden mallet used for grinding gold in one hand. Stonecrop was sprawled on the floor, blood gushing out of the back of his head. He'd been killed; his skull had been smashed. Sir Rauf was a strong man. I knelt down, felt Stonecrop's throat and looked up. Sir Rauf began to curse me. He called me a snooping, prying bitch who would undoubtedly use this against him. Before I could stop him, he had thrust the mallet into my hand. 'If I hang,' he declared, 'we'll both hang together. I'll go on oath and say you were with me when he was killed.' After that, well . . ." She shrugged prettily. "I collected some sacks from the cellar. We stripped the corpse, sheeted it up and dragged it out into the garden for burial."

"Did Lechlade find out?"

"No, he was in one of his drunken stupors, though I later told him about the map. The day after I was arrested, I was taken to the dungeons in the Guildhall. Lechlade visited me. I bribed him to search Sir Rauf's chamber for a map showing where treasure was hidden in Suffolk. He just gazed blearily at me. I told him that if he did find it he might become rich."

"Why did you ask Lechlade for help?" Ranulf asked. "Not Berengaria?"

"I'd grown wary of Berengaria — she even more so of me. I suspect she was frightened of being depicted as my accomplice." Lady Adelicia laughed sharply. "And Berengaria always looked after herself. I had my suspicions about her. I was also desperate," she confessed. "I needed certain things, comforts, luxuries. I also wanted to write letters to the King. Lechlade will do anything to buy ale. He hired a scribe and brought him to my dungeon. He also brought other things I needed: clothes, wraps, soap and money, at least Castledene permitted that. Once you are a prisoner, Master Ranulf, you have no right; silver and gold are the only language people understand."

"But surely you'd searched for the map before?"

"Of course, Sir Hugh. From that night onwards I was obsessed by it. I knew Stonecrop had brought something precious. When I went into the chamber I saw Sir Rauf holding a small scroll, yellowing with age, but since that night I have never seen it again. You must remember, Sir Hugh, Sir Rauf rarely left the house.

When he did, I would search everywhere, but I never found it."

"Did you talk to Wendover about it?"

"Of course I did. I suppose," Lady Adelicia blinked, "in the full moon of our passion we laid our plans and schemes. How we'd find that map, discover the great treasure, move away from Canterbury, begin a new life. Wendover was much taken by it."

"Do you think Wendover ever came back here to look for it?" Ranulf asked.

Lady Adelicia laughed thinly. "Sir Rauf would never allow a man like Wendover into his house, let alone to search his belongings. Moreover, Master Ranulf, Wendover is a thief."

Corbett stared at Lady Adelicia, who gazed coolly back. "We will leave Wendover for the moment. You know, Lady Adelicia," Corbett chose his words carefully, "the manner of your husband's death is truly mysterious. He was found in his chancery office, the back of his skull smashed, yet the door to that chamber was locked and secured. The lock is singular and special, I recognise that. It would be virtually impossible to replicate a key for it. Moreover, the key of this chamber was found on your husband's belt, as was the key to your chamber, the other one being held by you, and yet —"

"What do you mean, Sir Hugh?" Adelicia's voice was harsh.

"Well, mistress, why was your husband murdered? Nothing was stolen, nothing disturbed, so why kill him? And why make such a mystery of it?"

"Sir Hugh, I cannot answer that."

"No, madam, nor can I."

Corbett rose to his feet, left the parlour and went to sit in Sir Rauf's high-backed leather chair in the chancery chamber. He clutched the arms. Once again he felt those grooves beneath. Curious, he crouched down and studied them carefully. The weals or grooves were evenly placed in the wood on either arm, and freshly done. Corbett shook his head. There was some mystery here, but what? He sat down and gazed at the shelves and the manuscripts stacked there: the tagged rolls of vellum, the account books, the memoranda, all neatly filed and organised. He had no doubt that Sir Rauf had once owned the Cloister Map. Had he memorised it, then destroyed it? If that was the case, why hadn't he moved to discover the treasure? What had he been waiting for? "Of course!" Corbett exclaimed, beating the arms of the chair with his fists. "He was waiting —"

"He was waiting for what, master?" Ranulf stood in the doorway. He'd put his cloak around him and was standing with his thumbs pushed into his war belt.

"Come in." Corbett indicated the stool. Ranulf sat down. "I believe Sir Rauf had the Cloister Map. I suspect he memorised and destroyed it, but he was waiting. Clever man, Sir Rauf! He knew Castledene and Paulents were also searching for that treasure, not to mention Hubert the Monk. He was also wary of his prying wife. He allowed her to continue her trysts with Wendover, and took his revenge in accepting sexual favours from Berengaria. Eventually he would have applied to the Court of Consistory, an appeal to the Archbishop of Canterbury, demanding his marriage be annulled. Once he'd rid himself of Lady Adelicia, once he believed it was safe, he would have used his undoubted wealth, skill and secret knowledge to travel to Suffolk and hunt for that treasure. Sir Rauf was a cold-hearted man, he could bide his time."

"Anything else?"

"At this time, I don't know, Ranulf. I truly don't. We've discovered two new facts this morning. First, Servinus did not touch wine or any strong drink. I have to reflect on that. Second, Berengaria, a woman who lived on her wits, who had no more religion in her than perhaps . . ." he gestured at a coffer, "took a piece of charcoal and scrawled the word 'Nazareth' on her bedchamber wall. Why?"

Ranulf shook his head. "Do you think Wendover," he asked, "could have had a hand in Sir Rauf's death? He did leave Lady Adelicia early that day."

"Ah yes, our unfinished conversation." Corbett rose to his feet. He walked back in to where Lady Adelicia still sat staring into the fire. "You said Wendover was a thief?"

"Of course, Sir Hugh, and there's no honour amongst thieves. When I visited Wendover at The Chequer of Hope, I always took money. I have my own petty source of income, though my late husband took care of the rest. On frequent occasions I found something missing. Wendover and I lay together. He satisfied his lust as well as mine. I fell asleep. He always left before I did, claiming this duty or that."

"And he invariably stole?" Corbett asked.

"Yes, Sir Hugh, it is humiliating, isn't it? He took a coin or a bracelet, some small item he thought I wouldn't notice."

"Why?" Corbett asked.

"I don't know, Sir Hugh. Perhaps that was the nature of the man; perhaps he was like Berengaria, collecting money, wealth against the evil day."

"That is why he left early?"

"Of course it was, Sir Hugh, to steal and sneak away. When I woke there was no one to remonstrate with. I always thought I would but I never did. Perhaps it was pride. Our passion, Sir Hugh, was like a fire: it burned fiercely, then the flames died, leaving nothing but cold ash." She paused. "Sir Hugh, what will happen to me?"

"Madam, matters have become so confused, no judge could sit and listen to this case, yet there's a malignancy here which I must root out."

Corbett made his farewells still lost in his own thoughts. He and Ranulf dressed against the cold and waited for Chanson, who arrived from Maubisson declaring he'd discovered nothing new. They mounted their horses and made their way across the wasteland into the city. The break in the weather had brought everyone out. All the cocklebrains and twisted hearts, every rogue who swarmed in the King's city of Canterbury, had emerged looking for easy pickings. These mingled with the rich garbed in woollen robes wrapped firmly around well-lined bellies. Pilgrims flocked the streets, pale and wan after their days of abstinence, eager that Advent be over so they could give

266

up dry bread and brackish water to feast on wine, sweet manchet loaves and juicy meats. A prisoner recently released from the castle dungeons perched drunkenly on a cart, shaking the manacles on his hands, as he begged for alms and mockingly gave his last will and testament.

"To those in the trap" — he referred to fellow prisoners in the castle — "I give my mirror and the good graces of the gaoler's wife. To the castle, my window curtains spun from spiders' webs. To my comrades freezing at night and chained to the walls, a punch in the eye. To my barber, the clippings of my hair. To my cobbler, the holes in my shoes. To my costumer, my worn hose . . ."

The raucous speech had attracted the tavern-roisterers with their mulled wine and roasted chestnuts. They gathered around shouting abuse as the unfortunate begged and pleaded for pennies to take back so he and his fellow prisoners could celebrate the birth of Christ in some comfort. Corbett gave him some coins and passed on. He reached a crossroads and glimpsed Les Hommes Joyeuses now parading through Canterbury to advertise their coming pageant. The Gleeman had arranged a cavalcade of devils, all rigged with wolves', calves' and rams' skins laced and trimmed with sheeps' heads and feathers from which dangled cow and horse bells ringing out a horrid din. They held in their gauntleted hands burning pieces of wood, which gave off puffs of smoke and crackling sparks. The people flocked around them. The Gleeman would occasionally rein in and describe how the Mummers would meet here or there to tell the story of the Blessed Christ and His incarnation in the world of men.

Corbett urged his horse on, his ears dinned with the shouted bustle, the hoarse guffaws, the clink of steel, the pealing of bells, the raw scraping music of fiddlers, the shrieks of mopsies and prostitutes seeking customers. Stallholders shouted their goods whilst the sonorous, bellowing sermon of a stooped, black-garbed Dominican echoed across the streets. The preacher stood, one finger pointed to the sky, eyes gleaming in a pinched face, his nose scything the air. Shouted arguments between two dicecoggers echoed from a tavern door. A juggler screamed curses as he pushed his tame bear in a wheelbarrow, looking for space so the beast could dance. Market bailiffs moved around, shoving at the crowd with their steel-tipped staves. Corbett felt as if he was part of some bizarre pageant. He felt sick, slightly confused. He cursed as a pilgrim shot across his path to join the quarrel between a brothel-keeper and a fellow pilgrim who claimed he'd been cheated. Unsteady in the saddle, Corbett reined in and swiftly dismounted. He'd taken enough, he had to rest. He led his horse off the street into the quiet stable yard of The Gate to Paradise tavern. Ostlers ran up to take their mounts. Corbett left them and walked into the sweet, musty darkness of the tap room. He deliberately ignored the glittering, contemptuous eye of a courtesan standing in the entrance, a small posy of winter herbs in her gloved hand. Just within the doorway, a sign pointed down to the Painted Cellar, where The Father of Laughter ruled. Two men stood at the top of the steps, each cradling a pet weasel; they were shouting at the courtesan to join them below.

Corbett still felt as if he was in a dream. The tavern master hurried up looking all snug and cosy with a welcoming pot of wine. Corbett showed his warrant and demanded a private chamber for himself. Mine host bowed and swept him across the tap room, up broad, sturdy stairs into a long, well-furnished room. Coloured cloths hung across the walls, and a fire spluttered merrily in a hearth carved in the shape of a doorway. Above the ornamented mantel hung painted panels celebrating popular saints: Christopher, protector against sudden and violent death; Laurence, the patron of cooks; Julian, the patron of innkeepers. The tavern master waved Corbett and his companions to chairs and stools before the fire whilst he listed the food available: buttered capons and fowl; golden crusty pastries rich with dark tangy sauces; roast partridge; crackling pork served in a mushroom and onion sauce; soups rich with eggs and milk, all accompanied by the best wines of Bearn. Corbett half listened as he sank into the high-backed chair; he muttered that he wanted some wine. Ranulf sat next to him, highly anxious. He was alarmed at Corbett's drawn face, that haggard look when, as his master had admitted on previous occasions, his mind teemed, the thoughts flying thick and fast as flakes in a snowstorm. Nevertheless, he held his peace. A short while later a slattern served the wine. Corbett drank deep and relaxed.

"Master," Ranulf asked at last, "what is wrong?"

Corbett cradled the cup against his chest. "What is wrong, Ranulf?" He winked. "I'm confused. I feel like a man with a fever, wandering in that grey land between sleep and day. Questions come, jabbing at me like spear points. Who? What? Why and how?"

"And, master?" Ranulf wished to shake Corbett from his mood.

Sir Hugh glanced up at the painted panels. "Why? Well," he shrugged, "why has the Cloister Map disappeared? Undoubtedly it was taken from *The Waxman* by Stonecrop and brought to Sir Rauf, but what truly happened to it then? From what I gather, that house has been searched. You remarked on that, Ranulf, yet the Cloister Map has not been discovered. Did Decontet really destroy it? Secondly, why did the Cloister Map brought by Paulents prove to be meaningless? Even if you ignore these questions and move on to gruesome murder, why was Sir Rauf Decontet killed in such a fashion? Was it simply revenge, or something else? How was it done? Who was responsible? Why was Lady Adelicia cast as her husband's killer? How was that arranged?" Corbett sipped from his wine. "Who perpetrated those hideous murders at Maubisson? How was it done so swiftly, so mysteriously? Who killed Servinus in a fashion different from the rest, then ripped his belly open and stowed his corpse away? How could all this be done in a manor house so closely guarded?" Corbett paused as the reeling tune of pipes and the stamp of feet echoed from the tap room below. For a brief moment, in his fevered mind, he thought demons were dancing at his

270

frustration. He shook his head to free himself from such a macabre reverie, and turned, staring at his companion. "And Ranulf, what else is there?"

The Clerk of the Green Wax shifted uneasily in his chair. It was rare to find Sir Hugh so confused. "Well," he rolled the earthenware goblet between his hands, "you talk of who, why, what and how. Yet, master, surely the cause of this or that, the reason for everything, must be someone we have encountered, someone we know, who kills and kills again. Poor Berengaria, garrotted in that lonely church; she must have known her killer."

"And that word Berengaria etched on her chamber wall at Parson Warfeld's house?" Corbett added. "What was it? 'Nazareth', written as if to remind herself, but about what?"

"And the attack on Griskin," Ranulf added. "Who killed him?"

Corbett nodded. He did not wish to reply. Les Hommes Joyeuses was his secret. "Not to mention the attacks on us," he mused, "travelling back from Maubisson with Desroches, that crossbow bolt loosed at the shutters, another in the cloisters." He paused. "Then there's the wine."

"Master, what wine?"

Corbett quickly told him about the jugs left outside his chamber. Ranulf cursed under his breath, a shiver of cold fear pricking the nape of his neck. He glanced apprehensively over his shoulder at Chanson guarding the door. In truth Ranulf wanted to be away from here. He wanted to distance himself from the stretches of lonely, snow-draped fields, ice-rutted forest trackways, desolate, haunted wastelands, the abbey with its stone galleries and echoing, deserted passageways filled with juggling light and shifting shadows. He glanced at Corbett slouched low in the chair, staring into the fire.

"Master," Ranulf leaned over, "you have always warned me about the time lost staring into flames."

Corbett straightened up and grinned. "Not this time, Ranulf, it's . . ." He paused at the knock on the door. The tavern master bustled in with platters heaped high with bread, strips of pork and pots of boiling spiced sauce. Corbett and his companions sat round the table. They ate in silence. Chanson offered to sing, but Ranulf didn't reply, and the Clerk of the Stables' joke hung like a sombre sentence in the air. Corbett was about to return to his high-backed chair when there was a further knock on the door and the tavern master crept in.

"I have a message, sir. A tinker came into the tap room, asked for me, thrust this into my hand and fled."

Corbett took the tightly rolled piece of greasy parchment. He sensed the threat it contained. He moved a candle closer, undid the parchment and stared at the scrawled hand.

Hubert Fitzurse, the Man with the Far-Seeing Gaze, sends formal warning: King's man, be gone.

CHAPTER
THIRTEEN

Tempus erit quando frater cum fratre loquetur.
There will be a time when brother speaks to brother.
Arator

Corbett's anger rose at the mocking threat. He thrust the parchment into Ranulf's hand. "Burn it!" he whispered. "Read it, Ranulf, then burn it!"

He pushed back his chair. For a while he paced up and down the chamber, trying to marshal his thoughts. "I won't be gone!" He paused. "I am not going to flee! I swear this, Ranulf, Chanson: I'll see Hubert Fitzurse hang from the gallows! I have the power." He laughed bitterly. "All I need is the evidence to unmask him, tear off the pretence and see who he really is." He went back and sat in the chair, stretching out his legs and trying to relax. After a while he told Ranulf to open his chancery satchel and quickly dictated a short note on a scrap of parchment. He sealed it with some wax softened over the candle flame, impressing his ring hard against it.

"Chanson, take this to the clerks at the Guildhall. I demand certain records."

"About what?" Ranulf asked.

"You talked about the *causa omnis* — the cause of everything," Corbett declared. "I call it the *radix malorum omnium* — the root of all evils. It began with

273

that hideous attack on a small manor house in the year of Our Lord 1272. I want to find out more about who lived there."

"Why, master?"

"Nothing much." Corbett leaned against the table and stared across at Ranulf. "Just a feeling, a suspicion."

"What about Wendover?" Ranulf asked. "Is it possible he could be the killer?"

"Wendover." Corbett shook his head. "Wendover may have the Cloister Map. He may have some knowledge. Deep down, however, I suspect he is just a bully boy, a braggart, a thief. I wouldn't be surprised . . ."

"What?" Ranulf asked.

"I wouldn't be surprised if Master Wendover has decided to flee! He must be becoming very frightened. After all, an attempt was made to kill him at Sweetmead Manor, or I think there was. Anyway," Corbett straightened up, "Ranulf, settle accounts with the tavern master. Chanson, take this to the Guildhall, and meet us back at St Augustine's Abbey."

Corbett collected his belongings and went down into the cobbled yard. Ostlers brought out their horses and Corbett and Ranulf left The Gate to Paradise, going down narrow lanes, shadowed by the dusk. Doors were slammed, laughter rang out through casement windows. They reached the main thoroughfare and paused to allow a funeral cortege to make its way by in a glow of tapers, puffs of incense, chants and prayers. Corbett remained vigilant. He glimpsed a whore with a twisted nose, painted red lips and hard, dark eyes; she was clad in a fur-edged gown, her impudent face shrouded by a veil as she stood with her pimp, who proclaimed himself Master Pudding, at a tavern door. Corbett rode slowly on. The crowds were thinning, the stalls had ceased trading. Market bailiffs and beadles were busy. Pilgrims, some with a range of badges depicting all the shrines they had visited, still desperately tried to reach the cathedral before its doors were closed for Vespers. Corbett felt more settled. He had lost that frenetic anxiety, that heightened sense of danger. He must find and pick at a loose thread in the tapestry of lies before him, and as with all lies, there must be a weakness. Discover that, attack it, weaken it and the rest would tumble loose.

Once they'd reached the abbey, Corbett and Ranulf retired to the guesthouse. Both clerks checked it carefully, calling for the guest master, ensuring everything was as it should be. Ranulf busied himself with other tasks, trying to quell the tingling feeling in his stomach. He'd studied Master Long-Face for many a year. Corbett always reminded him of a hunting dog which would wildly cast about, grow agitated, but once he'd found the scent, ruthlessly adhere to it, pursuing its quarry to the death. Ranulf sensed this was about to happen.

Corbett went down into the yard, summoned a lay brother and gave him a message to take to Les Hommes Joyeuses, camped out near St Pancras. He made the young man repeat it time and again before thrusting a small purse into his hand.

"Make sure the mummer who calls himself the Pilgrim gets that, Brother, won't you?"

The lay brother smiled and held up his hand as if taking an oath.

"And this is for your pains." Corbett pressed a silver coin into his hand. "Brother, I beg you, tell the Pilgrim to be gone." He peered up at the sky. "Before darkness falls."

Corbett was about to turn away when two cowled figures came through the gateway. They shuffled through the slush carrying a makeshift bier; from the sacking thrown on top a clawed white hand trailed. A shock of black hair peeped out from the top. Corbett walked across. The two brothers paused.

"A beggar." One of them spoke before the clerk could ask. "Poor man, found frozen to death in the apple orchard. He's for the mortuary chapel."

Corbett whispered the Requiem, crossed himself and retired to his own chamber. He prepared his writing desk, laying out sheets of vellum, quills and ink horns. Chanson returned carrying a leather bag of documents. Corbett laid these out on the table and studied them carefully: the tax returns for Canterbury and the surrounding area between 1258 and 1272. He built up the braziers, wheeled them closer to the table, settled himself down and scrutinised the documents. About two hours later Ranulf and Chanson, lounging in their own chamber, heard Corbett shout with joy. Both hurried into his room. The clerk waved them away. "I apologise, gentlemen," he said, half turning in his chair, "but now and again when you go searching in the most unlikely places you always find a treasure, as the parable in the Gospels tells us about the woman searching for the lost coin." Corbett paused. "Nazareth, Nazareth," he repeated. "Ranulf, seek out the guest master. Ask if I can borrow a missal which contains the readings for last week, the Epistle and the Gospel. Tell him I want to keep it for a while. I've recalled something Berengaria told me, how carefully she listened to Scripture."

A short while later Ranulf returned with a leather bag containing the missal, which the guest master had described as "one of the Abbey's most precious possessions", so Corbett had to be careful. Sir Hugh nodded, opened the missal, pulling away the ribbon markers, and carefully sifted through the readings. At last he found the passage which described Jesus going back to his native town of Nazareth, and how the Saviour failed to perform any miracles there because of the inhabitants' lack of faith.

"Lack of faith," Corbett whispered. "Sweet Jesu Miserere — Lord, I believe, help my unbelief. I've found it!" Now he knew why Berengaria had scrawled that word on the wall of her bedchamber in Parson Warfeld's house. She had heard something from the Gospel, read in Latin but translated by Parson Warfeld in his short homily afterwards; this had been seized on by the sharp-witted Berengaria. She was going to use it, or perhaps she already had.

Corbett closed the missal, gave it back to Ranulf and sat back in his chair, plotting how he was to trap his killer. He idly wondered about Wendover. Perhaps they should have warned him, but what could be done? The Hours of Divine Office were rung; Corbett ignored them, fully intent on constructing his hypothesis before developing it, searching for proof. Only once did he pause in his study, putting on his boots and cloak to go down into the freezing night to join the good brothers in singing Compline. By then Ranulf and Chanson were fast asleep. Corbett returned and continued working through the night. Afterwards he sat warming his hands over the brazier, eyes heavy with sleep but still determined on forcing this problem to a solution, its logical conclusion? Sometimes he acted as a judge confronting an assassin, presenting him or her with the evidence. This was different; it was all so tenuous. He'd built this house on shifting sands. Would it withstand a storm of protests and counter-accusation? Yet if he failed, perhaps he would never get a second opportunity.

Corbett pushed the chair back and, taking his cloak, wrapped it about him and lay down on the bed, staring at the wall, wondering what to do. He recalled the corpse of that beggar man being brought in, then a verse from a psalm he'd sung at Compline, about God inviting all men, saint and sinner alike, to a banquet. Perhaps he should do that? He muttered a short prayer and, thinking of Maeve, fell into a deep sleep.

Wendover, captain of the city guard of Canterbury, was fully determined to put as much distance between himself and his native city as possible. He was a very frightened man. He recognised that his liaison with

278

Lady Adelicia would eventually cost him his post, once that prying clerk had finished his business. Sir Walter Castledene had made that very clear. Wendover would be asked certain questions, and if his replies were not acceptable, he would be summarily dismissed, his indenture with the city council torn up. He would become another landless man wandering the streets and alleyways of Canterbury, desperate for employment, and if he fell, what a fall! Wendover, with his bullying ways, had made many enemies in the city. Once his disgrace became public, all hands would turn against him, and he could expect little mercy or compassion. Lady Adelicia would have nothing to do with him. She had used him and that was the end of it, so where else could he turn? Moreover, he realised that Lady Adelicia suspected he was a thief, filching this item or that, the occasional coin from her purse as she slept after their love-making here in The Chequer of Hope. Might he be arrested and interrogated? Wendover was truly terrified by a further nameless fear, a deep sense of dread which made him drink more than usual. Every time he left The Chequer of Hope he would look over his shoulder, certain someone was watching him. He had decided to flee. The previous evening he'd packed his saddle bags with every possession, taking his pouches of paltry coins from their hiding place. As soon as day broke and the city gates were opened, he collected his horse from its stable and made his way towards Westgate. He'd go to London; he had relatives there who might shelter him whilst he secured fresh employment.

Once on the Whitstable Road, Wendover grew more relaxed. He joined other people who, despite the weather, were determined on their own journeys. The travellers crossed the Stour, making their way towards St Dunstan's church. Here Wendover decided to leave the main thoroughfare, following country lanes through the trees which would eventually take him on to the London road and safety. He was surprised at how quickly and easily he'd managed to escape, and his confidence grew; he had sword and dagger strapped to his war belt, a purse of coins hidden away, his saddle bags bulging. He comforted himself that he would soon find fresh employment. He let his horse make its way carefully along the woodland path, since the wine and ale he'd drunk the night before had made him mawmsy. Abruptly his horse paused and whinnied, hooves scrabbling on the ice. Wendover looked up in alarm, but it was too late. The stark, black-garbed figure standing in the middle of the trackway, arbalest raised, had already taken aim, and the barbed quarrel whirred through the air, hitting Wendover in the shoulder. He screamed at the hideous pain, his horse kicking under him, and then he fainted, crashing from the saddle.

When Wendover regained consciousness, he believed he was already in hell rather than on the road to it. The pain in his left shoulder was excruciating. He stared down in horror at the red-black wound, the feathers of the quarrel still sticking out. He felt faint and tasted the iron tang of blood at the back of his throat. He was also freezing. He'd been stripped of every item of clothing and now sat astride his horse, hands tied behind his back, feet fastened under the animal's withers. Someone was holding the reins. Wendover blinked and strained against the thick, coarse noose around his neck. The figure turned. Wendover moaned in disbelief at the black hood, the mask, the slits for eyes, nose and mouth. He cursed his own stupidity; he must have been followed from Canterbury. He smelt a faint perfume. Biting his lip against the waves of pain which swept through him, Wendover stared round. His saddle bags had been emptied, his clothes cut to shreds.

"Mercy!" he whispered.

The figure remained impassive, patting the horse gently along its neck.

"Mercy, Master Wendover, mercy for you? You were there when my brother was hanged. I have no mercy. You may buy your life for a price. I'll cut the ropes and let you go if you give me the Cloister Map stolen from Sir Rauf."

"I haven't got it!" Wendover pleaded. He winced as the horse moved; the pain in his left shoulder was unbearable. He was now fully aware of the cutting cold, the snow falling from the branches above him, the winter wind nipping at his flesh.

"The Cloister Map?" the voice insisted.

Wendover swallowed on the blood at the back of his throat. "I haven't got it, God is my witness I haven't, but I could —"

"No you couldn't," the voice interrupted. "You're a coward, Wendover. Ah well." The figure stepped back. Wendover was sure he recognised that voice. "I must go on my way and so must you." The nightmare figure passed Wendover, smacked the horse on the rump and stood for a while, watching Wendover kick and struggle until the naked figure hung still, twirling slightly on the end of that coarse hempen rope. Only then did Hubert Fitzurse, the Man with the Far-Seeing Gaze, slip silently away, leaving the horror hanging behind him.

Corbett sat in the guesthouse refectory. He'd risen early, washed, dressed and attended Lauds, followed by the Jesus Mass. Afterwards he'd strolled round the abbey as if studying the different styles of architecture. In truth he was calming his own mind, reaffirming the conclusions he'd reached the previous evening. He returned to the refectory to break his fast, and Chanson and Ranulf joined him. They were just about to leave when Sir Walter Castledene arrived with a retinue of city guards. The mayor bustled into the refectory, taking off his gloves and throwing his cloak back as he told Corbett the news. How a group of stick-gatherers had gone out to collect kindling and had found Wendover's naked corpse hanging from an elm tree on a woodland path leading to the London road, his possessions strewn all around, saddle bags ripped open, clothes shredded, his horse foraging for grass.

Corbett gestured for Castledene to sit, but the mayor shook his head and beckoned Corbett away from the rest towards the door of the refectory.

"Whoever it is," Castledene drew close, peering at Corbett whilst wiping the sweat from his face, "is also hunting us, Sir Hugh. What is to be done?"

"What is to be done?" Corbett put a hand on Sir Walter's shoulder and led him into the cobbled yard, where the noise and chatter from the city guards, the cries of the lay brothers and the neigh of horses drowned their conversation. "Sir Walter, I came here looking for the truth and you didn't tell me it."

"What do you mean, Sir Hugh?"

"In 1272," Corbett replied, "the year of His Grace's succession, the King's peace was violated here in Canterbury and other shires. The small manor house of Hubert Fitzurse and his half-brother Adam at Maison Dieu was attacked and looted, everyone found there killed. I ask you, Sir Walter," Corbett pressed his face closer, "as you will account to God, if not the King, for your life, were you one of those who attacked that manor house?"

"Sir Hugh, how dare you!"

Corbett gripped the man's wrist. "Guards or not, Sir Walter, I'll drag you into the abbey church and up the steps to its high altar. I'll get one of our good brothers to bring down the pyx and Bible. I'll put your hand over them and make you swear that you are innocent of any such crime."

Castledene's face paled. He chewed the corner of his lip, eyes darting, deeply regretting coming here to meet this sharp-tongued clerk.

"I'll tell you something," Corbett continued in a hoarse whisper. "It was not only you, Sir Walter; Rauf Decontet was also involved. It's the truth, isn't it?"

Castledene opened his mouth to reply. Corbett pressed his fingers against the man's mouth. This time Castledene didn't flinch.

"Don't lie, Sir Walter. About you I have much to say and much to condemn. You have crimes to answer for and answer for them you will! Now tell me, do I speak the truth?"

Castledene swayed on his feet. Face pale, he looked older, haggard. Corbett realised this secret sin must have haunted the merchant down the years.

"I was there." He turned sideways as if unable to meet Corbett's full gaze. "Rauf Decontet and I, we were two young men. There was a breakdown in law and order. Gangs of rifflers roamed the countryside. Decontet and I were so desperate to make our way in the world, we joined such a band. Most of them are now dead. We rode out to Fitzurse's manor. We went to plunder, drive off some livestock, that was all. However, on the way our coven, God save us, stopped at a tavern, and we all drank deep. It was dark when we reached the manor house. I thought we would go in, hooded and visored, to take what we wanted, but the ale fired our blood. Fitzurse's second wife was very pretty. I swear this, Sir Hugh, and on this I will take an oath, I tried to intervene but they wouldn't listen. I collected my horse and rode away. I sheltered amongst the trees and watched what happened, the screams, the flames. I thought everyone had been killed. I never rejoined that gang of rifflers, and as God is my witness, I never, ever talked to Decontet again." He shrugged. "At least not as a comrade."

"Did Decontet remind you of your dreadful secret when he petitioned the King for Lady Adelicia's hand in marriage? Ask for a favour, as you did when you sent the sottish Lechlade into his service? Two men who could put each other under duress?"

Castledene stared bleakly back.

"How many people died that night?" Corbett asked.

"Sir Hugh, I do not know. Some of the bodies were consumed in the flames. Fitzurse and his wife were found, and buried in St Mildred's. I knew they had boys. I was relieved when I heard that one was still at St Augustine's Abbey school, whilst the other had hidden away." Castledene shook his head. "I have made reparation. I have had Masses said. I have journeyed to St James's shrine at Compostela and the tomb of the Three Kings at Cologne. I would do anything to purge my guilt, to clean their blood from my hands."

"That is a matter for God to decide, Sir Walter, and remember, the mills of God grind exceedingly slow but they do grind exceedingly small. Christ's vengeance will ring out. Our blood-soaked earth is a constant insult to the Lord. He will repay. Theology aside, more importantly, Hubert Fitzurse, the Man with the Far-seeing Gaze, sees himself as the Judgement of God. You, Sir Walter, if you are not careful and prudent, will die the same way as Wendover."

"Sir Hugh, what is to be done?" Castledene's voice turned pleading. "How can this bloody mêlée be brought to an end?"

Corbett was about to reply but he no longer trusted this man. He still had to search for the proof, bring the killer to justice, and Castledene had a great deal to answer for.

"I tell you what I shall do, Sir Walter, tonight in this refectory." He pointed back towards the guesthouse. "I shall hold a feast. I am sending Ranulf and Chanson into London to seek certain information. You will summon on my behalf Lady Adelicia, Lechlade, Parson Warfeld and Physician Desroches for a sumptuous feast so I can make my farewells."

Castledene was puzzled. "But Sir Hugh . . ."

"Sir Walter!" Corbett retorted. "I don't care what you or they are doing. I will not tell you the whole truth, nor must you tell anyone of our conversation this morning. Bring them here. As the bells ring out for Vespers, the bells of God's justice will also toll. Oh, and Sir Walter, your presence is certainly required."

Corbett spun on his heel and walked back into the refectory. He summoned Ranulf and Chanson to his own chamber, where he gave them secret instructions. Ranulf looked concerned.

"But Sir Hugh, you'll be here by yourself."

"For a while," Corbett smiled, "and I'll be safe. You, Ranulf, Chanson, take the London road. It is now clear of snow. You see, Ranulf, certain malefactors, murderers, thieves and rifflers are brought to judgement by evidence in the King's court, but not this time. Our assassin is too cunning; he has to be trapped and I intend to do this. It's the only way. The King's justice will eventually be done, and, indeed, God's. Now, gentlemen," Corbett stepped back, "leave mid-afternoon, go through the city, let people see you ride away. I have other preparations to make."

Corbett left and searched out the guest master, who agreed to the arrangements but gasped when Corbett told him what else he wanted.

"His soul has gone to God," Corbett replied. "Do what I ask, Brother. Oh, by the way, once the banquet has begun and the meal has been served, neither you nor any of the good brothers must come anywhere near this guesthouse. Promise me."

The guest master made to protest. Corbett held out his hand, displaying the chancery ring on his finger. "On your loyalty to the King, Brother, you must do exactly what I ask."

The monk closed his eyes, sighed, crossed himself, and nodded. "As you say, Sir Hugh, whatever you want."

The rest of the day Corbett busied himself supervising the cooks in the abbey kitchens, making sure the refectory was prepared for the evening. The fires were built up. Freshly charged braziers sprinkled with herbs were wheeled in. Coloured drapes hung against the walls; the refectory table was covered with a samite cloth, candelabra placed along it, fresh candles fixed on their spigots. The Gleeman arrived to see Sir Hugh. He pretended to be a tinker, carrying a tray full of writing tablets, glass rosaries, pocket knives, amber signets, coloured ribbons, laces, tags, silks, steel pins, imitation jewellery — a veritable chapman, a pedlar of everything. Corbett met him in the yard, pretending to make some purchase as the Gleeman explained how the Pilgrim had now fled their camp.

"Like a dog on heat," the Gleeman whispered, "to the London road."

Corbett laughed, made his purchases, patted the Gleeman on the shoulder and returned to his own chamber. He took an arbalest and slid a bolt into the groove, winched back the cord making it secure and placed it on a stool near the door. He drew his sword and dagger, turning them, letting the sharpened pointed blades catch the light. He locked and barred the door and slept for a while, waking early in the afternoon to make his farewells to Ranulf and Chanson.

Later that day, just as the bells of the abbey tolled for Vespers, Corbett's guests began to arrive in the cobbled stable yard. Corbett waited for them in the refectory. He met each of them at the door and escorted them into a room now transformed into a small comfortable hall with its coloured cloths and turkey rugs, the trestle table laid down the centre covered with a shining white cloth, candelabra flaming brilliantly against the dark. Charcoal braziers spluttered while a fire roared merrily in the hearth. Corbett behaved as if relaxed, offering each guest a small cup of spiced wine before taking them to their seats around the table. The cooks had done themselves proud. Corbett made sure the wine jug circulated. At first the atmosphere was cold, even hostile. However, as the green almond soup was served, followed by oysters stewed in ale, crayfish, pork hash mixed with eggs, minces, roast capon in black sauce, venison in a pepper juice, and the wine jugs were refilled, the guests relaxed. Only Castledene remained

288

watchful, still pale-faced, nervous and anxious after his brief but blunt encounter with Corbett earlier that day.

"Sir Hugh," Parson Warfeld toasted with his cup, "this is most kind. What is the reason?"

"Why, sir . . ." Corbett slouched in his chair at the top of the table and gazed quickly at Lady Adelicia. She looked truly beautiful in a blue-mantled furred gown, her gorgeous hair pinned with a jewelled clasp almost, but not quite, hidden by an exquisite white veil. "Why, sir, because I'm leaving."

"Leaving?" Desroches pushed away his silver platter and gazed expectantly at Sir Hugh. "The King's business is finished here in Canterbury?"

"Yes, sir, the King's business truly is, thanks to a man called Edmund Groscote! Well, that's how he was baptised at the font." Corbett laughed. "He goes by the name of the Pilgrim and consorts with troubadours, mummers and moon people. Now the Pilgrim was once an outlaw hunted by that *venator hominum* Hubert Fitzurse. Through his own secret, sly ways, he managed to acquire a description of Hubert."

"And?" Lady Adelicia asked.

"At this moment in time, the Pilgrim is taking sanctuary in St Michael's church at Cornhill in London. He will speak only to me. I have sent Chanson and Ranulf along the icy roads to seize him and take him to the Tower or Newgate, or to bring him here. I suspect it will be the Tower. If the weather holds tomorrow, I shall certainly leave Canterbury. You see, the Pilgrim lived a chequered life. There are men and women who work for me. In a sense they are a secret society; I call them "the *ordinaires*". They collect mere trifles, snippets of information, bits and pieces; the Pilgrim is one of these and he has earned his keep."

"Who do you think . . ." Lechlade slurred from where he sat at the far end of the table. "Who do you think this Fitzurse is?"

"What he claims to be, Master Lechlade: an assassin who lurks in the shadows."

"And those grisly murders," Desroches asked, "at Maubisson and elsewhere?"

"I haven't solved them yet." Corbett lied. "Nor why that poor city guard was killed at Sweetmead or how Sir Rauf and Berengaria were murdered. Of course, you've heard the news about Wendover?" They replied that they had. Corbett glanced sharply at Lady Adelicia, who simply put her head down and picked up her knife to play with a piece of meat on her dish; embarrassed, she coughed, lifting her goblet to conceal her own confusion.

"When we seize Hubert," Corbett continued, "I am sure the King's interrogators will secure the truth, but more importantly," he smiled, "I have found the Cloister Map!" His words created immediate silence; even Lechlade glanced up sharply. "Ah yes," Corbett declared, "we know how Stonecrop, who betrayed Adam Blackstock, survived the sea battle off the Essex coast. He stole the map before *The Waxman* was taken. For a while he hid, then made his way inland. Stonecrop needed good silver to discover that treasure, so he approached Sir Rauf Decontet and brought him the map. Sir Rauf, however, murdered Stonecrop, stole the map, then hid it."

"Where?" Lady Adelicia asked.

Corbett sensed she was speaking for all, expressing their deep hunger for this marvellous ancient treasure. "Lady Adelicia," he asked, "where did your late husband spend most of his time?"

"In his chancery chamber."

"And?" Corbett asked.

"He sat at his desk, but I —"

"Oh, I am sure you looked for the map there," Corbett intervened. "But you were searching in the wrong place, Lady Adelicia, everybody was. You do remember me sitting in your late husband's chair? I did so every time I used his chamber?"

Lady Adelicia's face crumpled in disappointment.

"I found it," Corbett declared, "in a secret pocket of the seat beneath the quilted cushion. When you return home tonight, you'll find the gap, the aperture from which I drew it."

"I knew you searched his chamber . . ." Adelicia mumbled distractedly, "and sat in Sir Ralph's chair."

"Of course you did," Corbett agreed quickly. "At first I could not understand it, but the map is clear. I will be gone within the day. Soon it will be in the hands of the King's ministers. When spring comes, the royal household will go hunting in the wilds of Suffolk. True," Corbett picked up his goblet, "the murders of Paulents and others, Wendover and Sir Rauf, cannot be explained, but in time, royal justice will have its way and the felon responsible will go to the scaffold. Ladies and gentlemen, I thank you for your co-operation. I toast you . . ."

Corbett added that he would answer no further questions and deftly turned the conversation to other matters. Glancing around the table, he knew the effect he had created and pretended to celebrate by drinking copiously. The evening drew to an end. The guests made their hasty farewells and left. Castledene dallied for a while, but Sir Hugh refused to answer any of his questions or see him alone. Eventually the guesthouse and the stable yard outside fell silent, cloaked in darkness and, as Corbett had whispered to Ranulf just before he'd left, the dead gathered to witness God's judgement carried out . . .

CHAPTER
FOURTEEN

Ferreae virgae, metuende iudex.
Dreadful judge, your rod is of iron.

Sedulius Scottus

Shortly after midnight, the shadowy figure of the assassin slipped across the yard and in through the unlatched door of the guesthouse. Hooded and visored, knife in one hand, a small axe in the other, an arbalest hanging from a hook on his war belt, he gazed quickly round. One night flame still beckoned like a beacon, but the fire in the refectory was banked, the braziers capped, the candles snuffed, the table still littered with bits and pieces from the feast. The man started at the squeak of a rat; a dark shape scurried across the floor. He took a deep breath and softly climbed the stairs, pausing at every creak and groan of the weathered wood. Yet the night remained silent. He reached the stairwell and peered along the narrow gallery. One door was closed, the other slightly opened. He edged his way along, gripping the knife and axe tighter; he tiptoed closer, pushed the door open and crouched down, edging into the room. The chamber was still lighted; a candelabra stood on a table. One of the candles had guttered out but the other two still flickered beneath their metal caps. He gazed at the bed and glimpsed the outline of the sleeping clerk, his woollen jerkin, boots and hose strewn on the floor. The assassin smiled to himself. Corbett had drunk so much he must have staggered upstairs and fallen asleep, confident and secure that his task had been finished. The assassin raced towards the bed, stretched over the body and drove the dagger deep into the sleeper's chest. He heard a sound, whirled round and gazed in horror as Corbett walked from the shadows in the far corner, sword and dagger out.

The assassin looked at the open door. He sprang to his feet, kicked a stool towards Corbett and raced across. He scrambled down the stairs, Corbett in pursuit. Another figure abruptly appeared in the doorway at the bottom, hood drawn back, a primed arbalest ready. The bolt was loosed and took the would-be assassin in the chest. He crumpled to his knees, then fell, crashing down the stairs.

Corbett lowered his own sword and dagger and hurried down the stairs towards Physician Desroches, who was already lowering his crossbow. Corbett, gasping for breath, turned the corpse of the assassin over, pulling back the hood and mask to reveal Lechlade's ugly unshaven face. The man was dying, eyelids fluttering, blood bubbling between his lips. Corbett let him fall back and kicked him further down the stairs so that he landed at Physician Desroches' feet.

"Master Physician." Corbett walked down the stairs, sheathing both his sword and his dagger. He stretched out his hand. "I thank you. I owe you my life. Come."

He gripped Desroches' hand, making it clear he would accept no refusal. "You must come up for some wine. Fortify yourself, explain what happened." He waved Desroches up into his own chamber. The physician immediately went across to the bed and pulled back the sheet from the corpse Corbett had secretly taken from the mortuary house. He stared down at the pallid, pinched face of the beggar framed by a greasy mat of hair.

"You dressed him in your clothes?" Desroches declared, not turning round.

"Of course. I begged the guest master. I knew the death house had the corpse of a beggar found frozen to death in the abbey grounds. The rest is as you see. Lechlade thought I was asleep, drunk, wits fuddled by wine, so he struck. And what brought *you* here, Master Physician?"

"I watched Lechlade at your supper. He acted the drunk yet I always had my suspicions." Desroches flinched as the point of Corbett's sword pricked deep into the back of his neck.

"Turn round, Master Desroches, or, to be more precise, Hubert Fitzurse, the Man with the Far-Seeing Gaze. Turn round!" Corbett ordered.

Desroches did so, his hand going towards the belt under his cloak.

"Unbuckle it!" Corbett stood back, sword still raised. "Let it fall to the ground and move over there."

Desroches did so, sitting down on a stool. Corbett pulled another one across and picked up the primed arbalest, aiming it straight at Desroches' chest.

"Sir Hugh, you are making a mistake. I was watching Lechlade. I had had my suspicions for some time. I thought —"

"No you didn't," Corbett declared. "I too had my suspicions about Lechlade, but I also began to suspect that two killers were on the prowl, not one. Hubert Fitzurse, that is you, had an accomplice. What I believe, Master Hubert, is this. A gang of outlaws attacked your manor house many years ago and killed your parents. Decontet and Castledene were members of that coven. At Westminster you were visited by someone who told you that, a revelation which abruptly, very dramatically, changed your life. Your visitor was Lechlade. When I looked at the accounts for your parents' manor, I came across a list of those old enough to pay tax: your father was one, your stepmother another; the rest were servants, except for one other individual, John Brocare. I believe Brocare and Lechlade are one and the same person. Somehow Brocare escaped, concealed himself and re-emerged as Lechlade. From what I understand, he was a relative of your father, perhaps a cousin? Anyway, he discovered what had actually happened that night and brought the news to you at Westminster. In a way it was like a messenger from God, wasn't it? You learned that the very city which had helped you, men who were now its leading merchants and traders, had been involved in your parents' death. You decided to forsake God, your king, your order and become a hunter of men. I would wager you hunted down surviving members of that murderous coven, and, apart from Castledene, they are now probably all dead. You also shared Lechlade's startling revelation with your brother Adam, who, by then, had turned to a life of piracy. Little wonder that Adam Blackstock waged war on Castledene's ships.

"Then the Cloister Map emerged. Adam found it on one of Paulents' ships. He seized that and sent a message to you. He had not only stolen the map; he may also have deciphered it correctly. You and he were to meet along the Orwell, near the ruined hermitage with its chapel dedicated to St Simon of the Rocks; that's where you took your false name, isn't it: Peter Desroches? Desroches is French for 'of the rocks', whilst you changed the name Simon to Peter, as happened in the Gospels, just in case anyone remarked on the coincidence that you bore the same name in French as the hermitage where Adam Blackstock used to meet Hubert the Monk. The rest of the story you know better than I do. Stonecrop betrayed your brother. *The Waxman* was intercepted, your brother killed and gibbeted. I can only imagine your rage, which cooled into a deep desire for bloody revenge. You are a highly dangerous but very intelligent man, Master Hubert. It wouldn't be hard for the likes of you, who has always hidden deep in the shadows, to change character, shape-shift as they say. You ceased being Hubert, the *venator hominum*, the former monk, and became Monsieur Peter Desroches of Gascony, who'd studied at this university and that. You had acquired enough wealth as Hubert to finance such a clever deception."

Corbett paused and studied his adversary staring so coldly back at him, not a flicker of emotion in those hard eyes, no shift or twitch to his body; he sat perfectly composed, hands on his knees, scrutinising Corbett, searching for any weakness, any gap he might exploit.

"You are skilled enough to forge letters of accreditation, official seals, to be a physician from this school or a scholar of the other. You could study and absorb medical treatises; as a *venator* you'd also become skilled in the treatment of wounds and ailments. You'd soon learn the knowledge, customs and mannerisms of a physician, be it the treatment of Chanson's ulcers or the use of rats to test tainted food and drink. I suspect you're a finer physician than many a genuine one. After all, as a boy you'd displayed a talent to mimic, to imitate. Anyway, you pretended to be the wealthy physician who had studied abroad." Corbett paused. "When I talked to you and Lechlade, both of you mentioned how you had been a physician in Canterbury for over three years, some time before *The Waxman* was intercepted, but of course that is not strictly true, is it? It is just over three years ago that *The Waxman* was captured. Only after that did you arrive in Canterbury with your wealth, knowledge, expertise and pleasant diplomatic ways. Castledene accepted you, and so did others."

Corbett paused, shifting the arbalest for comfort's sake.

"Of course, you must ask why should they patronise you? Very easy." Corbett smiled. "Physicians are noted for their love of gold, their haughty ways, their

298

insistence on protocol. You played your own lure like a hunter with his snare: the easy-going, charming, knowledgeable Desroches who, perhaps, charged less than the rest. Tactful, diplomatic, you wormed your way into people's affections. You played the same affable physician for me, the man who didn't like weapons, who found it difficult to mount a horse."

Desroches snorted with laughter and flailed a hand, but his eyes remained watchful.

"You acted the physician very well, both for our good mayor and for Sir Rauf Decontet," Corbett continued. "You were in Canterbury for two purposes: first to wreak revenge, and second to discover the whereabouts of the true Cloister Map. You bided your time. When Castledene told you about Paulents coming to Canterbury, you laid your plans. Your confidant and accomplice Lechlade played his part. He too had assumed a new identity, a new guise. He was the lumbering, lurching, foul-mouthed, drunken sot whom Sir Rauf tolerated because it cost him next to nothing. In fact Lechlade was as sharp-witted as you, and equally bent on revenge." Corbett paused. "I reflected: in the past Lechlade may have been a toper, but revenge sobered him up. He would keep you informed of what was going on, be it Lady Adelicia playing the two-backed beast with Wendover and, above all, the whereabouts of that map. I realised two killers must be involved. When Paulents landed at Dover, he was given a warning; at the same time Castledene was threatened in Canterbury. It is possible for one man to travel from Dover to Canterbury, but I concluded it more likely that two people were involved: you in Canterbury, Lechlade in Dover. Your accomplice would find it easy to slip away: his master was murdered, Lady Adelicia held fast in prison and Berengaria safely lodged with Parson Warfeld, so who would be bothered about that drunken oaf? I also suspect Lechlade interfered with the food and drink served to Paulents and his family at the Dover tavern. Nothing serious, just enough to agitate the belly, to worsen the symptoms of a rough sea crossing. Paulents left for Canterbury. Lechlade also swiftly returned to the city before the snows set in."

"And what was the purpose of all this?" The question was taunting, yet brisk.

"Well, if Paulents and his family were unwell, naturally, as a city physician, you would meet them."

"Castledene could have hired someone else."

"I doubt it," Corbett replied drily. "As I've said, you'd proved to be most accommodating. Moreover, and I've asked Castledene this," he bluffed, "when Paulents and his family arrived in Canterbury, you happened to be in the Guildhall or nearby. Yes?" His adversary gazed stonily back. "You swiftly established a cordial relationship with Castledene's guests, assuring them that all was well. Paulents' wife was much taken with you and even asked you to stay at Maubisson. Of course, you refused; you had other plans. Now, Wendover was to guard Maubisson. However, our captain was deeply distracted, you knew that. He had been playing the fornicator, the adulterer with Lady Adelicia, who had now been arrested and lodged in the Guildhall dungeons for the murder of her husband. It would be easy for you, with your skill at disguise, to pretend to be a city guard dressed in his cloak, hood pulled up against the cold, and slip into Maubisson carrying this parcel or that."

"As easy as that, Sir Hugh?"

"Very much so! Wendover was distracted. Guards milled about. Who would notice you? Who would really care? No one suspected an assassin had crept in carrying the means to inflict bloody mayhem."

"And?" The self-proclaimed physician leaned forward. Corbett's fingers curled round the catch of the arbalest.

"A short while later Paulents and his family arrived. They locked themselves in. The guard was set, the fires lit, the food cooked, the wine served, and you emerged."

"Corbett, you are raving: too much time spent on idle speculation. How could I —"

"Very easily, Master Hubert. You'd learnt the guards' password; you pretended to leave. No one would give you a second glance either disguised as a guard or as the special friend of Castledene, the mayor of Canterbury. You made your farewells, went down the stairs, then slipped quickly into that cellar. Even if you'd been discovered, a remote possibility, you could have bluffed and lied your way out, but fortune favoured you. Paulents and his family wished to relax, Castledene to be gone, Wendover to reflect on his own troubles."

"If I emerged, as you put it, why wasn't the alarm raised?"

"Because Paulents would see you as a friend: the gentle physician who carried no weapons. You'd offer some pretence as to why you had been allowed to slip back into the manor. They must have thought Wendover had let you pass. You'd make up some story, how, perhaps, the mayor had given you a key to this postern door or that. You were the kindly physician, Castledene's close colleague: why on earth should they suspect you? You had the night in front of you. You reassured them that all was well; they would relax as you secretly mixed a sleeping potion with their wine. While they drank, you took Servinus outside on some pretext or other. You'd already established, when talking to them earlier, how Servinus did not drink alcohol, so he was brutally dispatched with a swift crossbow bolt to the chest. You laid his body down, turning it over so no blood dripped on to the floor, staunching it with a rag. By the time you returned to the hall, Paulents and his family were sleeping. You had the rope; it was simply a matter of dragging your hapless victims across to those iron brackets, putting a noose around their necks and hoisting them up. You are a strong man, Hubert; they eventually all dangled like corpses on a gallows. They never regained consciousness, slipping from sleep into death," Corbett snapped his fingers, "like that! Servinus was a different matter. In all this you had to be careful of time passing. You knew I was coming to Canterbury. Castledene told you that. Your business had to be done quickly, then you and Lechlade were to be gone. You slit Servinus's stomach so its foul vapours could escape

302

and thus slowed the stench of putrefaction, staunching the wound with more cloths and napkins."

"I know so much about physic, the bodily humours?"

"Of course you do, Master Hubert. You are highly intelligent and skilled. I wager you know as much about the art of healing as you do about killing! You've read books, the pharmacopoeia of the Ancients. You're probably more erudite than many a physician; you proved that when you treated Chanson's ulcer. After all, your expertise in physic as well as artful diplomacy had secured the patronage of Castledene and others."

"And what did I do with Servinus's corpse?"

Corbett eased the arbalest back. Hubert was waiting for him to tire.

"You dragged it down into the cellar, took the lid off that vat, having first run off some of the ale, lowered the corpse in and resealed the barrel. You carefully looked for any spilt blood. I can imagine you going along the floor with a candle, wiping away any stain of violence. You then returned to the hall. You took all the wine cups, emptied them, washed them and refilled them with fresh, untainted wine. Your task was completed. Servinus was dead and so was Paulents. Revenge had been carried out. You went to the merchant's chamber, took out the fresh copy of the Cloister Map and replaced it with another piece of parchment which was really nothing more than a farrago of nonsense."

"And how did I escape?" The prisoner on the stool moved his head to ease the tension at the back of his neck.

"Oh, that was quite easy for you, Hubert: a hunter of men, a skilled assassin. You had your city guard cloak which you had filched from somewhere. Wendover burst into the house; people were scurrying hither and thither, shouting the passcall; you were just another figure hurrying about. Nobody would think to stop a city guard during the immediate confusion. I did wonder, however, about Oseric killed out at Sweetmead Manor. Did he notice something untoward? Did you kill him, or did Lechlade on your order, because you wanted him dead, or was it just to create more terror? Whatever, Hubert, you slipped into that manor and hid yourself away. You were elated but you also had to be prudent: the King's man was coming, so you sent me warnings."

"Why?"

Corbett moved the arbalest. Hubert was whiling away the time, waiting, searching for a weakness, a mistake; the clerk strained to listen for any sound, but the guesthouse lay wrapped in an ominous silence.

"Because three people were involved in the death of your brother: Castledene, Paulents and His Grace the King. You already knew I was hunting you. You murdered poor Griskin, didn't you?" Corbett accused. "You discovered that he wasn't really a leper but an emissary from the Royal Chancery seeking out information, making enquiries in that part of Suffolk where the ancient treasure was supposed to be buried, about who had been there, why and when. Griskin had learnt something but it became garbled. He talked about Simon of the Rocks, a play on the name of the

304

physician from Canterbury who was making similar enquiries. Was that Griskin's way of concealing your true name? Or was it something else? Another alias used by you when you travelled into Suffolk? Had Griskin glimpsed you in the ruins of that lonely hermitage?" Corbett shook his head. "I cannot say."

"I never knew the time and place Griskin was supposed to meet you."

"Oh, Master Hubert." Corbett smiled at the consternation on his enemy's face as he realised his mistake. "Who said anything about the time and place of my meeting with Griskin? Did you find my letters giving such information, or did you torture him? We will never know. In the end you trapped him in some lonely alleyway or on some windblasted heath. You killed him, strung his corpse up on that gallows, cut off his hand, pickled it and sent it as a warning to me. You also took Griskin's chain; he would never be separated from that. You left it here in the chantry chapel of St Lazarus, a clear warning of the danger you posed. In the end you learnt about Griskin as I did about Edmund Groscote, also known as the Pilgrim. Oh yes, I've met him. He is a member of Les Hommes Joyeuses. He confessed everything. What I said to you at supper about what he knew of you was a mere fabrication, yet you believed it; hence your appearance tonight."

"And I could leave Canterbury for Suffolk just like that?" Hubert waved a hand, his voice betraying his growing desperation: "Go here, there?"

"Of course you could, Master Hubert. You are a master of disguise, a man of wealth, of status. You have no family, no wife, no maids or servants. No one has a clear description of you. Master Lechlade was always there to protect your back. So yes, when you were not pretending to be a physician in Canterbury, you made the occasional journey into Suffolk, your heart set on finding that treasure. Griskin found that out; perhaps not the full truth, but certainly enough information to threaten you, so you killed him. You enjoy such games, don't you? You like hunting men down. Griskin, me, Paulents and his family, we are just quarry in your eyes. You love giving yourself titles, sending out warnings; such power of life and death gladdens your heart!"

"And Sir Rauf Decontet?"

"Oh well, you had matters to settle with Sir Rauf, and what better time than when his wife was out playing the whore with Wendover. Again time was pressing. Paulents was coming to England, Decontet had that map. Lechlade undoubtedly found out about Stonecrop. He'd certainly have been aware of Lady Adelicia's furtive searches for the Cloister Map. Sometime on Thursday, the Feast of St Ambrose, he informed you that Lady Adelicia was leaving for one of her trysts with Wendover. You decided to visit Sir Rauf. Lechlade joined you. You bustled into the chamber in your role as Decontet's physician. Once inside, however, you locked the door and, assisted by Lechlade, tied Sir Rauf down in his chancery chair. I felt the marks of the rope on the wood beneath the quilted arm of that chair. You see," Corbett patted his own arm, "Sir Rauf was probably wearing a padded jerkin against the cold. The rope wouldn't show on his wrists, you'd be careful about that, but it did on the wood of the arms of the chair as he strained against his bonds.

"You questioned Decontet about what had happened to your brother. You taunted him. You demanded the Cloister Map, but of course that map no longer existed, did it? Sir Rauf, clever man, had memorised it carefully and burnt it. Oh yes, Master Hubert," Corbett smiled, "I never found any map. By now Lady Adelicia must have realised that. She'll have rushed into her late husband's chancery, only to discover no secret pocket in the quilted seat of that chair. Eventually you and Lechlade concluded that Decontet could not, or would not, tell you anything, so you killed him with a swift blow to the back of his head. You laid his corpse out, took his keys and locked the chancery chamber. Later on, after Parson Warfeld had arrived and the door had been forced, you secretly replaced the keyring. The good parson, distracted by Decontet's death and the administration of the last rites, simply saw what you wanted him to witness. I suspect that you or Lechlade replicated that small ring of keys, placing a similar one on his belt while you held the true one. You used these to lock the chamber after you opened Adelicia's, then, during the chaos that followed the forcing of Decontet's chamber, secretly replaced them.

"Once Decontet was dead, you left his chamber, but not before you had taken some napkins and stained them with his blood. Going up to Lady Adelicia's chamber, you unlocked the door, placed one bloodied napkin on the floor and the rest behind the bolsters. Later on you'd incriminate Lady Adelicia further: she'd left her cloak in the chancery chamber, an easy target for Lechlade to smear with blood when everybody else was distracted. You also used what time you had to search that house thoroughly. Ranulf noticed how things had been moved, but to your anger and frustration, no Cloister Map was found.

"The day was passing. The one person you and Lechlade had overlooked was Berengaria. Everybody makes mistakes, Hubert, even you with your far-seeing gaze. You must have been furious with Lechlade: he had not learnt of the maid's secret trysts with her master; she and Decontet had been very careful. Anyway, Berengaria came tripping back and saw something untoward involving you. Perhaps she saw you actually in the house when you later pretended to be locked outside. She also deceived me. She never actually approached the manor; she saw what she did from a distance, then fled back to Canterbury. Later on she decided to use her knowledge to blackmail you, the wealthy physician. Of course, she didn't perceive the full truth; just enough to upset your story. Nor did she want to explain to anyone else why she had returned home that Thursday afternoon. When we were all at Sweetmead, she probably hinted at blackmail. Of course, by then she had moved chambers from Decontet's household to Parson Warfeld's, where again, her skill in certain sexual matters advanced her cause. Naturally Parson Warfeld would ask for the proprieties to be observed so people wouldn't hint or gossip about scandal. Accordingly Berengaria attended daily Mass. The parson would read the Gospel and, as is the custom, deliver a short homily on it. Now a few days ago, during the very time Berengaria was staying with Parson Warfeld, the Gospel passage was about Jesus's return to his home town of Nazareth; Our Saviour expressed his astonishment at the lack of faith of his fellow citizens in an enigmatic remark. You must recall it?"

" 'Physician, heal thyself.' "

"Precisely. Berengaria, no Scripture scholar, was quick-witted enough to realise how such a phrase could also be applied to you, Master Hubert, and what truly happened on that fateful afternoon. Is that what she whispered to you at Sweetmead? 'Physician, heal thyself'? That is why she scrawled the word 'Nazareth' on her chamber wall, as an aid, a prick to her memory."

"But I was with Parson Warfeld when she was killed."

"Oh yes." Corbett eased himself back. "Worried about the souls of your dead parents. Did you take the name of Desroches, not only because of its links with that lonely hermitage but also because there was no one of that family alive in Canterbury to contradict you?"

"I was with Parson Warfeld!"

"But Lechlade wasn't. Most of the time he acted the drunken sot. However, when I questioned him at Sweetmead, my first suspicions were roused. Lechlade leaned across the table. On his breath I could smell the stew Ranulf had cooked, but no ale, yet he acted as if he was drenched in beer. On the morning Berengaria died, you distracted Parson Warfeld and took him away; Lechlade followed you. Lady Adelicia despised him. What would she care about his movements, slipping in and out of Sweetmead? The guards at the front of the manor were also there to watch the lady of the house, not her sottish servant. On that morning Lechlade furtively slipped into St Alphege's and Berengaria was quickly garrotted, her mouth closed for ever.

"Two killers must have been involved. You used that to protect yourself. When Berengaria was murdered, you were with Parson Warfeld. When Sir Rauf Decontet was found, you couldn't get through locked doors because Lechlade was asleep. No one could suspect you, especially when you called for Parson Warfeld to act as your witness. The same is true of other attacks. When I was journeying back from Maubisson to St Augustine's, a secret assassin loosed crossbow bolts at us from the trees. How could I suspect Physician Desroches? He was with me. It must be someone else. In truth it was Lechlade, who was also responsible for that warning bolt loosed at the shutters of my chamber as you were leaving the abbey. Strangely enough, by sheer coincidence, you were with Ranulf and Chanson in the refectory below when I came up to my chamber. If it hadn't been for the good Lord and our guest master, I would have drunk the tainted wine Lechlade undoubtedly arranged to be left outside. You insisted on accompanying us from Sweetmead. Lechlade secretly went ahead to prepare the poisoned wine, but it was a hasty job. Unable to use jugs from the abbey kitchen, he supplied his own, and of course, our guest master knows exactly to the last porringer what items are his and what belongs elsewhere." Corbett paused. "The same happened when I was attacked in the cloisters. You and Parson Warfeld were visiting the abbey. Our good priest definitely had business here, and so had you: the news about Lady Adelicia being enceinte. You decided to exploit that. You stayed with Ranulf and Chanson, Parson Warfeld went about his business, so who was lurking in the cloisters waiting for me to leave the abbey church after Vespers?" Corbett glared at this man who'd plotted so assiduously against him. "Why, Master Lechlade, your silent, stealthy accomplice."

Corbett drew a deep breath. "In truth I recalled that whenever anything happened, you were the one person who could account for his movements, be it the attack in the woods, the bolt loosed at my shutter, the poisoned wine, the death of Decontet, the murder of Berengaria, or the death of that poor city guard." He paused. "Oseric was killed in the garden. You were being questioned by me. Lechlade perpetrated that murder, opening the shutters of one of the rear windows. Why was that innocent man killed?" Corbett pulled a face. "To frighten Wendover, or just to establish your own alibi? You and Lechlade are killers to the bone. Who would suspect the drunken servant? In truth he was your murderous shadow, following you, ready to exploit any opportunity. On all these occasions Physician Desroches could have gone on oath that he could not possibly be involved. Such obvious innocence certainly made me suspicious. Moreover, you also had the means to travel to and from Suffolk. You were known to Paulents, his wife and his family. It's like a game of logic, isn't it, Master Hubert? What is common to all these events? Why, Physician Desroches!"

"If I stole the Cloister Map," Desroches replied, "why didn't I just escape?"

"Ah," Corbett nodded, "I thought of that, but of course you couldn't allow there to be two maps, could you? You had Paulents' copy, which you would certainly decipher, but you suspected Decontet still had the original. Moreover, you had unfinished business with him and others, including me. You wanted to make sure there'd be no other map, no rival hunter for that gold and silver. You realised the hour candle was burning away. Sooner or later you might make a mistake; sooner or later you would have to move, but you had to be certain. If Sir Rauf and Lady Adelicia didn't have the map, there was the possibility that Wendover, that braggart, that roaring boy, had it in his possession, so you watched him. He tried to flee Canterbury but you trapped him. You questioned him but he knew nothing, so he died. You and Lechlade then conferred on what might happen next. You had pushed matters to their logical conclusion — enough was enough, time was passing, the candle of opportunity was about to gutter out. Physician Desroches must suddenly disappear, Lechlade with him, but then you were invited to my supper. I dropped hints about Groscote, the *ordinaires* — the secret spies of the Chancery — as well as the possibility that I had found Decontet's map. You had to act. Ranulf and Chanson had left for London. You watched how much I drank. I was very careful; I also kept my cup covered: I didn't want a powder mixed with my wine. I begged the guest master for that poor man's corpse to do some good before it was interred in sacred ground. You sent Lechlade ahead whilst you guarded the door. He came in here, stabbed a body he thought was mine and fled. You are quick-witted, Desroches. Lechlade alive might incriminate you, so you killed him and pretended to be my noble rescuer."

Corbett paused at the faint sound of horses in the yard below. Voices echoed. Ranulf and Chanson had returned!

"Of course, my companions were never travelling to London." He moved the arbalest as Hubert leaned forward, but the man simply undid the clasp of his cloak and let it fall away.

"You have no evidence," Hubert said, "not really." He stretched out his hands in mock innocence.

"Oh, I think I have," Corbett retorted. "The logic of my argument; your presence here. Moreover, Master Hubert, Ranulf and Chanson merely journeyed to the other side of Canterbury and back. They carry royal warrants and have mustered the city watch. By now they have searched Lechlade's chamber and your house. I am sure they will find evidence enough."

Hubert Fitzurse, the Man with the Far-Seeing Gaze, slumped his shoulders; Corbett glimpsed the stricken look in his eye. "You never considered that, did you?" Corbett asked. "They too went hunting, and Ranulf is a good lurcher." He paused at the sound of footsteps on the stairs. "I am sure he has brought enough evidence to hang you, Fitzurse!" Corbett stretched out a hand. "The Cloister Map?"

Fitzurse smiled thinly. "Like Decontet," he murmured, tapping the side of his head, "I've memorised it. If you want to know, then I'll trade it for my life. I'll give you the map, I'll even accompany you there, but I'll demand a royal pardon and enough money to go where I want."

Corbett chewed the corner of his lip. He thought of Griskin dangling from the gallows, that hand of glory sent to him. Staring at the killer in front of him, he reflected on all the others who had died at Hubert's hands, especially Paulents and his family, strung up like a line of dead crows from those grim iron brackets in that ghostly hall at Maubisson.

"I don't think so." Corbett shook his head and watched the smile fade from his opponent's face.

"Sir Hugh?"

"In here, Ranulf," Corbett called.

Ranulf swaggered into the chamber, followed by Chanson. He threw a leather pannier at Corbett's feet.

"Enough?" Corbett asked.

"Yes, master, enough to hang him, but no Cloister Map. Documents, memoranda; the same at Lechlade's. He wasn't the toper he pretended to be."

"Very good." Corbett clicked his tongue, then gestured at Hubert. "Bind his hands, Ranulf. Chanson, you and I will go into Canterbury. I have a goldsmith to visit, whilst you rouse Sir Walter Castledene. Tell him that before the day is out, the King's Justice of Oyer and Terminer, Sir Hugh Corbett of Leighton, will sit in judgement."

Two days later, just before Christmas Eve, the execution party left Canterbury, making its way through the streets to the gallows erected outside the main entrance to Maubisson manor. The news of Hubert Fitzurse's summary trial, conviction and sentence had swept the city. Crowds had gathered to see justice carried out. Corbett, Ranulf and Chanson on either side, sat on his horse, cloaked and hooded. He watched Fitzurse be shriven by a friar. The prisoner thrust the priest aside and clambered to his feet, face towards Corbett.

"King's man," he bellowed, "I didn't ask to be created. I didn't ask to be redeemed. All I wanted was peace, my parents, my brother . . ."

Fitzurse was seized and pushed on to the cart beneath the gallows rope. Corbett felt a deep pang of sorrow and recalled what he'd said to Ranulf. They were now watching the hideous flowering of an evil, the roots of which stretched back over thirty years. The prisoner's hands were swiftly tied, the noose positioned around his neck, the knot placed expertly behind his left ear. The red-masked executioner jumped from the cart and looked at Corbett, who sat like a statue, left hand raised.

"Hubert Fitzurse," Corbett called out, "you have been justly tried. You have been found guilty of heinous crimes against the King, his peace and the city of

Canterbury. Do you have anything to say before sentence is carried out?"

"Yes," Fitzurse shouted back, twisting his head to where Castledene sat further along the line. "I'll be waiting for you, Master Mayor!"

Corbett dropped his hand. The cart creaked away. Fitzurse kicked and jerked for a while, then hung still.

"The King's justice has been done," Corbett called out. "Let everyone take careful note." He nodded at Sir Walter and turned his horse, determined to leave Canterbury as quickly as possible. Castledene and Lady Adelicia would have to wait until the weather thawed. Spring would come and so would a royal summons to both of them to account for their actions before the King's Bench at Westminster.

Once they were free of the crowd, Ranulf urged his own mount forward and placed his hand on Corbett's arm.

"Master, the Cloister Map?"

"I will tell the King the truth," Corbett murmured. "The treasure still lies there waiting to be found, but the map is gone."

Author's Note

This novel is woven with broad strands of historical truth. Piracy in the Channel and off the east coast of England became a common hazard during the reigns of Edward I and Edward II: pirates were actually nicknamed "sea monsters". The lost treasure of Suffolk is, of course, a reality and is now known to the world as Sutton Hoo, a beautiful Anglo-Saxon ship crammed with treasure buried beneath funeral barrows in south Suffolk. Legends about this treasure circulated for centuries, though the area wasn't excavated properly until after the Second World War. Edward I certainly recognised the value of treasure trove. By 1303 he was almost bankrupt: his commissioners even began to plunder parish chests in villages and towns up and down the country. Bounty-hunters were not just a feature of the Wild West; they also operated in medieval England: two of the most famous in the fourteenth century were Marmaduke Tweng and Giles of Spain.

A breakdown of law and order did occur in 1272, and royal clerks such as Corbett were given full mandate by the King to move into a city or shire to dispense royal justice. The treasures of St Thomas à

Becket's shrine at Canterbury are, of course, described in many chronicles.

One final note which may be of interest to modern readers: "chemical warfare" is not an invention of the modern era. In fact the use of lime features prominently in the capture of Eustace the Monk, a real pirate during Henry III's minority. His pirate ship, like that of Blackstock, was attacked and trapped by royal cogs who used lime and the direction of the wind to blind his crew. Eustace was overcome and immediately dispatched. Warfare at sea during this period was particularly cruel. Both sides adopted the proverb: "Dead men don't tell tales!"

Paul C. Doherty
April 2006
www.paulcdoherty.com

The Year of the Cobra

Paul Doherty

Egypt is in danger. The barbarous Hittites are rumoured
to be massing their armies in readiness for an onslaught.
And with Pharaoh Tutankhamen seriously ill, the country
appears powerless against its enemies. Apparently determined
to gain control over the threat, scheming Lord Ay sends
Mahu, Overseer of the House of Scribes and uncle to
the troubled young Pharaoh, to uncover the Hittites'
plan. But what Mahu discovers could have far more
devastating effects than any army . . .

When the masked messengers emerge to guide Mahu
on his journey, many unanswered questions begin to
reveal themselves: the truth about Lord Ay's devious
plotting and Pharaoh Akenhaten's disappearance; the
identity of the "Watchers" and secret knowledge about
the Aten. Mahu knows that his nation's future rests on
this knowledge, but he also knows that knowledge is
power . . .

ISBN 978-0-7531-7714-3 (hb)
ISBN 978-0-7531-7715-0 (pb)

The Gates of Hell

Paul Doherty

A campaign of murder as Alexander nears his greatest challenge

It is 334 BC. Alexander the Great and his troops march towards the strategically important city of Halicarnassus, with the aim of bringing it to its knees. But the city's commanders, Memnon of Rhodes, the Persian Orontobates and the Greek renegade, Ephialtes, plot to ensure that Alexander will meet his nemesis at their gates. A series of brutal killings begins proving that the Persians have infiltrated Alexander's court. With his lord facing the fight of his life, Alexander's boyhood friend Telamon must go through "the Gates of Hell" to find the traitors — but all the while the ever-cunning Alexander keeps his counsel and pursues his own plans to foil his enemies.

ISBN 978-0-7531-7163-9 (hb)
ISBN 978-0-7531-7164-6 (pb)

The House of Death

Paul Doherty

Spring 334 BC and the young Alexander is poised with his troops at the Hellespont, waiting to launch an invasion into the empire of the Persian King, Darius III.

Knowing he must win the approval of the gods, Alexander makes sacrifice after sacrifice but the smoke does not rise — the sacrifices are tainted. Worse, the guides hired to lead him through Persian territory are being brutally murdered, Persian spies are active in the camp and Alexander's own generals harbour secret ambitions.

Into this whirlpool of mistrust comes Telamon, a great friend from Alexander's boyhood. He sets abo revealing the secret enemies within the camp wh Alexander displays his true heroic stature, throwing fears and panics and leading a bloody attack on th Persian King.

ISBN 978-0-7531-6795-3 (hb)
ISBN 978-0-7531-6796-0 (pb)

The Godless Man

Paul Doherty

A Mystery of Alexander the Great

It is 334 BC. Alexander has smashed the armies of the great Darius III and is roaming through the Persian Empire, living up to his reputation as "the Wolf of Macedon".

Arriving at Ephesus, the success of his campaign is suddenly threatened by a series of violent murders carried out by a Persian spy known as "the Centaur". Then Alexander's old tutor Leonidas is found in a stagnant pool in the House of Medusa — no accident for the house was linked to a guild of assassins.

Once again, Telamon, the king's friend and physician, must set about unravelling a swirling mass of mysteries. He works hand in hand with Alexander's eerie Master of Secrets whilst coping with the unpredictable nature of Alexander himself — a consummate actor whose lust for glory matches the carnage and intrigue that dog his footsteps like the Furies themselves.

ISBN 978-0-7531-6869-1 (hb)
ISBN 978-0-7531-6870-7 (pb)